"I need to know what you're feeling. . . ."

"You fascinate me," he said, tracing the path of her eyebrow with his finger. "I don't know what to do with you." Patrick knew that wasn't what she was looking for.

"Try again, Patrick." Her voice told him she wanted him to find the words. Wanted him to give her what she needed. So she could give herself to him. She wanted it as badly as he. Patrick took a deep breath.

"I want you near. I want to be a . . . husband to you. I . . . I want to see if we really can be . . . something to each other." He couldn't spit the words out. "I never thought we could, but now . . . I want . . ." he fell off, convinced he'd muddled it.

"What if we can?" she said quietly, eyes wide. "What if you were a husband to me?" Her eyes fluttered as his hands found her hips.

"What if I did everything I was thinking?" Patrick was thinking of running his hand across her thigh at the moment. It made it a trifle difficult to talk.

"What if I let you?"

By Allie Shaw
Published by Ivy Books

THE IMPOSSIBLE TEXAN
THE IMPOSSIBLE BRIDE

THE IMPOSSIBLE BRIDE

Allie Shaw

IVY BOOKS • NEW YORK

An Ivy Book
Published by The Ballantine Publishing Group
Copyright © 2002 by Alyse Stanko Pleiter

www.ballantinebooks.com

ISBN 0-8041-1965-1

Manufactured in the United States of America

First Edition: July 2002

OPM 10 9 8 7 6 5 4 3 2 1

For Clarice

For Believing

⊱ Historical Note ⊰

While I have endeavored to base the Galveston portions of this book in actual historical settings, I feel compelled to point out that the Venezuelan natives in this book are entirely the work of my own imagination. A large, bloodred pearl does not (to my knowledge) exist, although I was delighted to discover while I thought I made up the idea of red pearls, it seems a marine animal called the horse conch had the idea long before I did. "La Roja," however, is entirely fictional. Therefore, I did not want to attach such a gem—and its legend—to an actual historical culture—although Margarita Island was in the midst of a tremendous pearl boom in the mid–nineteenth century.

⊰ Acknowledgments ⊱

When I am asked how my life has changed since I've become a published author, my answer is invariably this: "I'm much harder to live with now." It is to my family, then, that I owe the largest debt of gratitude for coexisting with this sophomore author and surviving to tell the tale. To my husband, Jeff, whose patience has been tried beyond the normal bounds of marriage yet continues to know when to tell me to just calm down and put my blasted fingers on the keyboard. I can write tales of true love because I live one. To my children, Mandy and CJ, who can spot the cover of *The Impossible Texan* a hundred yards out in any bookstore, who have endured "researching vacations," and who have let Mom take her laptop into countless McDonald's. I am deeply grateful to the members of both the Windy City and Chicago North chapters of the Romance Writers of America for their support, advice, and just plain showing up at booksignings (which means more than you can ever know!). Many thanks to the beautiful city of Galveston, Texas; the Galveston and Texas History Center; and the Rosenberg Library, for their hospitality and helpfulness as I researched this work. Thanks most of all to Margaret Doran, whose enthusiasm and sharp research eye has been a tremendous resource and a great blessing. The making of such friends is perhaps the best byproduct of book research. Thanks to my friends and the many members of my extended family, including my cousin David, who proves that sometimes the best research resources are hiding under your own family tree. My heartfelt appreciation to the team that keeps my career going: Karen Solem, Charlotte Herscher, Gilly Halpairn, Ballantine Books, and the many other talents that contribute to this book finding its way into your hands. Thanks, finally, to the many readers who have written to share their joy in my work—a connection that is perhaps the greatest satisfaction any writer could enjoy. God bless you all.

THE
IMPOSSIBLE
BRIDE

⊰ Chapter One ⊱

Serves you right, Trick O'Connor. If ye keep thinkin' the rules of this world don't apply to ye, then ye deserve to have it come back up and whack ye in the face now and then. Just look at her.

Patrick O'Connor stared hard at the woman standing alone beside the train tracks. She was so different than what he'd expected. He'd only caught a glimpse of her before, a few months earlier, but there was something about her now he was sure he hadn't seen before.

What were ye thinking, lad?

Patrick had grown used to his conscience—what little of a conscience he had—speaking to him in the lilting brogue of his late wife. There was rather a poetic justice to it.

Then again, there were times—such as this particular moment—where it bothered him immensely.

There Deborah Edgerton stood, the locomotive's great, greasy exhale billowing around her delicate form. Was it fair to instruct her to get off the train here rather than Galveston? No, it wasn't. There was

a great deal about this that was unfair, and he had
planned it that way.

Patrick watched her take in her surroundings. He
followed the gentle curve of her spine as she drew
herself up. She mustered her courage with more
grace than he had anticipated.

Damn.

She wasn't supposed to look like that. To be like
that.

It changed everything.

No, it doesn't, he told himself, but he was already
certain that he was wrong. He started toward her,
then stopped himself. He wasn't ready.

Why the hell wasn't he ready yet?

"Lovely welcome," she said to no one in particular, reaching down to brush the dust from her skirts.
She had pleasant hands.

Keep to the plan. Think, don't look.

He stepped into the sunlight and stood, waiting for
her gaze to find him. The way surprise lit up her eyes
was very nice indeed.

The plan, Trick. Remember the plan.

"And welcome to you, too," he finally said, pulling
himself up to his full height. Being a man of his size
had its advantages.

She eyed him above the rim of her spectacles.

He'd forgotten she wore spectacles, even though it
was highly unusual for a woman to have them. *Wait
for it,* he told himself. *She'll know.* Her eyes were
sharp and clear, even from this distance. He took two
steps toward her, watching the surprise slowly disap-

pear from her eyes to be replaced by an analytical stare. He touched a finger to the brim of his hat.

"Hello . . ." he continued, spoon-feeding her a response in the voice one might use to cue a small child.

She glared at him. She didn't understand yet. He expected this to produce a bit of fear, but she dismissed him instead with a wave suitable for gnats. Erect, she sidestepped him and headed for the station door.

Lord Almighty. He let out an astounded whistle over the train's parting churns. He heard her mutter something as she put her hand on the station door handle.

And then it came. He watched the wave of recognition start at her shoulders and travel down through her fingertips, right down into the pit of his own stomach. *Steady, man, steady.*

With an infuriation that was just plain delightful to watch, she strode back to dump her hatbox at his boots. He couldn't hold back a smile.

She knew.

"You're not!" she snapped out.

"I am." He thrust his hands into his pockets.

"You are *not* Pat O'Connor."

"Pat-*trick*. Patrick. Most everyone around here, though, calls me 'Trick'."

Without warning, she plunged the pointed end of her parasol into his gut. "I can see why! This is fraud!"

"Fraud?" No doubt about it, Deborah Edgerton was a damn far sight from what he had expected.

"I imagine this comes as no surprise to you, *Mr.*

O'Connor"—her voice pitched on the "Mr."—"but Pat O'Connor is supposed to be *female*."

"She is," he replied, rubbing the spot she'd skewered.

"You're not."

"A fact I deeply appreciate." The corner of his mouth sneaked up. *Well now, what do you know?* Still, it was best to keep an upper hand on the situation.

"I fail to appreciate it at the moment." She eyed him. "Mr. O'Connor, are you going to explain yourself or am I getting on the next train?"

"That depends, Miss Edgerton." He made a motion to pick up her hatbox.

She pinned the box to the ground with her parasol. "On what?"

Patrick looked up at her, cockeyed from holding the hatbox handle she still pinned to the ground. "On whether you're gonna poke me again."

"I admit it's tempting. But I shall restrain myself, depending on the explanation you *are* about to give me."

He dropped the hatbox handle, straightened, and drew his hand across his chin. "Pat O'Connor *is* a woman. She is my mother." *Now wait one minute.* The plan had been to explain as little as possible. How'd she pull that out of him so quickly?

"I don't suppose you'd mind telling me *which* Pat O'Connor has been corresponding with Senator Maxwell to arrange my employment?" Her expression told him she had already guessed the answer.

He pushed the hat up off his forehead a bit. "Well, now, that would be Pat*rick*."

"But—and I'm sure this again comes as no surprise to you, Mr. O'Connor—you are aware that the senator was under the impression he was corresponding with Patricia O'Connor?"

"In all honesty, I was counting on that fact, ma'am." Patrick was glad to feel his control returning. Today was a day for complete control.

"And *your* definition of fraud, Mr. O'Connor?"

My. He hadn't counted on wit. Despite his better judgment, Patrick replied, "Getting caught."

Patrick watched Miss Edgerton consider her options. They both knew there was no "next train." She had no idea that he knew she couldn't bear returning to Austin. Her options were nonexistent. He'd capitalized on the fact that she'd have to make the best of it—here—if she wanted any future away from everything she was fleeing in Austin. He squelched an unexpected curl of guilt, and heard his late wife clucking her tongue in the back of his mind.

With an unwarranted authority, she shoved her hatbox over onto his boot with the end of her parasol. "Mr. O'Connor, consider yourself caught." She glared at him, then pointed with her parasol at the small collection of trunks and bags that stood assembled on the platform.

He started after them, then stopped. He turned to look at her again, flat out amazed. He ought to have stayed gruff, but he couldn't help the whistle that slipped from his lips. A much softer whistle this time. "Damn," he said from the back of his throat. He regretted it instantly.

"Are you unaccustomed to having your bluff

called, Mr. O'Connor?" she asked confidently. Oh, she had no idea what was coming.

It was better to turn away before his face betrayed him. "Hardly," he called from over his shoulder as he made for the bags. He hoisted one of the trunks onto a shoulder and walked toward the wagon, but found he couldn't resist. Patrick stopped in front of her, one hip jutting out under the weight of the trunk. His eyes came to rest on hers. Crisp, clean eyes, framed with honey-colored lashes. He applied a cavalier expression, intending to unnerve her. "I just didn't count on you being so pretty."

She flushed despite her anger. "If you think . . ." she began, but Patrick had seen what he needed to see and had already turned toward the wagon.

Deborah Edgerton was dumbfounded. This had been a risky business to begin with, taking an unconventional post as a secretary to a family she knew almost nothing about. Now, before she'd gone a hundred yards from the train platform, things were spiraling out of control. Patrick O'Connor continued his conversation as he came around for another trunk. "Miss Edgerton, I'm not one to drum up a speech. You'll find I always say what I mean."

"Just as you meant everything you said to the senator? Deceiving him?"

He paused and looked at her, the glint of his coffee-colored eyes piercing her from under the shadow of his hat brim. "I meant to do that."

"You show a disturbing lack of remorse, Mr. O'Connor."

"Why, thank you ma'am." He slid a finger across his hat brim again and went for the next trunk.

Deborah simply couldn't let it go at that. Despite her efforts to keep reserved, she found herself walking all too quickly toward the wagon after him. "Just what was it you were expecting?"

His face showed he enjoyed her small pursuit. He scratched his cheek, crafting a response. His jaw was square and strong-lined, the set of his mouth sure and confident. A dusty rogue with an entirely too disarming smile. In any other setting she might have considered him handsome and powerful. And very much someone to be avoided. "Like I said," he eventually replied, one corner of his mouth angling up, "I wasn't counting on your being this pretty. I suppose I thought you'd be more practical-looking."

Deborah Marie Edgerton, who'd built a life on her practicality, found herself at a loss. "How very much like a man to assume beauty and practicality are mutually exclusive." *Beauty?* How had words like "beauty" come into this? She pursed her lips in frustration.

"You don't think highly of men, do you, Miss Edgerton?" he questioned from behind a box.

"What little regard I had is fleeing even as we speak."

"Damn."

Deborah sighed. "Mr. O'Connor, is such language absolutely necessary?"

"Not in the slightest." He didn't even look up as he hoisted the last of the heavy bags onto the buckboard with ease. "Are you ready, Miss Edgerton?"

"Not nearly."

He pushed the luggage in place and leaned back against the buckboard. He was considering a decision. Somehow it showed all over the man's face. Something in his eyes and the slant of his brows that disclosed a storm of thought. His gaze, an indulgent sort of stare that traveled up and down her body, flustered her thoughts.

O'Connor cleared his throat. "Miss Edgerton, no doubt you'd appreciate the chance to freshen up after your long journey, and, well, our arrival on the island might require more . . . formal attire." As if to punctuate this, he twisted to grab a small carpet bag from the wagon and produced a tie and vest. "Might you have something special in the way of a dress somewhere in these trunks?"

"Mr. O'Connor," she said slowly, "are you asking me to dress for my abduction?"

A broad laugh spilled out of him. An easy, rich laugh of genuine amusement. He sat his hands on his hips. "Why, yes, Miss Edgerton. I suppose I am. And may I say you've quite a way with words. I wouldn't care to get in an argument with you."

"I can hardly see where that's avoidable."

He stood there. "Well?"

"Well, what?"

"Which trunk is the dress in?"

Perhaps he was making a conciliatory attempt at hospitality. It had been a hot, dusty ride. She couldn't deny that the chance to change and wash would be a welcome one.

"The brown one."

O'Connor called out directions to a boy, who pulled the wagon into the street toward a hotel-ish—and that was an overstatement—looking building down the road a bit. He walked over to Deborah, made an overstated bow, and stuck out his elbow. Deborah swished past the gleam in his eyes and set out across the street on her own. Why was he looking at her like that?

"Damn." He cursed under his breath as he started out after her.

"I heard that."

"Damn."

The man staring at her and swearing in the parlor doorway looked quite different, now that he had shaved and dressed. He looked . . . well, Deborah had to admit he looked quite handsome. More magnetic than his change of clothes or clean face, however, was the spark in his eyes. As if it gave him great pleasure to look at her. She told herself it was just that it had been a very long time since anyone really noticed her, much less with *that* kind of expression on their face.

"Mr. O'Connor, would you *please* do something about your language!" she forced out, mostly because it seemed the safest thing to say.

"You're a sight, Miss Edgerton."

He made no effort to hide his enjoyment at looking at her. Deborah flustered despite her best efforts not to. She fussed with a button and managed a muffled, "Thank you."

"A damn fine dress, too. You are one damn surprise after another."

"*The language*, Mr. O'Connor!"

"Well, damn, I haven't got another word for it."

His look was easing toward unsavory. Exasperated, Deborah offered, "Pick a word, then. Any word. The first one that comes to mind."

"Potatoes." His hands shot into his pockets again, like a sassing schoolboy.

"Potatoes?"

He cocked his head toward the back of the house. "Potatoes. I smell potatoes frying in the kitchen."

Deborah eyed him from above her spectacles. "Hardly an improvement. It's far from—" She was cut short by having to move aside as the young lad and a companion struggled to lug her trunk down the hallway again out to the wagon.

"We'd best be going, Miss Edgerton. We've an appointment to keep."

Given the day's events, Deborah decided against inquiring about the appointment. Somehow she was sure she didn't want to know why he'd insisted she get off at the stop before Galveston when the train ran right onto the Island.

The ad for the rail line had read "Avoid dust, delays, and disaster." Strike three.

"*Poh-tay-toes!*" she heard him say from behind her, and was grateful he couldn't see the smile that spilled across her lips.

Although Patrick O'Connor had already lived up to his nickname, it seemed he did possess shreds of decency. Instead of the buckboard wagon, a nicely appointed surrey waited outside the hotel door.

He was gentle helping her into the wagon. The man had large hands, obviously strong, and yet his grasp was careful. Still, she slid as far over to the edge of the seat as she could manage. She set her parasol across her lap. With the pointed end aimed at one Patrick O'Connor.

They rode in uneasy silence for about half an hour. She tried to keep her gaze from him, but it proved difficult. Try as she might, the corner of her eye continued to catch his glance every once in a while. He was regarding her with fascination and puzzlement, the way a child would regard a new toy he liked very much but couldn't quite figure out how to work. As if he were deciding what to do now, as if his plans had somehow been altered by her arrival. And yet she knew, by the way he carried himself, that he had planned every detail of this scheme. The combination raised her pulse.

Deborah attempted to busy herself by watching the landscape lose its dusty color and gain a richer green in the grass and trees. It couldn't be that far to Galveston now. She wondered about this highly unusual secretary position at O'Connor Exporting. It had seemed like a godsend at the time, a chance to use her clerical skills for someone who would accept a woman to such a post. Deborah never expected to find such a position again—her post with the Maxwell family had been one-of-a-kind for a female. Now, everything she thought she knew about this new post had to be disregarded. It had been a poor decision to make the trip alone when Sister Agatha had taken ill and could not accompany her, but it felt as if every judgmental eye in Austin was closing in on her. She needed to leave.

That much had been accomplished. She was out of Austin. Granted, things were far from ideal, but she was here, on her own. She'd just have to improvise. She'd wanted a new life, away from the powerful family that had sheltered her most of her youth. If a life without the Maxwells meant change, she had better start getting used to change.

As the afternoon sun began to sink, they came to an intersection of dirt roads. Still she saw no sign of Galveston. In fact, she couldn't be sure they hadn't traveled farther inland rather than toward the coast.

O'Connor reined the horses to a stop. He leaned too close to her shoulder as he reached behind the seat into a small bag. His pulse was hammering in the sinews of his neck. She noticed a sizable diamond pin in his tie.

"Well, Miss Edgerton, this is where it gets interesting."

Deborah tightened her hands on her parasol. "I can hardly guess." She didn't know what to make of the tone in his voice.

When he held out a hand, she noticed a sparkling brown stone set in each of his newly donned cuff-links. "May I see your hands, please?"

Her hands? Why on earth did he need to see her hands? He sat very still, waiting for her to comply. Slowly, trying to read his eyes for some sign of what was to come, she raised up her hands.

Patrick grabbed them in a single move, and with a

powerful precision he swung them behind her back and began to tie them together.

"What?! Lord Almi—ouch! What do you think you're doing?" Deborah screeched. She began to squirm and kick as he finished off the knot.

"I'd imagine it's obvious." A heel struck home. "Damn! That hurt."

She kicked him again, glad to have a sharp shoe heel. "Untie me this minute! What on earth is going on here?"

"Well, I'd say—umph—'abduction' was a mighty accurate choice of—mmfgh—words on your part." The grunts came not from the strain of holding her down, but the acrobatics of dodging her feet.

She stopped the struggle to stare squarely at him. "Untie me or I'll scream."

Patrick held her with one hand, parking his free elbow on a jutting knee. "If it'd help, I invite you to. Might scare the horses a bit, but then again, a scared gallop would get us there a lot faster."

Deborah scowled at him, then screamed. Very loudly. At point-blank range. Into his right ear.

"Jesus—ow!" Patrick cringed, jerking her away with the hold he kept on her hands.

She screamed again. And one more time, until it became painfully apparent it would have no effect. He just sat there, pinning her to the seat, enduring the noise.

"Well I'll be," he declared when she finally fell silent. "This is going to be harder than I thought." He shook his head to clear the apparent ringing she'd caused. Still holding her and dodging, he climbed off the seat to stand behind the surrey. "It's going to be a lot more difficult to stay upright this way, but I'll be damned if I'll be wed with blood on my good trousers."

Deborah went stiff.

Patrick cursed fluently as he tied her hands to the back of the surrey bench.

"What?!" The word came out of Deborah's throat as a harsh gasp.

"I said," repeated Patrick, picking his hat up off the road and brushing it, "if you fail to calm yourself this is going to be the bloodiest wedding in Galveston County history."

"Wedding?"

He cocked an eyebrow at her, then looked around as if to make sure another groom hadn't magically appeared out of the brush. "Uh-hm." He pretended to inspect the rim of the buggy wheel.

"If you think I'll consent to *marry* you . . ." She was twisting, straining to find his face as he circled the buggy, examining things. He suddenly seemed too calm. Like the kind of man who might do anything. *Oh, Lord.*

"Consent?" He broke into her thoughts. "I'm no fool, Miss Edgerton. I never considered you would actually *consent* to this. But I'll admit," he reached down and rubbed one shin, "I didn't plan on you being so hard to force."

Deborah began to struggle harder, thrashing in a combination of rising panic and anger. "I . . . will . . . not . . . marry . . . you! I'd . . . rather . . . ummmph!" She lost her footing and tumbled sideways on the bench, skimming her head along the sideboard. It left a brown smear along her cheek and knocked her spectacles off. Her face grew hot and tight. "You're insane."

Patrick came around to the front of the surrey, standing quietly. "I've been called far worse by folk with far more colorful vocabularies. Now," he said in a quieter tone, "are you going to let me help you up?"

"No!" she spat out, angling her legs underneath her to bring herself erect. She watched O'Connor pick up her spectacles. He took a handkerchief from his pocket and carefully cleaned the lenses. In the odd way that fear heightens details, she noticed how tenderly he treated the frames. Deborah pressed her eyes shut when he leaned into her to return them to her face. He inspected them, then adjusted them. He let his finger linger along her cheek as he did so.

"Now," he began in a soft voice, "I figure there's only two ways to do this: either you cooperate and we make the best of this most . . . unusual . . . situation, or you fight tooth and nail and one of us ends up hurt."

Deborah opened her eyes to shoot him a look that let him know who she'd prefer to see end up hurt.

"Yes, well, I suppose I should expect no less." He cocked an eyebrow at her. "Would it help to get one last good scream in before we get started?"

Deborah simply stared straight ahead in silence. At some point he'd have to untie her to get her out of the surrey. She'd have her chance then. But Lord, he was so large. She felt like a mouse.

"Well now. That's a far sight better." He squinted and twisted a finger in one ear. "My ear is still ringing from the last one, besides."

Deborah braced her legs against the floorboards as the horse broke into a trot, neatly turning the corner toward a small clump of trees about a half-mile away. As they drew closer she could make out the profiles of three people in the sharp afternoon shadows.

"It will be a small ceremony, of course. But we'll aim to make it as civilized as possible." He called out cheerily to the tallest of the three men. "Afternoon, Judge Porter. How kind of you to come out all this way."

The spindly man snorted. "Kind, my backside, O'Connor. You're an hour late."

"Now, Judge, let's keep our language to that befitting a lady's company."

Deborah made a snorting sound of her own. *Abduct the lady, tie her up like so much cattle, force her to do God knows what, but mind your language?*

"Gentlemen, may I present Miss Deborah Edgerton."

Like boys in on a prank, they tipped their hats in a faltering chorus of "ma'am"s.

Deborah stared at Patrick. "You can't think I'll do this."

"Oh, my dear Miss Edgerton, I do indeed." He was actually confident about this outrage. Exceedingly confident.

For the first time, Deborah realized he might succeed. Her small prickle of fear now seemed to feed on itself. She watched him reach into the small bag and remove three leather pouches, tossing one to each of the three men.

Patrick turned to Deborah. "I need to ensure that your, shall we say, 'lack of enthusiasm' for the matter at hand stays private. In a small town like Galveston, silence can be downright expensive."

"You really expect them not to talk because you've *paid* them?"

"Honey," began the lanky judge as he peered into the pouch, "For this much loot I'd tell the world y'had three arms." The trio snickered.

"I'll offer you double." Deborah suddenly blurted out. "Whatever he's paid you. When Senator Maxwell hears about this he'll . . . he'll . . ." The amused look on the men's faces stopped her short.

Patrick seemed actually pleased, whistling through his teeth again. "My goodness, who'd have thought you'd have such fight in you?"

"You're abominable." She tugged again, but the rough ropes were beginning to hurt. Panic snatched at her breath.

"Well, now, that's always been one of my favorites. If I may say so again, Miss Edgerton, you do have a fine vocabulary."

One of the other two men finally spoke up, flailing at a fly that buzzed around his face. "For God's sake, Trick," he whined, "git on with it."

"Indeed." Patrick swung out of the surrey, whistling as he came around to the ropes that bound Deborah's hands. He undid the knot that lashed her hands to the bench, but didn't untie her hands.

Deborah felt sweat slide down her back. He plucked
her easily from the seat. He took his time bringing her
to the ground, staring into her eyes as he lowered her.

"I won't do it," she declared as calmly as she
could, as he turned the two of them toward the trio.
"I'd rather . . ." The poke of a small, cool circle in
her back cut off her words. A panicked little yelp escaped her.

"Yes, ma'am," Patrick's voice was low and soft behind her ear. She could smell the soap on his skin.
"What do you suppose that is? I'd say you're smart
enough to know that now might not be the best time
for anything rash." She heard him shift his weight
behind her. "I'm going to untie those lovely hands,
Miss Edgerton, and you are going to cooperate. Is
that clear?"

Deborah could only nod. She couldn't draw
enough air to come close to speaking.

Everything blurred together after that. She could
hear the judge's drawl but not his words. She could
feel Patrick O'Connor's hand clasped around her elbow and the smooth circle of his incentive aimed just
below her ribcage. She could smell the dust in the
clumps of grass and the whiskied tang of the trio in
front of her. She could hear her breath sputter in and
out of her body above a pounding heartbeat. She
could not, however, bring it all into focus until she
heard a voice say, "Do you, Deborah . . . Eh . . .
Eb . . . what was it, Trick?"

"Edgerton, Wiley. Miss Deborah Marie Edgerton."

"Do you, Miss Deborah Egg-derton, take Trick O'Connor to be . . ."

"*Patrick*. And it's Edgerton. Get it right, Wiley. You're being well enough paid for it."

Wiley sounded insulted. "Do you, Miss Deborah *Edgerton*, take *Patrick* O'Connor to be your husband?"

A hot tear leaked down the brown smudge on her cheek. Deborah refused the handkerchief O'Connor offered, choking on the unspoken words. When the metal nudged her from behind, her hands flailed a bit at her side and only a small, ugly sound came out of the back of her throat.

"She does," O'Connor pronounced.

Deborah Edgerton was outnumbered. She had a gun to her back. She was ill from the ride, scared to death, standing out in the middle of nowhere with not a soul to help her. She was probably going to die.

How could any woman not be queasy in such a dire situation?

Most women, however, wouldn't have had the gumption to get ill onto his shoes. In that regard she surprised even herself.

"Hell, Trick," called one of the trio, swallowing a laugh. "She don't look like she does to me."

⊰ Chapter Two ⊱

"Why?!"

Of course she'd ask that. She'd asked it of him four times in the last twenty minutes. There'd been far too many surprises in the last two hours, he was damned if he was going to go into the murky waters of telling her "why" now.

"No." Patrick settled his hat farther down over his eyes and jostled the reins.

"I've a right to know!" Deborah demanded.

"I suppose you do," he replied. Well, of course she did. Which was precisely why he wasn't going to tell her. This woman made it blasted difficult to keep the upper hand. Improvising, Patrick chose to respond by shooting her a look designed to convey she had no rights whatsoever at the moment. He hoped his expression suggested she'd asked the question one too many times.

She fell silent, but he knew she was still waiting for some explanation. You could see the woman think. Her eyes would narrow, her lips—a very delicate, rose-petal color, they were—would purse just the slightest, and her head would cock slightly to the side. He could almost guess her thoughts. Her mind straining for some indication as to why he'd done it. Grasping to conjure up any reason why a man should go to such extremes to obtain a wife. It was an intriguing thing to watch.

"Are you going to tell me?" she asked finally, turning to face him after avoiding his eyes for several minutes.

"No."

She pulled against the ropes in exasperation, sucking in her breath with a hiss when the cords cut into her wrists. "Was it really necessary," she moaned, "to tie me up again? It hurts."

Patrick switched the reins to his other hand. "You have my word, I'll untie you when the time comes."

Deborah snorted. "I don't put much stock in your word, Mr. O'Connor."

With that Patrick pulled the surrey to a stop. He pushed his hat up and looked her straight in the eyes. "All right now, we'd best settle this up right here. 'Mr. O'Connor' is just not going to hold water from here on in. You're going to have to call me 'Trick' like everyone else."

Deborah leveled her eyes at him. "No."

Oh, hell. He stared out over the dusty landscape. She stared at her shoes.

"Well then, Patrick, if you please." He watched her smile with a hint of victory until he added "Deborah." It was pleasing to say her name. He clicked his tongue and set the horses off again, rolling the name over in his mind. Deborah O'Connor had a nice ring to it. A clean, true, ring. *Ring . . .* the ring!

He pulled the horses up short again suddenly, slapping a hand to his vest pocket. "Dam—potatoes! I almost forgot." He dangled a small red velvet pouch from his fingers. "You startled me so much by . . . well, your *episode* back there I clean forgot about the ring."

Deborah's eyes widened in disbelief. "The ring?"

"It doesn't seem right to get married without a ring. It'd be uncivilized. 'Specially with all you've been through."

"Mr. O'Conn—" she started until Patrick held up a scolding finger. "Oh all right for God's sake—Patrick," she emphasized his name sharply, "you have just kidnapped me by fraud, married me against my will, and you're worried about jewelry?"

"I am a man of details." Stuffing his fingers into the small pouch, he produced a gold band. He had admired its age and delicacy in a store window just the week before. The winding ivy etching had caught his eye. "Pretty, isn't it?"

She glared at it. "That, sir, is no token of affection."

Patrick was indignant. "Well, alright then, consider it a consolation gift."

She thought some more. Then, to his surprise, she smiled just a bit and nodded. "Accepted."

Well, there now. That wasn't so difficult, was it? The woman had sense. "Can I trust you enough to untie your hands?" Patrick palmed the ring and put the pouch back into his pocket.

"Please," she said quietly.

It took Patrick only two swift movements to free

the ropes. Sighing, she brought her hands around to rub the disturbingly red rings that circled her wrists. *Tying her. Hell, Trick, was that really necessary?* He noticed her hands were puffy from the binding. Slowly, with some effort, she extended her left hand.

Deborah stared at her hand, lost in this man's enormous grasp. She felt the prick of Patrick's callused skin as he lined the ring up with her fourth finger. An involuntary gulp escaped her when he slid it up her knuckle. The ring was warm and smooth.

And huge. It hung off her small finger, even swollen as it was. When she moved her hand, the ring slid off into her lap.

"Quite an ill omen, don't you think?" she quipped before she could stop herself. It seemed only appropriate that the ring didn't come close to fitting.

Patrick stared for a moment at the circlet in her lap. He reached into his pocket again. "Nonsense," he proclaimed, "just in need of adjustment."

He undid the knot of the slim leather thong around the pouch's top. Picking up the ring, he deftly whipped the thong around the ring, forming a band of leather around a small segment, and tied it off neatly. He bit the ends of the thong off and held it up for her inspection. "I'm guessing it will fit fine now." Taking her hand this time, he slipped it onto her finger. "There now. Consider it a metaphor."

Deborah tried to stay as calm as possible, remembering her new plan. She'd agreed to don the ring so that he would free her hands. She couldn't arouse any further suspicion now.

Keep him talking. "A metaphor?" she asked.

"It's like us. Takes a bit of adjustment to make it work." He admired the doctored ring on her hand.

What kind of man are you? "It is a lovely—if ill-fitting—ring. I suppose I should thank you for the thought."

He nodded. "I suppose you should."

Deborah simply returned her gaze to the landscape and said nothing.

She felt his eyes on her for a long moment. Then he shook his head and snapped the reins. "Deborah. Deborah O'Connor. Fine ring to it."

Stay calm, Deborah reminded herself. After a calculated time, she kept her voice causal as she asked, "May I please have my parasol back? It's still quite bright." She shielded her eyes for effect.

Patrick turned to her suspiciously. "Are you going to skewer me?"

Deborah pasted a slightly helpless look on her face. "I can't see where that would have any use now."

"Indeed. I'd just like to keep my ribs where they are, thank you." He considered her for a moment. Deborah wondered how eyes of such a muted color could be so bright. Sharp. Mischievous, even. Deborah tried to make herself squint a bit more for emphasis. It wasn't hard. "I swear," he said, reaching back behind the surrey seat, "If the sharp end of this comes anywhere near my liver, I'll not be a gentleman about it."

"You have my word." That much was true. She accepted the parasol and carefully opened it. With a slight panic she realized her plan needed the parasol to be closed, not open. Her lie wouldn't hold if she didn't keep it open for at least a while. *Stay calm,* she told herself, trying to ignore that each moment brought the surrey closer to wherever he was taking her, *you'll think of something.*

They couldn't yet be near Galveston. Galveston was an island, and there was no body of water in sight. He must have taken her far out of their way to stage that charade of a wedding. *A few minutes more might take you nearer to help. You're out here in the middle of nowhere. Stay calm and think. You'll be all right.* She settled the parasol over the shoulder farthest from Patrick O'Connor.

Impatient, she mentally recited every verse she could think of to "The Yellow Rose of Texas" to pass the time. Two verses weren't much of a help. She had resorted to "O God Our Help in Ages Past" when she saw a small building on the horizon. A tiny, fenced homestead, run-down but hopefully occupied by someone outside of Patrick O'Connor's bribing influence. Trying to appear casual, she folded the parasol. Patrick watched her. With a cocked eyebrow she laid it down with the point away from him. He nodded in appreciation and jostled the reins again. *Good. Easy, now. You'll only get one chance.*

Deborah leaned ever so slightly over toward the edge of the surrey, gauging the distance. She fidgeted her fingers on the parasol, the leather-wrapped ring banging awkwardly against the handle. She shut her eyes for a brief moment, forcing a deep breath into her lungs. Then, with all the power her small body could command, she leaned over and thrust the parasol back over the side into the spinning surrey wheels. The power of the turning spokes ripped the parasol from her hands, but not before it had produced its intended effect, for the sound of splintering wood filled her ears as she hung onto the lurching surrey.

Patrick let out a seaworthy stream of curses, fighting to keep the horse in line as the vehicle rumbled and fell toward the side of the wounded wheel. "What in the name of heaven . . ."

Deborah waited only until the carriage slowed just enough, then threw herself out of the seat and began to run in the direction of the hut.

"Sweet mother of God . . ." She heard Patrick scramble across the surrey bench. The rest was lost above the thunder of her breath. She grabbed at her skirts, hoisting them up far enough to allow her a good run. She refused to look back, despite the torrent of angry sounds coming from Patrick and the surrey. She fixed her eyes on the hope that waited beyond the crude fence.

A yell came out behind her, and suddenly an unseen force grabbed at her ankles. Its yank catapulted her to the ground. With a wail, she smacked against the hard dry earth. Patrick was shouting behind her. She realized she'd exceeded his patience. Deborah thrust her hands down to whatever was holding her feet.

It was a rope. And at the other end loomed Patrick O'Connor. All the civilized wise-cracking was gone.

"Do you have any idea how much I *didn't* want to do that? I don't know what I'm going to do with . . ." Patrick was closing the distance between them.

With a yelp she pulled her foot from her boot and scrambled upright. She lunged for the fence gate, calling for help.

"God damn it, woman, stop!" came Patrick's voice just behind her shoulder.

"Help! Is there anyone . . . ?" Her plea was cut short as Patrick all but tackled her from behind. He locked his hands across her chest, pinning her arms and trapping her against his frame.

"Hell fire, God-damned woman, hold still."

"Help in there! I will not hold still you deplorable . . ."

"Oh Lord, what are you going to call me now? You've tried me beyond . . . umph . . . my considerable patience, Deborah . . . ouch!" He struggled to contain her flailing.

"Get away from me!" Deborah fought his grasp even though she was soundly overpowered. With a sinking ache she realized no one was coming from the meager little homestead. She put her head down and fought harder. "What is it you want from me? Just go ahead and shoot me. You were ready to earlier, what's stopping you now?"

"Blasted woman, why on earth would I shoot you? Do you think I'm . . . umph . . . itching to be a widower on my wedding day? You're going to hurt yourself. For God's sake, *stop it.*"

With the last words he let her loose and began to pace the ground in front of the fence. He seemed to realize, as did she, that there was nowhere for her to run. The wide open space and the accuracy of his roping skills trapped her neatly.

"Are you God-damned blasted well finished?" he bellowed, not even looking at her. "Because I am God-damned blasted well tired of doing this!"

"No!" Deborah shouted back, her own anger getting the best of her. "How on earth could you *expect* me to be finished? How on earth could you expect *any* woman to do this?"

He spun and glared at her, formulating an answer. Instead, he turned, let out a frustrated groan, and walked back slowly to the place where her boot was. He returned, snapping the rope into a coil as he went.

He placed the boot at her feet. "It's ripped, but it'll have to do. It's too dangerous to walk around here without shoes on. I've got to go figure out what the devil I'm going to do about your little bit of handiwork back there." He walked away, grumbling.

Deborah stared at the vacuum of land, the sheer absence of any help to be found, and felt tears steal down her cheeks. She flung herself on the hut's log block of a step, thrusting the laces through their hooks as the tears overtook her. She looked up once, only to see him staring at her from the distance of the wagon. She met his eyes. He looked disconcerted. Angry at himself and her. For a fraction of a moment there was something faintly like remorse. Then he shook his head and turned his attention to the destroyed wheel.

This was absolutely, positively acres beyond what he had in mind.

Patrick stared at the splintered wheel. How could he have misjudged this so? Patrick O'Connor was an uncanny judge of character. He was one of the best exporters on the Island because he was the sharpest negotiator on the Island.

And he'd been wildly, astoundingly wrong about her.

When he'd heard her story on a trip to Austin last fall, the idea to bring her here burst into his head. She was a young woman, making her way in life without family. Suddenly, she was forced to have a past mistake plastered across Austin's newspapers, purely because of her close association with a powerful political family. Austin society wasn't forgiving to unwed mothers, and she had no pedigree with which to leverage the mercy of the gossips. When he'd caught a glimpse of her that fall, weary and beaten down by the scandal, something tugged at him. Patrick O'Connor understood lethal mistakes. She seemed to him an odd combination of wounded prey and a phoenix yet to rise from the ashes.

Still, there was nothing heroic about the scheme he'd concocted to bring her to Galveston. Why not just propose the arrangement to her outright? In his more egotistical moments, he told himself the deception was because he didn't want a woman who would willingly consent to such a marriage. Cooperation born of sheer desperation. When he was honest with himself, however, he knew the abduction was really a way to ensure his wife would welcome the emotional and physical distance he'd keep between them.

The horse's snort fought for his attention, and he began the arduous task of freeing the horse from the surrey's rigging. The wagon wasn't going anywhere soon, thanks to the hurricane of a bride he'd just married. With each slap of the leather his frustration rose until he was whipping the straps around, rushing through the process as he berated himself.

He undid the last buckle and let the rigging drop from the horse. "You're off, Poker my boy," he grunted, thinking the animal was the only one who'd come out the better for the day's escapade. He swung the reins over Poker's head and looped them around his hand as he led the beast over to the fence.

He heard it as he got nearer the shed. The small, sad sound of Deborah's crying. Seeing the fight she'd shown, it made it infinitely worse to hear her giving up. Even if just for the moment. He slipped for a minute and allowed himself the mistake of considering all he'd just done to her.

Truly, lad, came his ghost of a wife's voice inside his head, *did it not occur to ye how cruel a thing it is you've done? Did I teach ye nothin' of love and marriage?*

Oh, Moira, his heart groaned in reply, *too much.*

He snapped the rein again, pushing the thoughts away. This was supposed to be a scientific, precise operation. Get a wife, period. It made his chest burn to think it was exploding into something else. *Don't let it,* he told himself. *Get a hold of yourself, Trick my boy. Keep on the goal here.* He had almost convinced himself, and was walking past her, when she spoke.

"Why?" It was more a wail than a question. A sharp, painful wail that cut into him far too much for his liking.

He stopped tying up the horse but made sure he did not look at her.

"I have my reasons."

A thread of strength came back into her voice. "What reason could you possibly have to do this?"

"Plenty." He tied off the reins tighter than necessary. He'd already decided it was better she didn't know. Yet. The less she knew, the better. And damn it, these days Trick O'Connor didn't explain anything to anyone.

Much less a wife.

She fiddled with her boots in silence.

"Are you going to shoot me?" she asked suddenly. It wasn't a desperate plea, it was a sensible, courageous attempt to prepare for her own death. That bothered him immensely.

"I have no intention of shooting you."

She stood up. "You married me at gunpoint and you have no intention of shooting me? Forgive me if I don't believe you."

Patrick's agitation grew again. "I did *not* marry you at gunpoint."

She pushed the hair back out of her eyes. "You held a gun to me back there!"

"I did no such thing!" He pushed his hat up off his forehead.

"How can you stand there and deny it?"

"This!" Patrick pulled a short length of copper piping from his pocket and tossed it at her feet. "I would never turn a gun on an unarmed woman. Only make her think I did."

It should have felt good to remember the one part of his plan where she *did* act as he anticipated.

It didn't. Not at all.

She stared at him, wide eyed with betrayal. "You vile animal!" She picked up the pipe and threw it at him, not caring that he dodged it easily. "God damn you, Patrick O'Connor! Damn all of it! All of it!"

He'd reduced her to cursing. The words stung in his ears despite every effort to remind himself that he had what he needed and that's all that mattered. "Mrs. O'Connor, watch your language," he said, to prove to himself that he could. He walked toward the surrey so he wouldn't have to look at her.

"I hate you!" she yelled.

"Fine!"

An hour's worth of attempts could not render the wagon operative. The parasol had snapped through too many spokes to allow the wheel to hold any weight. With dusk coming soon, there wasn't any point in trying again. With a groan of frustration, Patrick hurled the wheel across the yard to watch it splinter into pieces on impact. They'd have to ride. Together. She'd be right up there next to him. Close to him. Her soft shoulders right there in front of him.

He'd probably have to hold her to keep her on the damn horse. *Oh, hell.*

He found Deborah sitting on a rickety stool inside the house, braiding thin strips of what he guessed was her petticoat hem into a lace to hold the torn boot together. Her best dress—the one she'd donned at his request—fit her pleasingly but was now grimy and torn in a few places. She had—what had his mother always called it?—a "quiet beauty" about her. He always found that phrase trite before, yet it truly applied to this woman. No airs. No rehearsed charms. Just the unadorned grace and strength of a woman who'd been to hell and back again. Her face was strong and defiant behind the dusty smudges.

"Well, Mrs. O'Connor, you've blasted the surrey wheel to kindling. We'll have to ride all the way to Galveston on horseback."

Her eyes blazed up over the spectacles. "Surely you don't expect me to get up on that horse with you?"

For the first time he noticed their pale shade of lavender. He didn't realize eyes came in that color.

"I do. And you will."

"Or what? You'll *pipe* me?" She tied off the lace knot with a snap.

Patrick had to admire the retort, exasperating as it was. "You'll get the *potatoes* up on that horse if I have to tie you up to do it." He stabbed a finger at her for emphasis. He darkened the tone of his voice, making sure to hide any hint of amusement. "And you already appreciate my roping skills."

"I don't and you won't."

"Wouldn't I?" He crossed his arms over his chest.

"A man who paid good money to keep people from knowing how 'uncooperative' I was can hardly ride into town with his wife in chains, can he?" She crossed her own arms, declaring the value of her point.

Damnation.

"*Ropes,* my lady. And it's a long way to Galveston. I'd only have to untie you just before we hit town. That would make for a long, uncomfortable ride until then." He put his hat back on. "The way I figure it, you can either ride upright like a lady or over Poker's rump like a saddlebag." It was an idle threat, and he knew it the moment he made it. To cover, he added, "And I've the opinion that you're far too pretty to be a saddlebag."

"You are a Visigoth, Mr. O'Connor."

"My, now that's one I don't believe I've heard before." It would be a long ride. She'd be up there next to him for hours. Her neck just in front of him. There was this spot on her neck, a certain curve . . .

He pushed open the door. "You can tell me what it means while we ride. Come on."

"It means," said Deborah as she went through the doorway, "exactly what you think it means."

"I wouldn't count on it, Mrs. O'Connor. I've quite a vivid imagination."

"In that case whatever is the worst you can come up with should suffice."

⊰ Chapter Three ⊱

It couldn't get worse.

Deborah considered her present circumstances. They were absurd to the point of epic. The stuff of dime-store novels. And the farthest cry imaginable from the new life she had expected to launch when she got off the train.

They'd been riding for several hours. Patrick had gotten off twice to rest the horse, but had allowed her to ride the entire time. Now, though, they must be nearing Galveston, for the landscape began to take on coastal characteristics. The breeze picked up, the greenery increased, and the first hints of sea spiced the air.

As Patrick picked up the horse's pace, she tried to twist around to gain her bearings. It was a mistake, for the shift of her weight sent her off balance yet again.

"I keep telling you," he said as his strong grip pulled her back into place easily, "With no saddle you've got to lean your weight against me to stay up." His hand slid back around her waist. She was keenly aware of its warm pressure against her stomach. "I don't want you falling off this horse and getting hurt." When she registered surprise at this display of concern, he added quickly, "Or ruining your dress further. I take a particular interest in my wife's appearance." Patrick brushed some dirt off her shoulder for emphasis. Something happened when he touched her that way. Just as it had when he put on her glasses. Something that made no sense given their situation, but pulled at her all the same.

Now wait just a moment. That's pure nonsense. Give a thought to where you are right now, what he's done, and see how charming you find that!

Her indignation rose with the thought. "How do you expect me to quietly play the bride when you arrive at your home, Mr. O'Connor?" It was a taunt rather than a question.

"Don't call me Mr. O'Connor."

"Very well, then, Patrick. What makes you think I'll cooperate without the benefit of guns and ropes?" She tried to catch his reaction in her side vision, but couldn't. She didn't want to twist around again and risk falling into him.

He waited a long moment before answering. She realized the sensation she felt on the back of her neck was his breath. "You will."

Deborah straightened, startled by the recognition of their proximity. "You seem rather sure of yourself for a man undermined by a well-placed parasol." Deborah knew by the way his body shifted that she had hit the mark.

"I am," he murmured.

In another twenty minutes Galveston Bay came into view. Deborah began fidgeting uneasily, growing nervous of whatever awaited her once they reached Patrick's home.

He must have sensed it, for Patrick shifted his own weight and cleared his throat in the same way he had just before his speech in the hotel. Deborah held her breath. It surely meant something was on its way.

"Mrs. O'C—Deborah, you strike me as a mighty smart lady. I've some introductions to make this evening, so I believe now's a good time to help you recall some important facts. We're married. Which means, I'm sure you understand, that you are now my wife. Now, Texas law affords you precious few legal rights as a wife. Crude as it sounds, you are essentially my property. Your testimony is only viable in a court if I give you permission to speak—which I won't. There are no respectable men in Galveston who'd aid you behind my back if you chose to attempt a legal end to our little arrangement. It'd be prudent to remember I have the legal right to treat you however I see fit.

"Now in one respect, you're right; I can't force you in any visible way to cooperate once we're in town. But I'm guessing you've intelligence in you, and I respect that. So I'll just let the facts speak for themselves."

Deborah fought the lump in her throat. She tried to edge her body away from his on the horse. Instead, she felt his hand wrap around her to hold her firmly in place. His face was right behind her ear. "Crossing me is a highly regrettable experience."

At that moment, Deborah had no doubt that it was.

As they neared the town, Patrick stopped the horse beside a small well. He slid down off the horse. It was the first time in a long while that they had the opportunity to come face to face. He stared up at her. The gleam in his coffee eyes held a double edge of amusement and control.

Going over to the well, he pulled a handkerchief from his pocket, wet it, and offered it to her. "I imagine you'd welcome the chance to wash up. It's not much, but do the best you can now. There won't be another chance until we get to the house."

Remembering what had happened the last time he'd asked her to clean up, she took the cloth and did what washing could be done under the circumstances. He touched her hand when she handed it back to him. "That ring looks mighty nice on your hand," he said. "I'll be sure to have it sized to fit those little fingers right away."

He dipped the cloth again, wiping his own face. He pulled his large hands through the uncooperative tangle of his wavy hair. It struck her that his hair was the same warm brown as his eyes. How could such warm features host such a cold and calculating nature? The unpredictability of the contrast disturbed her.

Patrick replaced his hat, adjusted his tie, and proceeded to walk the horse toward a ferry crossing the bay. It was well past dark, and the streets were not particularly full. Swaying ships' masts stuck out from behind the outlines of buildings. The array of small coastal sounds—so different from Austin's nights— fluttered from the outskirts of her vision. Birds, shouts, clanging and banging things, the soft clap of evening waves slapping against docks and boats. The ferry across to Galveston Island contained only one other passenger who said nothing to her and Patrick as they crossed. It was quiet and noisy at the same time. Much like this man who had confiscated her life.

Once on the Island, more people appeared, several of whom seemed to know him. She was alone in his world. With a wash of resignation Deborah realized Patrick's "facts" rang true in her ears. Until she could find a way to get word back to Austin, there was precious little she could do except stay alert. The gold band on her finger had the power of a stockade.

And so it was with an amazing absence of feeling that she smiled and nodded each time Patrick introduced her to a passerby in town.

When they turned a particular corner, Deborah noticed a change in Patrick. The timbre of his steps changed, and a stronger set came over his shoulders. He glanced around more frequently, but most obviously at the buildings at the block's far end. His hand fiddled with the reins. Deborah recognized the emotion: anticipation. It was not the same thing as nervousness or anxiety—there was a strange, welcome tint to his energy. Patrick O'Connor was looking forward to something. A jolt spread through her stomach as she considered the possibility he was looking

forward to getting her alone. To expand his definition of "wife." She remembered the warmth of his
hand on her waist.

Her more logical side dismissed the thought—
they'd been alone and out of public view for hours in
the surrey. Surely if he had anything in mind it would
have happened out there. No, this anticipation was
directed at whatever was waiting at the end of the
block. And he was trying hard to hide it from her.

His house was four houses from the end. A stately,
upright home, with grand, double-level verandas
bursting with elegant wood trim. Long windows
poured light out onto the street from between sets of
shutters. A wrought-iron fence opened into a gate in
front of wide stairs. At the top of the stairs stood a
high green door, running the full length of the first
story so that its top molding touched the second-
story veranda. It was all buoyant, vertical lines,
standing out in contrast to the random curves of the
trees in the yard. Patrick stopped at the gate. "Your
new home, Mrs. O'Connor."

He gestured behind him, displaying the house. It
was a lovely house, to be sure, but he couldn't expect
her to be pleased by the architecture of her new confinement.

Evidently, he did. He paused and raised an eyebrow, waiting for her to say something akin to "It's
lovely." Deborah refused to compliment her well-
appointed prison.

She watched his brow fall. The man's eyes had a
way of pulling your glance to him whether you

wished it or not. A faint smile crept to his lips as his eyes narrowed. Something was coming.

He spoke in a declaring, almost public tone. As if giving a speech. "Right here is where it gets the most interesting of all. I have given this considerable thought. . . ." He reached up and plucked Deborah from the horse. Suspended mid-air by his enormous hands, she again realized how physically powerful he was. He took his time bringing her down off the horse, slowly arcing her body away from the beast until he lowered her close—*very* close in front of him. ". . . And I must admit I've rather looked forward to this part." With one hand still around her waist, he removed his hat. He fixed his arm around her shoulder. *Oh, Lord.* With a gulp she realized his intent. "So given the circumstances I can't take any reluctance you might have into consideration when I . . ." Patrick tightened the hold on her and brought his head down.

He kissed her.

In actuality, kissing was an overstatement of his actions, for he had simply locked his body around hers and planted his mouth atop hers. And locked it was. The man was a human fortress. Solid and enormous.

It was a strange kiss. Understated for a man of his extreme nature. Carefully controlled. Under other circumstances Deborah might have considered it respectful. Protective. But this kiss had the odd air of a *posture.* Patrick O'Connor was kissing her to be *seen* kissing her.

At least it started out that way. Then something

happened. His sudden touch pulled her sensibilities off balance and sent the ground spinning under her feet. Shock. It must have been the shock of it, of being kissed. But she felt a reaction in him as well. For one split second, she felt him soften his grip and inhale. As if giving in.

Suddenly light flooded in on them. And the something she'd felt—or thought she'd felt—was gone. Surely it was only shock.

Patrick angled his face up to see the house's curtains part. The wedge of light revealed a silhouetted profile.

"Well, now," said Patrick, his voice showing only a hint of whatever had just happened. He pulled away slightly, but kept a tight hold on her. "I imagine that ought to suffice."

Suffice? Deborah stared at him, baffled, groping for a reaction. The man had just kissed her. It should have been awful, frightening given the day's events, but it wasn't. He had kissed her carefully, the way he wiped her cheek or handed her the boot or cleaned her glasses. The carefulness of it made her want to blink and shake her head. They looked at each other for a long, vacant second. "Mr. O'Connor, you had—"

"Well, no, now that I think of it, that just won't do at all." Before she had a chance to object, Patrick's hand stole back around her shoulders while the other arm pulled her waist to him. In a split second he had swept her into an embrace. No hard lock of arms, but the pulsing, moving contact of an embrace. Softer and yet still much tighter than the first.

He stared at her, bending her back off her balance. My Lord, those eyes were practically liquid. He took a deep breath, as if giving himself one last chance to reconsider. And then he kissed her. A *real* kiss. Impassioned. Extreme. There was nothing careful about it. The distinction shot through Deborah like a thunderbolt.

One hand spread across her back and shoulders, while the other wandered up her back to let his fingers play in the nape of her neck. The sensation rippled down, curling her spine and stealing her breath. She couldn't stop it. No amount of impropriety stifled the spark that leapt up in her chest as his mouth slid across hers. It was a broad, warm mouth. With a low sound, he deepened his kiss, the friction of his tongue nearly stopping her pulse. Unfathomable. A lock of his hair fell to graze her temple. This reckless kiss made Deborah want to explode from shock and panic and a chemistry that surely couldn't exist until . . .

Patrick pulled his head away, wide-eyed, shocked as she.

"I . . ." Deborah fought for composure that simply wouldn't come.

He had dropped his hat. He just stood there, staring at her. Stunned.

"You . . ." Both of them were at a complete loss.

"Mr. O'Connor, sir?" A female voice called from the now-opened front door. "Might that really be you coming home at this hour?" The thick brogue held a schoolteacher's disdain.

"Indeed," he almost stammered, still staring at

Deborah like she had just kissed him instead of the other way around. "It is indeed, Mrs. Doyle."

"Dear God, for the life of me we'd begun to think somethin'd happened to you!" She came down the steps, wiping her hands on her apron. Her stereotypical appearance—practically textbook in its recognizability—labeled her as the family housekeeper. "Oh my goodness, there she is. There she is. Saints! She's standing right in front o' me." Deborah could honestly not tell whether the woman was glad or disappointed to see her. Friend or foe? Deborah was unsure. What was obvious was her doubt—or perhaps it was more accurate to say disbelief—of Patrick's married status.

"Mrs. Doyle, may I present my wife, Deborah. Dear," said Patrick, regaining his composure and slipping his arm around her waist, "may I present my—*our* housekeeper, Mrs. Doyle."

Deborah's throat was too tight to speak. *What in heaven's name had just happened?* She managed a nod.

"Well for goodness sakes, look at the two of you. You look as if the devil's been at ya. Had a bit of trouble on the journey, did you?"

Patrick cut in efficiently. "Broken surrey wheel. It's been one blasted surprise after another since the train."

Well, now, that's certainly the truth, thought Deborah. She caught Patrick's gaze looking over Mrs. Doyle's shoulder into the house.

"Asleep, sir." Mrs. Doyle replied to an unasked question.

"No I'm not!" came a small voice from inside. The sound of the voice brought an astounding, instantaneous change over Patrick's features. He broke into a brilliant smile, one that infused Patrick's face with such light and warmth that Deborah could hardly believe it was the same man.

A small white blur barreled down the steps to collide with Patrick in a flurry of arms and legs. "Pa! I've been waiting for you all day till I thought I'd die from it!"

Pa.

Deborah watched his shoulders sink into a heartfelt embrace of the child, watched the impulsive dip of Patrick's head to bury itself in the small outstretched arms. The power of the moment, the sheer undiluted affection it displayed, caught her up short. As if their kiss had not thrown her sufficiently into confusion. How could this man have been the same one who abducted her into marriage?

Up from the bundle of bedclothes popped a miniature pair of Patrick's penetrating eyes. They were coffee-colored and sparkling like his father's, and just as wide with disbelief. A circle of dark hair tumbled across the boy's head. He drew one sleeve across his eyes and blinked.

"Damn!" the boy cursed. With alarming ease.

Patrick's face registered an amused guilt while Deborah's eyebrows shot miles above her spectacles.

"Yes, well, we'll have to work on that, won't we?" remarked Patrick. Heavens, even the man's voice had changed, warmed with affection.

Deborah stared at the boy. He must have been

about five. She could see the resemblance to Patrick, but the clear castings of another, darker parent—his mother, she guessed—played across his face. The eyes were all his father's. They fixed on her, with the same potency as his father's.

"She's real," the boy gasped. The pure, unadulterated amazement of his voice and eyes held Deborah's heartbeat. "Pa, you gotta tell me. She's real?"

Patrick nodded. As if her body had lost a will of its own, Deborah felt her head dip and rise as well.

"Damn, Pa, but she's pretty. Didn't tell me that part."

Deborah shut her eyes for a moment, confounded.

"Duncan, you'd better clean up your language a bit. I don't think she takes kindly to such talk."

"Awright. Sorry, ma'am." He was still staring at her. "You're real," he repeated, poking an exploratory little finger at her sleeve. "M'gosh, Pa, you did it. Before tomorrow n'everyfing." The boy finally pulled his gaze away from Deborah to stare at Patrick. "Pa . . ." the single syllable seeped with *I love you you're amazing you are the absolute center of my universe my hero*. He pulled his father's head closer. "Mrs. Doyle was mad you were kissing her!" he whispered.

Patrick nuzzled up to the boy. "Mrs. Doyle's nosy." The conspiracy sent the boy into a torrent of giggles.

Deborah watched Patrick pull himself back into control as he lowered the boy to the ground. "In with you, Dunc. It's late." He swatted the boy's backside gently and the flurry of white tumbled back up the stairs. Duncan stopped at Mrs. Doyle, chin up in the king-sized defiance of a child.

"She's *here*, Mrs. Doyle. Told 'ya."

Mrs. Doyle arched an eyebrow in a *we'll see about that* expression before walking the boy upstairs.

Patrick stood still for a moment, then began dealing with the horse. Deborah stared at him, grasping to put all these new pieces together. Finally, she started with a simple question. " 'Before tomorrow and everything'?"

Patrick looked up calmly. "Duncan's six tomorrow."

Deborah's mouth fell open. In absolute shock she said slowly, "Am I a *birthday present?*"

"No," replied Patrick. "That's in the stables getting groomed for tomorrow. Apple may be a fun pony, but she's nowhere near as pretty." He smiled at her. He'd grinned before, smirked even, but never the kind of smile he gave her now. It felt like being handed a lit stick of dynamite. "You're more of a promise."

"A what?"

"I told you I'm a man of my word. I promised Duncan he'd have a mum by the time he was six. A mite under the wire, but we made it."

"So you went out and *stole* one?"

Patrick settled his hat back on his head. "That's a harsh word, Deborah. I'll admit to unconventional methods, but I'm still mighty pleased with the outcome."

"You can't be serious! This is ludicrous!"

Patrick pulled a bag down from the horse. "You do have such a fine vocabulary."

Deborah walked up to him. "You expect me to walk up those stairs and play house so that your son doesn't have a disappointing birthday?"

"Yes, as a matter of fact, I do." He tied the horse up. Turning to her, he cocked out his elbow to escort her.

"You're mad."

"That's a disappointing one. I much prefer 'extreme'."

She wouldn't budge.

Deborah watched an idea flash across his face. He removed his hat again. "Of course, how forgetful of me. Try not to scream too loudly and wake Mother up, will you?" With that he ducked down and scooped Deborah up in a steel grip and started up the stairs. She opened her mouth to scream but he pulled her head to his and planted his mouth on top of hers to stifle it. Without a word to anyone—neither the two servants gaping in the hall nor the agitated Mrs. Doyle nor Duncan pulling at his pant leg—he marched through the doors and up the stairs. Mouth still muffling her cries, Patrick bumped open a door, kicked it closed behind them, and tossed Deborah down on a bed. In seconds he pinned her arms above her head and angled his knee across her legs, trapping her.

He pulled his mouth back only an inch or so, boring into her eyes, panting from what Deborah hoped was only the exertion. All the warmth was gone.

"I've been nice, but I don't have to be. If you 'play house' tomorrow, you might keep alive the chance that you can weasel out of this someday. Then again, you intrigue me. I could easily make this marriage good and legal right here and now. I respect intelligence, but I also enjoy a feisty woman."

"You wouldn't!"

"I'd like to think I wouldn't, Deborah, but you've a mighty fine talent for exceeding my patience."

Deborah struggled against him. Uselessly. He was huge. She shut her eyes in resignation as a tear escaped down the side of her face. She gave just the hint of a nod.

"Excellent."

Deborah kept her eyes shut. After an excruciating pause, she suddenly felt Patrick leave a gentle kiss where the tear had trailed. She whipped her head away from him.

He pushed himself up off the bed, freeing her hands and legs. Deborah kept her eyes shut and pulled her fists in to cover her face. She curled over to one side, away from the sound of Patrick's footsteps.

"I'll have your things and some food brought up in half an hour. I'll make sure you're left alone until then." She heard his hand on the door latch. "Good night, Deborah O'Connor. And thank you."

Thank you?! Thank you?! Deborah's anger flared at the cavalier remark. With a predatory growl she grabbed the pillow next to her and flung it in the direction of the shutting door.

❧ Chapter Four ❧

"Pa?"

"Yes?" Patrick tugged the coverlet farther up until it reached his chin. Duncan's jiggling feet sent small ripples across the bottom of the linens.

"Were you ever five, Pa?"

The question's serious tone made Patrick grin. "I was. A mighty long time ago." He had to admit, though, that lately he felt older than his thirty-one years.

Duncan's eyebrows bent in a five-year-old's quiet, pronounced consideration of the facts. Again he looked up. "Pa?"

"Yes?" Patrick had to fight the temptation to sound weary of the questioning. Duncan was too riled up to be obediently tucked into bed tonight. The inquisition was merely a stalling tactic. What child could sleep on the eve of his birthday with a magic lady just doors away? If Duncan avoided sleep tonight, it was Patrick's own doing.

"Were you five for a hundred years 'fore you got t'be six?"

Patrick's hands swept through the dark locks of his son's hair. "A hundred and ten."

Content to know his father understood his impatience, Duncan settled down farther into the linens. The jiggling limited itself to only one foot, then faded off all together. Patrick watched his son's eyes take on the soft, faraway look of near sleep. There was a constant, daily magic about this moment that made him reluctant to ever relinquish the task of tucking Duncan in to anyone else.

"Pa?" It was more quiet this time, almost a sigh.

"Yes, Dunc?"

"Is she real? Really?"

For the look in Duncan's eyes he would have kidnapped a hundred razor-tongued parasol-poking ladies. "Really."

"Damn."

His son's vocabulary would have been troubling had it not echoed his own thoughts precisely.

Once downstairs, Patrick pushed open the back pantry door with a sigh. He reached up to a wooden spool of rope that was suspended across the top shelves by a length of pipe. *Pipe.* He thought about the short length of pipe still in his pocket, the one he had used on Deborah. It had been a cruel trick to poke it in her back. Patrick supposed, with a chuckle, that he deserved having his shoes ruined for that one. He hadn't ever considered using a gun, but he hadn't ever considered she'd put up such a fight.

She'd surprised him. Oh, Lord, had she surprised him. He reached up and spun the spool, sending the

thin rope cascading down. He calculated a suitable
length of rope and cut it with a pearl-handled knife
fished from his pocket. She was here. He'd done that
much. He coiled the rope into a handful of loops and
set off for the front parlor. Mrs. Doyle was just extin-
guishing the kitchen lamp when he passed.

"Everything ready for tomorrow, Mrs. Doyle?"

" 'Tis, sir. Quite." Her manner was curt.

"Good night then, Mrs. Doyle."

"Good night to you, sir." She stared at the rope in
his hands. Her expression revealed she knew tonight's rope was longer than usual.

What of it? This could be a hundred-knot-night for
any number of reasons. He couldn't leave it be. Not
when she was so delightfully irritated. "Oh, Mrs.
Doyle?"

"Sir?" Even she caught the mischief in his voice.

"Have breakfast brought up to me tomorrow. I'll
take it to the missus myself."

"Indeed, sir." She strung the word out, one eyebrow arched.

Satisfied at having ruffled her, he strolled out to the
front room and pulled the stopper from the brandy
decanter. Patrick poured an extra finger—in *celebration*, he declared, not anxiety. He'd done it. Pulled
off the impossible for Duncan's sake. So much de-
pended on him keeping this promise. So much more
than most people knew. And he'd kept it. *Well, almost*. The situation had some troublesome hitches,
some unexpected turns, but nothing Trick O'Connor
couldn't manage. Handily.

So why was he pouring a fourth finger? And why was tonight's rope so damned long?

Her position disturbed him. Sprawled across the bed, fully clothed, her limbs were folded at sharp angles that spoke of turmoil rather than rest. Her hands—small, lovely hands—held twisted, wrinkled sheets, as though she'd been gripping them tightly and only exhaustion had loosened her hold.

Pulling the door shut, he took the opportunity to look at her. Here was a chance to take in her features unobserved. Lord, but he had not remembered her looking this way. She seemed small and frail when he had seen her in Austin. The kind of woman he could—with some effort, granted—coerce into this odd scheme he'd concocted.

But he knew now, looking at her strong shoulders, the set of her jaw, that she wasn't any of those things. She wouldn't give in that way.

Did it occur to ye that ye ought not to be coercin' her at all? Well, yes, of course it did. It was a costly plan, to be sure. He was well aware of the consequences.

And how are those consequences lookin' to ye now?

Patrick stood for a moment, regarding Deborah and the strange collection of emotions she seemed to pull from him. He should never have threatened her like that, but he'd lost his control. She'd managed to unnerve him a dozen times since this afternoon. And when he kissed her . . . why the hell had he kissed her? Then kissed her a second time? What had she done to him? He wasn't used to it—things, especially women, weren't supposed to unnerve Trick O'Connor.

With a practiced quiet he pulled a chair from the corner and set it down in front of the doorway.

What have ye done?

The only thing that could be done.

Are ye truly sure? Patrick set the brandy down on the floor beside him and let the rope uncoil around his ankles.

Yes I'm sure, he defended. His fingers began to work the rope, twisting and looping the line until a first knot appeared. This knot-tying had become a nightly ritual, a meditation of sorts. It relaxed him, took him back to the sailing days of his youth. Yes, tonight it might take a hundred knots.

He'd made an outlandish promise, one that required a drastic fulfillment. He didn't want a woman from the Island. A clean transaction—no history, no emotion, no relatives, nothing to cloud things up. Patrick drained the snifter in a single gulp.

Clean? Or unfair? Have ye really given Duncan anything but a prank? A second knot found its way onto the rope.

They'll be fine. If she gave up her son so many years ago, then maybe there's a poetic justice in giving her one back. They'll be good for each other. He snapped off a third and fourth knot. He could already see it in the way Duncan looked at her. Fifth knot. It had been a goddamned tiring day. Sixth.

If ye believe that, Trick, you're not the man I married.

Go away, he told Moira's voice. He wasn't hearing voices, not of Moira's, nor God, nor wee fairy fold. He was just hearing the brandy after a long day. But he'd done it. Seventh. It was worth anything to keep that promise. Eighth. And he'd kept it. He'd kept Duncan believing in him and that was all that mattered. Ninth. Tenth . . .

Patrick opened his eyes to find Deborah sitting on the edge of the bed staring at him. He inhaled slowly, drawing his gaze up to meet her eyes. "Well, now," he said softly. How had he fallen asleep? *God bloody damn.*

"Why?" The woman knew how to be direct.

He knew but asked anyway. "Why what?"

"Why?" she repeated, grinding it out.

How far would she push? He couldn't tell just yet. "You already know."

"I'm guessing I don't even know the half of it. And you're going to tell me right here, right now."

Patrick considered the advantages. To have her know more might gain her further cooperation. Duncan obviously had an effect on her—the story might be useful in keeping her here. Not knowing, however, kept her edgy and unsure; that had its usefulness, too. *Let her know only as much as she needs to get her guard down.* He'd need every advantage her cooperation could give him.

"Why?" She gave the word a sharp, insistent edge.

"Because I had to." That much was true.

"I find that difficult to believe."

Patrick pressed his hands to his forehead. "Well, if it helps matters, I find it tough to latch onto myself. I'd best start at the beginning if you're going to understand this at all." Her shoulders softened a fraction of an inch. "Duncan's mother took ill when he was just turning four. A fever I brought back from one of my exporting trips. She was always afraid of me catching something. It seemed unfair that she . . . well . . . She just kept getting sicker, and Duncan kept getting more scared. It got worse. She was ebbing away right in front of me. It got to where I couldn't hide it any longer, and Duncan saw my fear and panicked. He was beside himself, and scared to lose his Ma. There was no way to make him feel better. I'd already called in the best doctor I could find, and they were telling me there wasn't much hope. I couldn't bear to watch him like that when I was already so . . . So I did the only damn thing I thought would help him. I promised him his Ma would get better."

Patrick looked up at Deborah, judging her expression. He could see in her eyes that she knew the folly of such a promise just as he did. But there was a hint of understanding just behind the scowl.

"I know it was a senseless thing to do but I didn't see how anything else would calm him down. I didn't want Moira to see him that way. If he had hope, then she would." The scene washed up over Patrick's memory the way it always did, complete with the little details that made his heart ache: the way Duncan's tiny fingers dug into his arms, the way he'd start to choke when he couldn't stop crying, the way he rocked back and forth when he felt the coldness of his mother's weak hand. "I was sorry the minute I'd made it. I couldn't take it back, not with the way he looked at me when I said it." Patrick stopped. He wanted more control before he went further.

"She died," offered Deborah. There was a catch to her voice.

Patrick nodded. The room was silent for a moment. "It was a nasty, lingering way to go. She deserved better." He paused. "Dunc deserved better than to watch his mother melt away in front of his eyes. I expected him to get angry, but instead he just shut down in a way. We both shut down." Patrick took in a breath. He was saying more than he planned. Straightening up, he put a more factual tone into his voice. "So things were rather solemn for about a year until Duncan's fifth birthday. We'd planned a big dinner to try and brighten things up and all."

Patrick picked up the rope and began to tie more knots into it. "But when the day came, I just couldn't stand the thought of celebrating without Moira. So I went out like a fool and got falling down drunk. I missed the dinner, I missed Duncan's birthday, and he tore into me something fierce when I finally did creep back home. He told me it was all my fault. That I'd made his mother sick, that I'd broken every promise I'd ever made to him since she took ill. And, damn it, he was right."

He looked up, expecting Deborah to chide him for swearing again. She didn't.

"I was still half sauced and angry at myself when I did it. I promised him he'd have a new mother by his sixth birthday and I swore on Moira's memory that I'd never break a promise to him ever again." He coiled the rope tightly around his hand. He didn't want to talk about it anymore. It was harder than he guessed it would be to tell the story. With a shock he realized that he'd never actually told it to anyone before. It felt odd to hear it spoken aloud.

Deborah's hard, clear gaze held his eyes. She looked different without the spectacles on. Inside the lavender of her eyes was a remarkable silver tint that was lost behind the lenses. A simple soft curve to her features that had been hidden before. "That was an impossible promise to make to a boy."

Patrick drew his ankle up across his knee. "No, it wasn't. You're here."

"You promised Duncan a mother. All he has right now is a *prank*."

Her use of Moira's word sparked his anger. "What Duncan *has*," he shot back, "is enough of a start. A tiny piece of magic to think the world might not be such a nasty place and that people can keep their promises." He put his leg back down and leaned into her. "And I'll make damn sure he gets to hold on to it."

"You're feeding him lies. I won't be part of this a moment longer."

She stood up and made straight for the door, ignoring the fact that he was blocking it. Patrick stood up, knocking the chair over, and grabbed her.

The last pin in her hair fell out as she fought toward the door, sending her hair cascading down her back. It wasn't a particularly stunning color—not something you'd notice from across a room—but it had a gentle wave to it, like a wheat field. He held her fast, cursing himself for what the defiance in those lavender eyes could do to him. For the second time today she'd pushed him beyond his boiling point. "You've already seen the lengths I'll go to keep this promise," he warned.

He felt her wedding ring under his grip. *Too far, Trick, too far.* He stared at her eyes for a moment and allowed himself to remember what it had been like to kiss her in the middle of Tremont Street. To recognize the split second where her body had responded despite her outrage.

He regained his control and exhaled. "I will not let you leave." She was pulling against his grip, jutting her chin out at him. He pulled her in tighter, so that their faces nearly touched. It had been so very long since anyone had surprised him the way she did. Unnerved him so repeatedly. It appealed to him in a way that seemed rather unwise.

She narrowed her eyes at him. "You would lie so much to your son?"

With ease he transferred both her wrists into one hand, leaving his other one free. With one finger he pulled a lock of hair from her face. She sucked in her breath, just as she had done when he put her glasses back on out in the surrey. *Tenderness.* He guessed she hadn't seen much of it in her lifetime. He ran the

finger down her cheek. "I will make him the truth he
needs." Ignoring the impulse that it was going too
far, he held her head still while he planted a soft kiss
on her cheek. A tender, slow brush of lips to counter-
act the vice-grip he had on her wrists. He held his
face against hers as he whispered, "And *you* will,
too."

Deborah shot across the room the second he eased
up on her wrists. This man seemed to know just how
to unnerve her, how to elicit the strongest reaction
with the least amount of effort. She felt as if he knew
far too much about her, and she knew far too little
about him. What he wanted. How he planned to get
whatever it was he wanted. His face was telling and
yet unreadable at the same time. He just stared at
her, his shirt half undone and his sleeves cuffed up,
looking a bit wild and rather unpredictable. She
clung to the bedpost, wanting to keep an obstacle between them. Deborah's cheek still burned from the
path of his finger, her response a disconcerting mix of
anger and . . . no, it *couldn't* be anything else. She
fought to clear the lingering trace of his last soft kiss
from her mind.

Eyes still locked on her, he slowly approached.
"Turn around," he said, in a voice as smooth as silk.

Deborah's throat knotted up like that blasted rope
he had around his hand. *Oh, God. Oh, dear Almighty God.* She backed up against the bedpost.

"Turn around, Mrs. O'Connor. Please."

Please? That made it worse. How could he be so
civilized about it? She glanced around for anything

to defend herself, but nothing useful was within reach, not even a buttonhook.

"No." She wanted to shout it at him, but the word came out as a weak, thin whisper instead.

"You mind telling me how you're going to get out of that corset alone? You're trussed up like a turkey in that thing. I imagine you'll be blue by morning if you try to sleep in it."

What?

"I did not spend seven years as a married man without witnessing what it is you all go through to get that dam—*potatoes* of a contraption on. Now, I have no plans to send Mrs. Doyle or anyone else up here tonight so if you want to take a deep breath anytime in the near future, I suggest you let me help you out of that thing."

Deborah stared at him in utter disbelief. Was he going to—how did he put it—"make this marriage good and legal" or just unlace her corset? Or both?

A wicked look flashed across his eyes. She didn't like the way he seemed to know what she was thinking.

"Well, now, I admit that did cross my mind," he replied to her silence with such an uncanny accuracy that Deborah had to wonder if she'd been thinking aloud. "It does pose an attraction with all that wavy hair of yours down. You should wear it down again. It suits you." She watched his eyes wander over her hair. He paused before adding, "But my only intention at the moment is to get you unlaced, not undressed."

Deborah felt the heat rise through her cheeks. His

words were civilized enough, but his gaze continued to roam over her body as if she were standing in nothing but a fig leaf. No one had ever looked at her like that before. An unbidden, irrational ember ignited somewhere down in the pit of her stomach. He said the word "unlaced" with a particular emphasis, as if unlacing a corset was something he'd enjoyed. Something he'd done often in the past and was looking forward to again. She watched his fingers rub casually against the rope in his hands. She thought about the way he'd touched her cheek.

What's gotten into you? Stop such thinking. He's holding you prisoner, how could you let him get to you so? Bringing his eyes very slowly back up her body to her face, Patrick cocked one eyebrow and motioned with a spinning finger for her to turn around. A slight flush colored his cheeks. *Oh, dear.* Her anxiety rose, but Deborah didn't see how she had much choice.

Deborah shut her eyes, held her breath, and turned around. Her skin prickled. The ember in her stomach continued to glow despite every effort to squelch it.

Nothing happened.

She clenched her fists and waited, thinking he had changed his mind and was now shrugging off his shirt to take her like the visigoth he was. But there was no sound, only the brassy chime of a far-off ship's bell.

"I can't hardly unlace that thing if you don't take care of those buttons. I'm not going to ravage you."

Deborah's hands moved toward the top button.

"At least not tonight."

With a shiver she peeled the shirtwaist down off her torso. She thought she heard his exhale when she exposed the laces of her corset.

After a pause, his hands touched her back. His touch was light. She heard the *whip-whip* of the laces being pulled through the grommets and gave an involuntary sigh as the garment's grip came loose off her ribcage. She could feel his eyes on her shoulders, her arms, the back of her neck. As he got farther down the grommets, Deborah felt his breath on her neck and the unmistakable lingering in his fingers. Every once in a while the rhythm of his unlacing would slow down, then speed up again. As if he was trying to be casual about it but not succeeding.

It was such an intimate, *married* kind of exchange. As if he were brushing her hair or helping her with the clasp of a necklace. Or . . .

"There." His voice was soft and heavy, just over her shoulder. Miles from the threat he'd whispered in her ear just moments earlier. And there was something in it. Something that spoke of . . . well, more than unlacing a corset for comfort's sake.

Thinking he was expecting it, she gave out a quiet "Thank you," but didn't turn around.

Patrick lay one finger on the nape of her neck. One pinpoint of touch, intense and cautious. If the smile had been a lit stick of dynamite, this touch was the explosion. As she fought to control her breath, her hands grasping the bedpost, he slid his finger over one shoulder in a slow curve. A solitary finger that spoke of a hundred lush thoughts, just as it had done on her cheek. "My pleasure," he said, with a tone that dissolved her composure.

He let his finger start down the arc of her shoulder blade, then drew it away with a quick hiss of breath. Without another word, he left. Deborah held onto the bedpost until she heard his boots head off down the hall.

⇥ Chapter Five ⇤

"That's no way to look at your husband. Especially when he goes through the trouble of bringing you breakfast." Patrick was standing just inside the doorway, a silver tray in his hands. He was not yet dressed for the day, and his hair stood out at odd angles, unbrushed and disobedient. His tousled appearance and mischievous grin made him look exactly like Duncan.

Deborah pulled the sheets up farther, pressing her back against the pillow.

"Good morning . . ." he cued, in the same voice he'd used on the train platform.

She leveled her eyes at him. "This charade looks no better in the light of day, I assure you." *How could he just stand there, as if this were a perfectly natural circumstance? As if men abducted brides on a daily basis?*

Patrick brought the tray over and sat on the bed corner. "Thanks to the ingenuity of a certain . . . lady, we failed to arrive in time for dinner last night. I'd imagine you're rather hungry right about now."

It did smell delicious. Deborah's stomach gave a betraying growl.

"One stomach and one husband to one wife. You're outnumbered, Mrs. O'Connor," he remarked, staring at her belly under the covers. "Eat." He unfolded the napkin and handed it to her.

Did he have to keep calling her that? If he was intending to make her more aware of the situation, it was hardly necessary. She was acutely aware. The effect was rather unnerving. That's most certainly why he did it.

He sat there, quietly, watching her eat breakfast. Despite his large size, he had an extraordinary command of his body. He should have looked huge and lumbering on the lacy bedclothes, but his demeanor conveyed only confidence. How could he do the unbelievable things he did and still manage to look anything but . . . no, no . . . *no! He is not attractive. Captors are not attractive! Have you lost your senses?*

She forced her attentions to breakfast. Halfway into the egg, however, she couldn't keep silent any longer and asked the question that had been gnawing away at her for hours. "Just how do you intend to maintain this . . . this illusion today? It won't succeed."

Patrick sat back against the bedpost—the one she'd clung to just after he ran that single, warm finger down her shoulder when he'd unlaced her corset—and crossed his arms.

"It will," he said, all too softly.

"I have no intention of cooperating." Deborah

tried to stab her eggs with something she hoped looked like resolve.

"Oh, that's mighty clear. But, you see, intent isn't always what's necessary. You had no *intention* of marrying me, now, did you?"

Deborah put her fork down.

"But here you are, my bride. And the pride and joy of Duncan O'Connor, who is turning six today believing the world just might be a nice place to live. Intention's a funny thing. Can't always count on it to get you what you want."

"I *intend* to walk out that door and leave," she said slowly.

"No, you don't." His voice took on an edge. "If you intended that, you'd be long gone by now because you'd have already discovered I left your bedroom door unlocked after I left last night."

Deborah pulled a breath in through her clenched teeth. It was infuriating to be toyed with so.

"No, you're not going anywhere because you're a smart woman, and you've figured out that there isn't a place on this island where you can go. Safely, that is. And you've already figured out that you're safe with me. You're very valuable to me now that I've introduced you to young Duncan down there. He thinks we're in love, so as long as you keep up our little—what'd you call it?—*charade*, you can count on me treating you like a queen. If you clue him in to how you really came to be Mrs. Patrick O'Connor, then the magic will be gone and he'll be so mad at me it won't matter one hoot how I treat you."

The eggs in Deborah's mouth were taking on the consistency of shoe leather.

"Am I following your thinking, ma'am?"

A reply hardly seemed necessary.

"You know, I just knew a little gesture like bringing you breakfast would get our day off to a fine start. And it's a big day, mind you. I've had all your dresses hung up and aired out so they'd be ready to wear. Have you a watch?"

"Pardon me?" Did it really matter if a captive had any sense of punctuality?

"Do you have a watch?" he repeated.

"Yes," Deborah replied, letting her exasperation show.

"Good. It's half past nine now. You'd best get up and get washed and such. I'll be back in at quarter past ten with a dress. We eat at eleven o'clock. And Duncan is just clamoring to get another look at his new mother. It's high time you met the other Pat O'Connor as well. I think Mother will take to you just grand." Patrick eased up off the bed.

"You're insane," she said quietly.

"You've used that one twice already. No, just highly irregular and more than a little determined. By the way, your hair does look mighty fine in the morning light. I do find it appealing down around your face like that. You're a pleasing woman to look at, Deborah. Mind you be ready at quarter past," he called almost cheerfully as he strode toward the door. "I don't want to keep Duncan and Mother waiting."

She heard him whistling as he set off down the

hall. Letting out a groan of frustration, Deborah tore into a piece of toast and launched herself out of the bed to pace the room. *How can he do this? How can he think this is possible? Did the man have any capacity for reason? People just didn't do this sort of thing!*

As her hand wrapped around the bedpost, it came to her. All last night she couldn't shake the notion that Patrick was wrestling with something. She saw it again this morning. Her brain wove the pieces together. He didn't *want* to like her. He thought he'd kidnapped a damsel in distress and couldn't help his fascination when she just didn't submit. That must be it. He'd been looking for a meek, mild woman who'd just sit there and hate him for what he'd done. Who wouldn't cause trouble. And now he'd gotten more fight than he'd asked for.

And was starting to enjoy it.

That's it! her mind cried as she pulled off her nightgown and reached for her shift. *He thought he wanted a meek woman, and your actions only prove him wrong. Don't you see he's fascinated by how you defy him? Keep this up and you'll never get out of here.*

For the first time in a day, Deborah felt a smile coming across her face. Well, yes, it was rather appealing to think she fascinated a man such as Patrick beyond his own resistance, but that wasn't the point. Now she had an advantage. Now she could give Trick O'Connor a trick of his own. When he walked back through that door, he was going to find the most acquiescent, meek, obedient woman Deborah could create. It would buy her time to think, to plan a way out of this mess without him continuing to throw new obstacles in her path. But most importantly, it might just buy her the upper hand. And that was worth a great deal. She pulled her petticoats on with a flourish and went to finish her egg.

Patricia O'Connor looked just like her son. Her coloring was soft and warm, her face was cut from clean, sharp lines, and she had the same astounding caramel-brown eyes. Patrick's wild personality also seemed to be a family trait. Patricia had the air of someone who wasn't quite in the same room with everyone else. When a young woman introduced as Fiona brought her in to breakfast, it was in an ornate cane wheelchair. Patricia must have been in her seventies, and rather frail. In her lap were about half a dozen red socks, a ball of red yarn, and knitting needles. As the old woman stuffed the needlework into a tapestry bag, she was having an animated conversation. Only it wasn't with the young woman. It wasn't with anybody. Patricia conversed with the thin air.

"Quite a day, eh, Shamus?" She eyed a sock critically. "We're going to meet Patrick's new wife today. Such a day. Hard to believe." She directed her gaze somewhere to her left. "Indeed?" she said after a slight pause, "I'd have to say so, you're quite right. Quite right."

Deborah stared at the woman, dumbfounded. She sent a questioning glance over to Patrick, who seemed to be enjoying it all.

"Good morning, Mother," he said. From his tone

of voice, his mother's conversing with no one in particular seemed to be an everyday occurrence. *They're all mad. The whole lot of them.*

"Hmm? What's that?" replied Patricia. Her eyes swept unsteadily around the room until they landed on Patrick. "Oh, excuse me, Shamus—good morning, Patrick. Where? Where's that new bride of yours, son?"

Patrick rose and walked toward her. "Here, Mother. Right here." With a wave of his hand, he motioned for Deborah to come toward the old woman.

Deborah guessed the woman's field of vision only extended about ten feet because when she got that close, suddenly Patricia's eyes lit up.

"Begorrah! It *is* her. Mary Mother of God, son, I can hardly believe it." She extended a gnarled hand. "How are you dear? How *are* you?"

At a loss for anything else to say, Deborah replied a simple, "Fine, thank you."

"She's lovely, Patrick dear. Lovely." Her eyes wandered to the left again. "Oh, thank you, Shamus, I think she'll do just fine as well. Hmm? Of course! How smart of you to ask!"

Patricia's eyes focused on Deborah again. "And tell me, what is your name, dear?"

"Deborah."

A broad, appealing smile spread across her face. "A good name. Solid. Graceful. Names are extremely important, you know. It's why I didn't mind when Moira chose a Scottish name for Duncan. It has a Celtic strength any Irishman can appreciate, don't you think? Deborah. Strong. Rooted. Names are important you know. Vital."

"She's beautiful, isn't she, Mother?" Patrick interrupted, his voice tinted with a touch of wonder. Deborah knew the comment had been directed more at her than at Patricia. In fact, Patrick had been looking right at her when he made it. He'd done it again. Complimented her in the middle of a completely absurd situation. It unnerved her. Again.

"Well, she's your wife," cut in Patricia, clearly amused at Patrick's downright doting expression. "I daresay there'd be hell to pay if ye *didn't* think so. But Shamus here agrees with you. I do, too. You're a fine bride, Deborah O'Connor." She strung the name out, as if inspecting how it rolled off her tongue. "Oh my. It is a beauty to say it, it is. A true ring. And names are important, you know. Extremely." The old woman gave her imaginary companion a knowing wink.

Taking a meal with these people was starting to feel like being invited to the circus.

"Eat something, son, or you'll never make it to seven," Patrick reminded his son for the tenth time. The boy just sat there staring at Deborah, his mouth open, a joyful awe on his face. Patrick was just about busting out of his shirt with gratification at having given his son back a slice of hope and trust. He was trying not to let it bother him that the boy had barely looked at him in an hour, just kept gazing at his new mother with a look that belonged in a painting. Could he really blame Duncan? He was having a hard time not staring at Deborah himself. "Duncan . . ."

"I know, Pa, I know." Without taking eyes off Deborah, the boy groped across his plate until his fingers found a biscuit. He took an obedient, unenthusiastic bite, even though the cheese biscuits were his favorite.

Deborah smiled at Duncan and said "Happy birthday" for the tenth time. It reduced Duncan to smiling giggles just as it had the other nine times.

She'd changed something. There was an attitude about her that he didn't like but couldn't name. She was, however, playing her new role to perfection. Perhaps he had less to be worried about now. The more time she spent with Duncan the harder it would be for her to break his heart by leaving. There was no denying she liked the boy. And Duncan certainly liked her.

"Finish up, now, Dunc, Miss Cooney will be here any minute. She's told me she's come up with quite a gift for you this year, so you'll want to be ready."

That got his attention. With a hurried "uh-huh," Duncan dragged his napkin across his mouth and slid off his chair to shoot from the room. Patrick smiled.

Until Duncan burst back in the room to tug at Deborah's sleeve. "You're gonna come, right? You gotta be there. Miz Cooney's *amazing*."

So why was Patrick less than pleased when he watched Deborah place her hand—her hand with his ring on it—atop the boy's and whisper, "of course."

This is what he'd wanted, right? Compliance. Why didn't it feel better?

Amazing *was* a good way to describe Miss Cooney, Deborah thought as the woman swept into the room. Deborah was expecting a young, teacher-like woman; not the diva who appeared at the door in an outfit that belonged more on a showgirl than a woman in her sixties.

"Where is he?" she called. "Where's that hand-some young six-year-old I hear tell lives in this house?" Her drawl was so thick, 'where' came out in three syllables. "Someone bettuh tell him he don't want to miss this present!"

The giggles from behind the parlor settee were all too revealing, but Miss Cooney swooshed around the room anyway, pretending to search by opening cabinet doors and calling through doorways. She was a slim woman, but with no hint of frailty. In fact, Deborah guessed she had more energy than Duncan. Her bun had the orange-white tint of hair that had once been bright red. With a wink at Patrick, she stood right over Duncan.

"Well," she declared, "I'll have to find *anuthuh* boy to play with this brand new, high falutin' model train set. Shame, don't you think?"

"Miss Cooney!" Duncan shot up practically into the woman's face. "I'm right here. Here!"

The woman's ring-encrusted hands flew up in mock surprise. "Duncan, honey! Don't scare Miss Cooney like that. I ain't a young woman, you know."

Duncan simply couldn't seem more pleased with himself. "Nufin scares you, Miss Cooney."

"Oh honey," said Miss Cooney in a low, silken voice that spoke like she'd seen a great deal of this world, "you'd be surprised."

Duncan tugged on her sleeve. "A train? Really? Lemme see!"

"You do have your father's way of gettin' to the point, now don't you, hon?" She ran a hand across the boy's hair. He gave an oversized nod. Deborah fought the urge to send a darting glance at Patrick. "I'd bet that big box over there with your name on it is a good place to start."

Duncan raced across the room to a box behind Patrick, but not before his father deftly snatched his elbow, stopping him in his tracks. Patrick raised one eyebrow. "Oh, right," said Duncan, throwing his head back in Miss Cooney's direction. "Thank you, Mizz Cooney."

"You're so very welcome, honey." It was only then that the woman turned her attention to Patrick and Deborah. Or more precisely, to Deborah. "Now, I confess Duncan is far from the only O'Connor I've been itchin' to see this morning." She swept her glance over Deborah from top to bottom. She put her hand to her breast and let out a deep breath. Her dress was low cut, but Deborah had to admit she had the figure to pull it off even with her advanced years. She must have been a stunning woman in her youth. She still was. "Trick," she said, after a dramatic batting of her eyes, "I'm speechless. I didn't think you had it in ya."

Patrick stepped forward, bringing Deborah with him by a hand around her waist. "Madge, may I present my wife Deborah. Deborah, this is Margaret Cooney. But I expect she'll want you to call her 'Madge' like the rest of the Island."

"You expect right, Trick dear. *Well*," the word came out as more of a sigh, "Deborah, welcome to Galveston. Do you have any idea what you're in for, sugar?" She took Deborah's hand in both of hers. Her many bracelets let out a chiming sound as she gave it a tight, friendly shake.

"Hardly," Deborah gulped out, taken back by the eerie pertinence of the question.

"Now, Madge, don't go makin' up stories just to get Deborah's dander up. She's been through enough already." He winked.

Madge kept a hold of Deborah's hand. "Y'all had a frightful trip in, then?"

"Most alarming," said Deborah, looking at Patrick.

"Well, dear," said Madge, pulling Deborah's hand into the crook of her arm and leading her toward the couch, "I reckon Trick can't do things any other way." She studied Deborah's face as they sat down. Slowly and carefully, like a gypsy reading a palm. "Mmm . . . I do believe you *do* know what you're in for. Well, that's good. But even so, I'd venture anything you've expected is still only the half of it. Our Trick here is not a man given to calm, rational behavior, now, is he?"

"No," replied Deborah, trying to keep the astonishment out of her voice. *How much does she know?*

"Well, I never could see the point in a husband all these years—not that I haven't had my share of companionship, mind you," she added with a scandalous wink, "but I do find the institution of marriage a fine thing. Fine thing. I have to say I'm glad to see Trick gettin' back in the saddle. This house has been far too quiet for too long." She raised her gaze over Deborah's shoulder. "Trick, honey?"

"Yes, Madge?"

"Why don't you take Duncan and that new railroad empire of his upstairs to the nursery so I can have a nice talk with your new wife."

Ha! thought Deborah. *Cornered!* "Why yes, Patrick dear," she added in a sweet voice. "I'd like that." She turned her head to catch his eye, gloating just a bit before she remembered she had opted to play it meek and quiet.

Patrick came over and laid a hand on her shoulder. He caressed it, letting his hand wander up the side of her neck. The sudden, intimate touch did completely inappropriate things to Deborah's train of thought. *How did he do that?* "I'm not so sure I'm ready to let my bride out of my sight just yet, Madge."

"Nonsense!" Madge countered, shooing him away. "Y'all have the rest of your lives to get cozy. I imagine you've been cozy enough as it is. Now, take your manly, possessive airs upstairs and let us be."

Patrick, truly cornered and not helped by Duncan's insistent pulling on his arm, gave in. He sent a warning glance to Deborah before allowing Duncan to drag him from the room.

"I swear! Sometimes I just don't have the patience

to deal with men. They are a lovely distraction and all, but they can get downright uppity about their women in my opinion. As if we were *their* women."

Deborah was hardly hearing her, concentrating so hard on pushing Patrick's touch out of her mind so she could take advantage of her current privacy. Did Madge know anything? That 'cozy' remark could be taken either way. Might Madge be willing to help her? It was best to go slowly, to tread carefully.

"Miss Cooney . . ."

"Call me Madge, honey. Everyone does. Everyone I like, anyway. The preacher's the only one I make call me Miss Cooney. We don't get on well." Deborah didn't find that hard to believe. She looked like she could drink half the town under the table. From the size of her jewels, she had enough money to do just about whatever she wanted. And she struck Deborah as the type of woman who did just that.

"Madge," began Deborah, trying to make it sound conversational, "just how much has Patrick told you about me?"

"Not much, honey. Just that he'd found you in Austin and that you were coming. He doesn't talk much about such things since Moira passed. You know men, they feel if they let on that they might possess even a shred of emotion that we'll all go running for the hills. Honestly, I didn't press him. He's been a sad man, honey. I sure am glad you're here."

Deborah concluded that Madge didn't know. She couldn't decide if that was helpful or harmful.

"Madge, I . . ." she ventured.

"Look, love, y'all don't need to say any more. I can see it plain as the nose on my face that you haven't known each other all that long."

Deborah stiffened in surprise. "I don't think you . . ."

"Oh, you'd be surprised what I know," she interrupted, making Deborah's heart skip a beat. "I know what it's like to face a marriage you're not sure of. I said I never had a husband. That's not to say I haven't come close a time or two. No, I'm guessing you two haven't been courtin' long, and I'm sure I don't know what all there is between you, but I'm here to tell you that it's gonna be just fine. Not a woman in the world that hasn't gone through this, so don't you let that worry get the best of you." She pulled her face close and lowered her voice. "He hasn't been rough with you, has he?"

Deborah's eyes shot wide open. He'd been a thousand things, but she wasn't sure rough was one of them. Not in the violent sense. Not unless you counted being tied up or having a gun which wasn't really a gun put to your back, which definitely counted in her view. Yet Madge's comforting was the closest thing to sympathy she'd encountered since this entire mess erupted. She yearned to blurt the whole thing out, but was frightened that the truth might somehow scare Madge away. She was too desperate for an ally to even risk it.

"Not really," she managed, thinking herself a coward for not risking an escape this very minute. She was surprised at the emotion welling up in her throat. Just as she said it she realized Madge was referring to "rough" in the *married* sense of the word. The *bedroom* sense of the word. Her face went red. "No," she added meekly.

"Well don't you worry," Madge replied, putting a hand softly on Deborah's shoulder. "It gets better."

Deborah was sure her face was turning scarlet.

"If you're lucky, hon, it gets *delicious*." Madge's eyes gained an expression that would have made Jezebel blush. Deborah gulped.

"I have an idea, Deborah darlin'. Y'all are gonna come to dinner tonight. We'll throw ourselves a little shindig in your honor. That way I can see to it that you find yourself a few friends on this Island. Lovely people, Islanders, but they can be a bit slow to warm up unless you kick 'em in the backsides so as they remember their manners. Let's give them a nice, big, fancy kick, shall we?"

Madge didn't even bother to see what Deborah thought. Deborah got the distinct impression that it didn't much matter at this point. Madge Cooney did exactly as she pleased, and it was best not to fight it. "I'll just go and see Herself now. You run on up and tell Trick he's got a dinner engagement."

"Herself?"

Madge looked surprised. "Why Patricia, of course. I expect she doesn't get too many visitors these days. Trick's one of the only souls left who treats her like a human being any more, seems to me. You know, hon, you can tell a lot about a man by the way he treats his mother. You remember that. Now come on by at eight. I'll have you introduced to the whole

Island by Friday. Y'all look sharp now, this is your big debut." She looked like she was going to pinch Deborah on the cheek, but instead just touched her shoulder in an affectionate way. With the same splendor as her entrance, she swept out into the hall.

⊰ Chapter Six ⊱

For a split second, Deborah considered just walking out the front door. She was alone in the parlor,
with no one to see her leave. But go where? To
whom? There was a pastor in town—which meant
probably at least one church, if not more. Surely she
could flee to the Catholic parish, throw herself on the
mercy of the Sisters, and have them aid her return to
St. George's where she had sought refuge in Austin.

Yet as quickly as the plan came to her, the aversion
to return to Austin rose with equal strength. These
were not the circumstances she wanted, surely, but at
the same time she could not—would not—crawl
back to Austin defeated. She had sworn to rise above
that tainted past. It had been bad enough to have her
life's darker hours plastered all over the *Austin City
News'* front page. Giving up her son had been the
most difficult decision she had ever made. She loved
William enough to give him a better life than what
she could have made for him alone. Not to mention
the pain of an uninterested father.

Giving William up had been awful, but Deborah
had managed to come to peace with her choice. To

suddenly have it all publicly displayed in an attempt to bring down her senator employer pulled the wound open again. As if that were not enough, the man to bring all this to public light was someone who professed to love her.

No, there was nothing in Austin worth returning to. Even her best friend there, the senator's daughter Marlena, was now so happily in love with her new husband—expecting a child, even—that it hurt to be with her. Until there was somewhere else to go, her best chances at a new life remained as the ill-begotten bride of Patrick O'Connor. At least until she could devise a means of escape that did not include Austin or her former family-cum-employers, the mighty Maxwell family. They'd helped her enough. More than enough. Deborah was tired of a life under the shadow of someone else's name.

She wasn't feeling like life had much of anything to offer as she climbed the stairs toward the sounds of the nursery. With mixed emotions, she remembered how she had mounted these stairs just last night. Struggling in Patrick's arms with his mouth planted atop hers. She paused on the landing to consider the memory. Yes, it was wrong for her to be hauled into captivity like that, but . . . something about it refused to let her go. Unsettling as it was, she could not deny the spark of Patrick's kiss. He kissed her so . . . so recklessly. He was trying to keep it all showmanship, but something inexplicable had passed between them. To be swept up like something out of a pirate story was, well, it was enthralling. Impossible as he was, there was a certain quality deep inside Patrick

O'Connor—carefully hidden, mind you, but there all the same—that intrigued her. Something in the way he looked at her. She had come to expect tolerance, indifference, or even scorn when people looked at her. If people looked at her at all. When Patrick looked at her, there was fascination, surprise, even a sense of frustration, but he *looked* at her. Stared at her. Couldn't stop staring at her.

Patrick was intense. Excessive. He loved his son to irrational extremes. Such a devotion pulled at Deborah. Uncovered a hunger she thought had been extinguished. What would it feel like to have someone go to such extremes for her?

What's gotten into you? Her rational side roared out above the powerful emotions swirling inside her. *Think about where you are, why you're here, Deborah. You're a means to an end. Nothing more than a birthday present wrapped up in something that can hardly even be qualified as good intentions.*

With that reminder her anger returned, and she began marching up the remaining flight of stairs until she remembered her earlier plan. *No defiance, stay in control.* Deborah softened her steps as she followed the sounds of Patrick and Duncan to the door at the far end of the hall. Realizing that this was her first chance to observe Patrick unawares, she crept carefully toward the door. She tilted her head inside just enough to see but not enough to attract their attention.

Deborah didn't know what she was expecting, but this wasn't it. Patrick was sprawled on the floor next to his son, the two of them looking more like playmates than parent and child. With their faces so closely aligned, the similarities between them were striking. There, unchecked in Patrick's eyes, was the warm look she'd seen when Duncan shot out of the house last night into his father's arms. A powerfully total affection. Delight in his son.

Son.

The word tolled in her stomach like a great, deep bell. The memory of the tiny, bawling baby boy came back to her. She had only a short glimpse of the child, whisked away before she could hold him "because it would be easier that way." Spirited off to an upstanding worthy family. She had had no chance to love her son, to play with him the way Patrick played with Duncan.

Here, she thought, is the complete opposite of the situation that had brought William into the world. This was a father who desperately loved his son. Who desperately wanted his son to love him despite the grief-wrought mistakes that had been made. A wave of yearning for all she had not had, all she could not give William, tightened her throat. Her heart stung inside her chest.

Patrick was pulling an engine up over the bridge, making *chug-chug* sounds, basking in his son's glee. Duncan's eyes were transfixed on his father. Adoring. She nearly burst out laughing when she noticed both Patrick and Duncan wore red socks. Obviously knitted by Patricia. However strange, this was a *family*.

"And here it comes. The village has been waiting, waiting for their train. Aye, don't ye' see the crowds of happy families line the station . . ." Patrick had adopted a leprechaun-worthy brogue as he narrated the action. With every rolled "r" Duncan erupted into new giggles. "Even the dogs are wagging their tails. And the cats, who never come to look at anything, couldn't stay away. The train is coming through! The train is coming through!"

"Hooray!" shouted Duncan, "Everybody's happy! It's the birfday train! Whoo-whoo!" He pulled an imaginary whistle, sending Patrick into laughter of his own. With a new torrent of *chug-chugs* Patrick rolled onto his back, grabbed Duncan by the waist and hoisted him into the air over him.

This was pure joy. There was no thought of propriety, of not soiling one's good clothes, of good manners. This was just *being*. The rarity of it struck Deborah with force. The Maxwells, who had cared for her since she was not much older than Duncan, loved each other, but she'd never seen them act this way. Senator Maxwell loved his daughters as much as any man she'd ever known, but he'd never been so open, so connected with them. The memories of her own father, even though they were strong and warm, never included such unabashed affection. There was something potent and magical about it. Patrick O'Connor was a man capable of a powerful love. Magnetic. Irrepressible. The kind of force that would make a man go out and do something unheard of.

At that instant Patrick's head turned enough to catch sight of Deborah. There was a fierce warmth still in his eyes as he looked at her. He was panting from the effort of hoisting Duncan, his hair falling across his eyes, his expression exuberant. The caramel color in his eyes became shot through with sparks of gold. It dropped through to her stomach, and she knew—in a strange connection of a moment—that she'd glimpsed his heart.

Duncan tumbled out of his father's arms to come running toward her. A child's instant, uncontainable affection. For a moment, with the exuberance of Duncan wrapping itself around the sharp regret of William, Deborah understood what drove Patrick to extremes.

Duncan hit her full speed, almost knocking her over before he grabbed her arm and began dragging her toward the train set. "Oh you gotta see this! You gotta! It's the best damn train set I ever seen!"

Behind the lump in her throat, Deborah cocked an eyebrow at Patrick. *What kind of father teaches his son such language?*

"Duncan," pronounced Patrick in his best fatherly voice as he stood up, "We're going to have to do something about your language with a lady in the house now."

Didn't Patrick think there were ladies in the house before? Mrs. Doyle? Fiona? *His own mother?*

"Oh yeah. Fergot." Duncan's shiny dark eyes caught Deborah's gaze. "Sorry."

"Well," said Patrick, looking at Deborah, "she had a fine solution for this. Worked for me. I imagine it oughta do just fine for you, too." He peeled Duncan off Deborah's skirts and leaned down. With the air of a secret, he pulled the boy's face close and whispered, "Potatoes."

"What?"

"Potatoes. Whenever I'm thinking about a word I ought not to say . . ."

"Like damn?" the boy cut in.

"Yes," said Patrick, rolling his eyes a bit, "that's just the one I was thinking of. Whenever I'm thinking of that one, I say 'potatoes' instead."

"Potatoes? That's silly. I don't even like 'em."

Deborah couldn't help but smile.

"Well, that's true." Patrick ruffled the boy's hair. "And that's what makes it work. It's silly enough to remember." He pulled the boy closer still, whispering in his ear, "and it makes her laugh."

Duncan pushed himself off his father, walked up to Deborah, and with his fisted hands on his hips, he tried it out. "Potatoes!"

A laugh escaped her despite every effort to stifle it.

"It does!" Duncan proclaimed as if he'd been given a new toy. He turned to Patrick. "Does it work on Mrs. Doyle and Miss Fiona, too?"

"I don't think so," replied Deborah quickly. "All the same I think they'd much rather hear that than such bad language." She directed the last three words at Patrick.

"Aye now, she has a point, don't you think?" There was a hint of the leprechaun voice back in Patrick's question.

"S'pose," replied Duncan. " 'Specially Mamó." He cast a sideways glance at his father.

Before Deborah even drew breath to ask the question, Patrick offered, "That would be Patricia."

"I gathered," said Deborah.

"Come here already," whined Duncan as he pulled

Deborah by the skirts over to the train. "It's got a caboose n'evryfing. Look! Up over the bridge it goes! Whoo-whoo!"

Patrick watched Deborah kneel down, nodding now and then at the endless narration Duncan supplied. She'd been different this morning. For this one moment, he allowed himself to admit how much she intrigued him.

Patrick watched Deborah absentmindedly tuck a stray curl behind her ear. The ring, still bearing the leather thong that held it to her tiny finger, glinted in the sunlight. She smiled at some silly sound Duncan had made. She *smiled*.

She hadn't smiled last night. She hadn't smiled for even a second yesterday. Neither had she broken down, even though he had expected her to do so. *Surprise, Trick, this woman is strong.* Unbeckoned, the memory came to him of what it was like to unlace her corset. To feel her shiver and gulp her breath. To run a single finger down the hidden curve of her shoulder blade and feel the muscles work underneath. The potent sound of her first deep inhale once that blasted vice of a contraption fell off her ribs and let the softness come free.

I could, you know. A dark, needy thought whispered in his brain. He felt his body entertain the possibilities of the soft curves beneath the corset. *She is my wife.*

Could you now? He chased the thought back down to the place where he kept it hidden. *And what goddamned blasted good would that do you?*

"Pleeeeease!" Duncan's voice interrupted his thoughts. "Pleeeease come down to the stables to see the new pony?" He was tugging on Deborah's arm as if it were the front door bell.

"I'll let you know right now, Duncan O'Connor, that tone of voice will get you nowhere with me." She adjusted her spectacles. "If you ask like a gentleman, however, I might consider it." She crossed her arms, prepared to wait for his concession.

Duncan's own arms crossed. He thought about it. He stubbed his toe against the train track a time or two. "Would you? Please?" he said quietly. Patrick slid his hands in his pockets, watching.

"After I talk with your father. Why don't you go tell Miss Cooney how much you like this present while you're waiting. She's in with your grandmother."

Duncan nodded and stuffed his hands in his pockets in a way that was so much a mimic that Patrick pulled his hands from his own pockets. As Duncan made for the door, he stopped just past Patrick, angling his face up at him. "Did'ja know she was gonna be so tough?" he asked in the most grown up–sounding voice he could muster.

Patrick only shrugged, because he couldn't decide if yes or no was the correct answer. *How could she be getting to him so?* He watched Duncan shuffle through the door, ignoring the sensation his indecision was causing. When he turned to look at Deborah again, she was seated carefully on a low ottoman, fingering a wooden sheep from the train set.

"Madge asked me to tell you that you now have

dinner plans." She leaned over and put the sheep down beside a piece of wooden fence.

"Can't say as I'm surprised." He could tell by the line of her mouth that she was biting down the urge to say more. He gave her the wide-open door of a hefty silence, but she held her tongue. He realized he was glad to be alone with her again. No, this was not going according to his plan at all. Unsettled, he pushed the issue. "So which would you rather, Mrs. O'Connor? An evening in the safety of the public eye, or a night alone in this house with just us?" *Was it really necessary to make that sound like a threat, Trick?*

"I should like to accept the invitation," she said quietly. Trick waited for her to add something about her opinion not mattering much anyway, but again she remained silent. Had he really frightened her that much? He doubted it.

It hit him like a freight train: she was playing with him.

Damnation, she'd sensed that he enjoyed sparring with her even before he knew it himself. And now she was being meek to frustrate him. And much as he hated to admit it, it was working.

Just then, Patrick heard the unmistakable sound of Mrs. Doyle's shoes on the stairway. A smile spread across his face. *Oh no you don't. You'll not get the upper hand on me, madam.* He sent a knowing glance Deborah's way, glad to see the shock that flashed through her eyes.

"Of course, darling, I think it's a fine idea," he said loudly enough for Mrs. Doyle's eavesdropping ears.

He moved toward her. She kicked the sheep over with her shoe as she moved back on the ottoman. *Two can play.* In two strides he was at her toes. She thrust her chin back, straining to look up at him against the sharp sunlight. "I confess I'm eager to show off the new Mrs. O'Connor," he continued. "I'm eager for a whole host of things." Within a second, he pulled Deborah up, plucked off her spectacles and tossed them on the ottoman, and clasped her to his chest.

Ah, there it is. The defiance returned to her eyes. She knew she'd been caught. As he heard Mrs. Doyle tiptoeing toward the doorway, he pulled Deborah close and clamped his mouth down on any protest she was thinking of offering. She pushed against him, pressing her mouth shut, but he arched her back and put her off balance like he'd done the night before, wrapping himself around her so tightly she could barely move. He had her angled perfectly so that Mrs. Doyle could only see him, not Deborah's fighting hands.

It was supposed to be another display. A public kiss like the one he'd given her in front of the house last night. But, like last night, it hurled itself into something much more before he could stop it. She pushed against him. He arched her back farther, hoping to stop her pushing, but that was a huge mistake. Instead, the deeper angle forced her to cling to him. To clutch at his shirt with her small hands. His head clouded at the sensation. She'd used the lavender soap and dusting powder he'd set out for her. He tightened against her, refusing to admit he craved the contact. There it was, Lord, it *was* there. A spark, something aching behind all the resistance. For a moment, an unbelievable, intoxicating moment, she softened against him. He felt her suck in her breath and still her hands against him. *Damn.* Patrick felt his own breath begin to catch. When his fingers on her back felt the bumps of her corset lacings, things got out of hand. He gave her mouth one last, luscious pass—just to prove to himself that he was still in control—and discovered he wasn't. Not nearly.

Mrs. Doyle cleared her throat loudly in the doorway. Forcing back his composure, Patrick pulled them both upright and turned toward the door. Deborah let out a stunned gasp as she pushed away from him.

"I didn't mean to intrude, sir," Mrs. Doyle said curtly.

"Of course," replied Patrick, inserting calm into his voice. *The hell you didn't, Mrs. Doyle.* It was the first time in perhaps years that he'd been grateful for Mrs. Doyle's excessive nosiness.

"Mrs. Doyle, you must . . ." began Deborah in a panicked voice. She was going to ask for help. He'd pushed her over the edge. Well, hell, a minute ago he'd been a little closer to the edge than he planned himself.

". . . help her find something suitable to wear to Miss Cooney's tonight," he finished for Deborah. "She's threatening to spend the evening at home alone with me if we can't get her properly dressed."

Deborah wasn't giving in yet. "Mrs. Doyle, you've got to . . ." Deborah started. He'd better do something fast.

Putting a playful smile on his face, he came around to stand behind her and put his hand over her mouth. "Mrs. Doyle," he began, his voice dripping with affection, "much as I'd like to keep Deborah to myself, I think it's best we step out tonight. Would you please go get the dress we had made for Deborah?"

Mrs. Doyle looked like she didn't quite know what to make of the situation. For a moment, Patrick worried his playful face wouldn't cover Deborah's actions. She was squirming under his grip, making pleading noises from under his hand. In situations like these, though, Patrick's outlandish personality worked in his favor. People expected outlandish things from him, so he found he could get away with quite a bit. He wrapped his hands around Deborah's waist and pulled her against him. He tried not to notice how neatly she fit inside his arms, how he could feel the rhythm of her breath against his chest. *Come on, Mrs. Doyle, take the bait.*

Mrs. Doyle shook her head and reached for the ring of keys at her shirtwaist. "Saints, Mr. O'Connor, it's a wonder any woman would put up with the likes of you at all." She eyed him and he knew he'd succeeded. "And I should hope you've better manners somewhere in that chest of yours than to be pawing her so in polite company tonight. Indecent, it is." She directed her gaze to Deborah. "See if you can hold him off until I return, lass, aye?"

⊰ Chapter Seven ⊱

"Fine fish, don't you think?"

Deborah could barely answer. Every bite tasted more or less like burlap to her. It all seemed rather dreamlike, this meal, these people, this situation in which she found herself.

Madge's table was resplendent with a spectacular collection of food, flowers, and tableware. Deborah felt like she was on display here as much as the pansies that spilled from a massive silver bowl at the table's center.

Disconcerting as it was, Deborah couldn't help but give in to the excitement of it all. Her last months in Austin she'd been stared at—no, gawked at—anytime she left the front doors of St. George's convent. Even though she had no intention of joining the sisterhood, St. George's had taken her in just to give her a place to heal. Austin society, however, wasn't eager to remove the scars. It wasn't anything blatant or cruel, just a constant undertone of disdain. People averting their eyes, or staring while they whispered, or being terribly curt and careful about what they said.

Here, people didn't stare at her with disdain. They stared, but it was more with wonder. Curiosity. As if she were someone they'd be interested to meet. The attraction of all that made it too easy for Deborah to hold her tongue. Yes, she'd been brought here by an atrocious collection of events. A tiny voice inside her heart warned that the gawks could come back if she spoke up now. *Just for a night, despite everything, let it be,* the voice pleaded. *It's been so long since no one glared. So very long.*

"You'll find," came Patrick's voice to her left, drawing her out of her thoughts, "that Galveston boasts some of the best seafood you've ever tasted. We take our local fare mighty seriously, my dear."

Deborah caught Madge's eyes on her. The woman clearly expected a positive critique of her meal. She didn't seem like the type to take kindly to anything but praise, so Deborah attempted an offer of "It's delicious. You're quite right."

"Madge, your table and food are a sight, but you'll have to forgive my complete attention being drawn to my lovely wife here. I'm obliged to say she outshines them all, wouldn't you agree?"

"Lord, Trick, but you did always have a talent for flattery!" teased Madge. After a warm smile she added, "Make sure you keep it up, hon. Ain't a woman on the planet who don't want to hear that kind of talk over and over."

Deborah stared at the lace adorning her sleeve. The gown was exquisite. Her every attempt to resent it was no match for the smooth feel of the silk and the sky-blue color. It was the loveliest dress she'd ever worn. She hadn't owned a stunning array of clothes in her lifetime—mostly good, sensible dresses. But this was the most beautiful thing she'd ever seen. The extravagance of satin. The delicate, frothy lace. It was the very latest fashion, adorned with mother-of-pearl buttons and graced with a small, smart bustle.

She'd caught her breath when Patrick had plucked it out of Mrs. Doyle's hands and into the room. It'd been far too early to put it on, so Patrick had laid it out while she stood there, panting from the exertion of their struggle, trying to make sense of the nonsense that had filled her life in the last twenty-four hours. After that Patrick had corralled her throughout the day; to the stables to admire Apple, back to another surreal conversation with Patricia and her entourage of little invisible men, then walking down to the gulf. Several times she had turned to catch him staring at her. The man was acting downright besotted, lavishing her with compliments as they walked down the street. Not hiding for one instant the look on his face when she finally appeared in the dress to leave for Madge's. He had, in fact, looked like he would devour her on the spot. His eyes pulled at her resistance, daring her to feel as though this might be more fairy tale than farce. But it couldn't be, could it? He was simply using her, wasn't he? As the day wore on, she became less and less sure of anything.

Then there was Duncan. He took to her instantly, and she to him. He was a bright, boisterous child, free with his affection and in awe of the world around him. She was powerless to deny that the keeping of this promise, her being here, had somehow given him hope. There was a tremendous power in how happy her presence made the boy. His joy, in turn, affected her deeply. Some of it made sense; any fool could draw the comparison and see that he wasn't that much younger than what her own son would be. But it was fast becoming more than that. Duncan's spell over her had much to do with William, but it also had much to do with Duncan.

"To Deborah Marie O'Connor." Patrick hoisted his wineglass into her field of vision, his toast snapping her out of her thoughts. "The finest wife a man could never expect."

"Trick, whatever on earth do you mean by that?" came a teasing question from a rather round man across the table.

"That, Morton, you will never know." With that Patrick wrapped his arm around Deborah and pulled her close to plant a lingering kiss on her jaw line. She felt the heat rise up through her chest. Evidently it showed, for a flurry of mildly disapproving-but-they-are-newlyweds-after-all laughter rose up around the room.

"All the same, I'd rather you not show me at the table, Trick," came Morton's reply. Yet even as she blushed, Deborah remembered what had happened the last time she'd believed a complimenting gentleman. Samuel Hasten, a reporter for the *Austin City News*, had courted her like a Romeo. He'd professed devotion. Brought her gifts. Told her she was beautiful. Proposed marriage. Finally, in an effort to be forthright with the man who would be her husband, she told him of the son she had given up years ago for adoption. Sam had told her he understood. That he loved her all the more for her courage to start over after such an ordeal.

And then Samuel Hasten had plastered the story all over the front page.

It was an underhanded attempt to bring down her employer, Senator Maxwell, in an election year. *Even my own scandal,* thought Deborah with a sharp stab of pain, *was for someone else's benefit. I was only a pawn.*

And what are you now?

Only a means to an end. Again. She thought of a piece of driftwood she'd seen this afternoon. Tossed about by the tides, dashed back and forth across the beach by the dueling currents. Helpless.

Stop it. You're not helpless. You're just truly on your own for the first time. If you let this be the end, what was the use of all the rest? Why even bother to leave St. George's? You're far from dead. You're not injured. You're at a blasted dinner party, for God's sake. Gather your strength, Deborah, and work your way out of this. You'll get nowhere until he trusts you enough to let you be alone, so play along. You're in a room full of people who could be helpful to you soon. Pay attention.

With that, Deborah resolutely dove into the conversation. She asked questions, laughed at jokes good and bad, attempted to be charming, and tried to deflect the compliments Patrick continued to lavish her way. Not to mention the toasts he made. Champagne wasn't exactly daily fare at the convent, and Deborah had to work to fight off the giddy feel-

ing of a bit too much alcohol. As the dessert course
was served, Deborah anticipated the customary sepa-
ration of men and ladies—the women to the parlor,
the men to cigars and brandy in the library. Surely
there would be an opportunity there.

She was wrong. Instead, Patrick pleaded the besotted newlywed, and rather than join the men in the
study, he convinced Madge to let him wander the
balcony with his "lovely bride." Before she could get
a protest in edgewise, Patrick had swept her out the
French doors with another bottle of champagne and
two glasses.

"What do you think of my friends?" he asked,
pouring the glasses as they sat on an ornate wrought-
iron bench. He leaned back and drank, awaiting her
response.

"I'm surprised you even asked my opinion," she
replied sharply, still a bit angry and not a little anxious at being alone with him. That tangle of brown
hair, pulled neatly back, made him a gentleman
rather than the dusty cowboy who had abducted her.
His powerful physique gained a refined grace inside
the formal attire.

"I admit I get my own way most times," he said,
"but this time I've a mind to know what you think."
He was staring at her again.

Feeling suddenly warm, Deborah decided now was
a good time to let Patrick know what she really
thought. She inched away from him in her chair and
started to count the dinner guests off on her fingers.

"Madge," she began, "thinks of you as the son she
never had. She's upset that she didn't know more

about me, but is pleased at being one of the few people who knew you were *importing*"—Deborah chose to emphasize the word—"a wife from Austin. She'll leave you and Duncan a lovely chunk of her estate if you play your cards right." She checked Patrick's response. His look of surprise pleased her.

Deborah ticked off the second and third finger. "The Mortons have eyes on your exporting business. They think it might be useful to their mercantile. Anna thinks you're wonderful if a bit dangerous, but Archibald is reserving judgement. I think he believes there's some great scheme up your sleeve. He wants to see how it plays out before he starts approaching you about becoming partners."

Patrick had stopped drinking and set the glass down. That fascinated look was coming over him again.

Deborah kept talking, speeding up a bit. "Lila Hollister sees you as a schoolboy who needs to grow up. She probably thinks marriage might calm you down, but she doesn't care one bit for the way you've gone about it. I'd wager she has an eligible daughter or some other reason to be upset—that is, if your own scandalous conduct isn't sufficient." She paused a moment, out of breath, before she added softly, "which, of course, it is."

Patrick's eyes were deep and warm, unraveling her thoughts. Deborah allowed herself a drink to pull herself together before she continued. "Nate Hollister is wondering how to write this up in the local paper. He's worried your behavior might reflect badly on the Island." Oh, heavens, she wished he'd stop looking like that. "That . . . that's Island with a capital "I" around here, isn't it?" He didn't even nod. "He's glad you married, even more pleased that it's not to his daughter. I imagine if he has a daughter, she's made the unfortunate choice to express some kind of interest"—Deborah tried not to trip over the word—"in you—but disturbed that you went off the Island to find a wife. Feels you've made some kind of statement as to the unsuitability of Galveston's maiden population. He's wondering if an announcement or a denouncement of your marriage will sell more papers."

"Potatoes!" swore Patrick, still staring. He leaned in a bit toward her. "And Hal Bosworth?" he prompted, looking like he'd have said anything to keep her talking.

"Sorry to have been asked to dinner. He probably feels now he'll have to have us over and introduce us around. I'm sure Madge will see to it that he does."

"Addy Bosworth?" Closer still.

"Even sorrier. She doesn't care for you one bit. I imagine she must owe Madge a favor or some such thing."

"Captain Hornsdell?"

"Was more interested in the food than anything else," Deborah replied. "I'd wager his housekeeper is a monstrous cook. He sees you as some kind of pirate. Someone to give a wide berth. He's correct, of course," she inserted, almost as a defense against the power of Patrick's gaze. "But he'll come if we ask him to dinner."

"Damn!"

"Pota—" she started to correct.

"Damn," he insisted. "You're a damn fine woman, Deborah O'Connor. Amazing."

It was getting hard to breathe. Scrambling, she brought up the one thing that had bothered her most all evening. "However I'm of the distinct impression that there is something they all are wondering if I know. Something they feel I ought to know about you but are afraid to ask because they don't want to be the one to tell me." She crossed her arms.

Patrick narrowed his eyes. "Indeed there is."

Deborah held her breath. She didn't like the way he said that. It made her anxious and reluctant to know at the same time.

Patrick leaned in over her, sending her off balance. Before she could stop him, he wrapped his hands in around her shoulders and leaned her back against the bench. He hovered over her, still giving no answer to her question. His hands were warm on her shoulders. His caramel eyes gave her a long, searing look that seemed to see right down inside her. And yet, there was more in his gaze. A struggle to reconcile what both of them were feeling—wait one minute, had she just thought "both of them"?—with the impossible situation. She could see that he was a shred nervous at the accuracy of her assessments. His eyes revealed that her question had struck very close to home. She'd hit a tender nerve.

His voice was pure silk as he said, "I abduct my wives."

"Well," gulped Deborah, finding her voice, "they needn't worry about being the first to tell me that, do they?" She knew at that moment that there *was* something. And that he wasn't going to tell her.

Although he was doing his best to look commanding, Deborah could see he wasn't completely sure what his next move would be. He looked like he might kiss her. Suddenly, Deborah wondered what kind of kiss this man would give if no one was looking. He made no move for a long, expectant moment. She felt his breath on her neck. His fingers flexed on her shoulders. The muscles in his jaw flexed.

He pulled back and set her upright.

She watched him reapply his control. The sharp, almost teasing edge came back into his voice. "I've a gift for you." He reached into his pocket.

Deborah exhaled, raising a doubtful eyebrow. She didn't hold much stock in Patrick O'Connor's idea of presents.

Patrick took a piece of dark red velvet out of his coat pocket. He pulled her hand out to hold it as he unwrapped the square of cloth to reveal a beautiful pearl bracelet. The two rows of pearls were all the same small, delicate size, yet they had a subtle rainbow of colors to them. Some were rose-colored, others had a more yellow sheen, still others held tints of blue or violet. They looked at once classic and exotic. The paired circlets met in a clasp shaped like a Celtic cross. It was exquisite. And not at all what she was expecting. "My," she whispered involuntarily.

Patrick picked up the bracelet, twirling it around in the evening light so that the pearls glowed like moonbeams. "These are my favorites from my last three trips. The white ones are always in high demand, but it's the ones with the hints of color that catch my eye." His enchantment with the gems was evident.

"You import pearls?" Deborah asked.

Patrick caught her gaze out of the corner of his eye. "Import some things, export others. Cloth, spices, wood," he paused for a moment before adding, "and wives."

"From which do you gain the most profit?"

"Right now I'm thinking it might be the wives." Patrick set the cloth on the bench and pulled her hand to him. "Let's see how *this* fits." With that he set about securing the bracelet's clasp around her wrist. His huge fingers were amazingly deft with such a tiny thing. There was an alluring friction when the roughness of his fingers grazed the inside of her arm. As they had with the corset lacings, his fingers paused on her skin for a moment, then resumed their task. Something flashed between them. Unlike the wedding band, the bracelet had been sized well, and it hung gracefully around her wrist.

Patrick stared at the bracelet on Deborah's wrist. He told himself this feeling must be the champagne. The sight of those tiny pearls circling her wrist like a whirlpool of moonlight pulled him under. There was something about the sight of them, *his* pearls, on *her* hand. Where his fingers had just been. Where her skin was so pale, so soft. Something that cracked the smallest fissure in a place Patrick wanted to leave walled up forever. What was going on? What kind of faery magic did this woman possess that unnerved Trick O'Connor? The man with nerves of iron? With a heart of . . . no, he wasn't going to even think about that. That was not an option.

He stared at her. Hard. Trying to figure out what it was that she did to him.

It disturbed him beyond reason that he couldn't.

She'd assessed every dinner guest with an uncanny accuracy. He'd never met a woman who could do that. It made him wonder . . .

"Take off your glasses," he said. He needed to know more. Needed to see those eyes clearly when she answered his question.

"Pardon?" Deborah looked up from fingering the bracelet.

"Would you please take those spectacles off for a moment?"

She looked like she was going to refuse. Then, after a moment, she quietly removed them.

Oh, Lord. Those eyes. He stared into them for a moment, searching. "There was one more guest at that table. I'm much inclined to hear your thoughts on him."

Deborah's eyes looked away and he watched her mentally count the dinner guests. He waited for her to realize he was talking about himself. Her eyes snapped back, and he knew she understood. Then her eyes narrowed, telling him she was giving careful consideration to her answer.

"Are you quite sure you want to know?"

With another tiny crack, Patrick discovered that he did.

Very much.

Deborah steepled her hands. Patrick watched the bracelet. His own body felt the friction as it slid down to settle a few inches below her wrist. He reasserted his resolve. "I've already told you, woman, that I rarely say things I don't mean."

She spoke slowly, as if choosing her words carefully. "He's pleased at his accomplishment. Satisfied that his strategy has proven successful. Even more successful, I'd wager, than he anticipated." She paused, and Patrick doubled his efforts to hide any response, for he knew she was trying to gauge it. She continued. "He'd never dream of taking on a partner like Archibald Morton; he prefers to work alone. But he is a lonely man. He likes Madge's outlandishness, and wishes he had enough money to enjoy her total disregard for society's sharp tongue. And someday he might. He loves his son more than any man I have ever known. And he gives less care to the propriety of his conduct than any man I have ever known. He is extravagant in the worst . . . and the best sense of the word."

Patrick willed himself to harden his stare and defied his throat to swallow the betraying lump hovering there. She uncovered something in him. Something he wasn't at all ready to show. And yet, for the first time in what seemed like decades, the void that had been so filled with blackness felt open and empty instead. In an impulse, without first considering its advantage or strategy, forgetting his plans altogether, he heard himself saying, "And he's going to kiss his wife here and now. Because he can and he wants to."

"Regardless of her objections?" Her voice had a very definite catch to it.

"Absolutely." He moved in, watching her breath quicken. Her hand tightened around the spectacles. Her lashes were a shade or two darker than her hair color. There was a faint splash of freckles across her cheeks—her face must have been full of them as a child.

"I should expect no less." Her voice was hushed.

"No, madam," Patrick said with a husky growl, "you should expect far more." In the moment his lips touched hers, Patrick felt something he'd never expected: panic. An instant, deep jolt of fear that things had just leapt out of his control. He'd planned to kiss her soundly, to let his tongue wander over that delicate mouth until she couldn't see straight, but he found he couldn't. She certainly seemed to be expecting it, seemed almost ready to fight it, for he felt his own shreds of panic echoed in her shoulders. Their lips touched just a moment, like a hand pulling away from a spark.

A very powerful, very dangerous spark.

Patrick pulled away, scrambling to hide his astonishment. He wouldn't even look at her, for he knew her face would only hold the same frightened wonder. No. He wasn't ready for this. It would only complicate matters. No.

Trick O'Connor wasn't about to get himself in too deep when the current was so damn strong. He couldn't afford it. More importantly, he wasn't sure he could control it.

"We'd best get inside," he nearly stammered, hardly even turning around to look at her before shooting back through the balcony doors.

❧ Chapter Eight ❧

" 'Tis a fine dress, it is," Fiona remarked as she worked her way down Deborah's corset laces. A subtle sharp edge hid inside her voice.

"Beautiful," replied Deborah. She rolled her shoulders, moaning at the stiffness that had settled in them. It was obvious Fiona didn't share her mother's bemused tolerance for the new lady of the house. Was she put out about having to play dressmaid to yet another Mrs. O'Connor? Or was there something else about Deborah's presence that bothered her? It was worth finding out.

It had been an unsettling evening. Deborah ventured her comments further. "He has a penchant for extravagant gifts, doesn't he?"

"I wouldn't know, ma'am." The woman snapped the last lace through the grommet with a bit more zeal. Yes, there it was. A tender nerve. It could merely be that Fiona was feeling uncertain of her position given Deborah's arrival as lady of the house. Or it might be something more personal.

Deborah turned around. She took a good look at the woman. Her features were dark Irish: black hair, fair skin, and green eyes. She wasn't beautiful, nor plain, but lean and strong-looking. Her brogue was not as heavy as her mother's, but still colored her speech with musical tones.

"I'll put this away, then." Fiona reached for the gown to put it in the armoire.

Deborah put out a hand to stop her. "No, really, I'll do that. I don't want a lady's maid, just a hand with the corsets and such." She watched Fiona's eyes fall on the bracelet at her wrist. The woman's back straightened.

"Another of his grand gestures," Deborah explained, watching Fiona's response.

"Lovely."

"I have to admit, it is." Deborah sat down on the bed. "Fiona, may I talk with you for a moment?"

Fiona was appropriately startled by the request for conversation with a member of the house staff, but Deborah gave her a pleading look. Fiona paused a bit before shifting her weight to rest against the bedpost.

Deborah fingered the dress, selecting words carefully. "You've served Duncan and Mrs. O'Connor a good long time, haven't you?"

"Six years," Fiona replied. Deborah quickly calculated and knew it meant that Fiona had known Patrick's former wife. She filed that information away for future use.

"I've a feeling it comes as no surprise to you that Mr. O'Connor and I had a rather . . . shall we say . . . unusual courtship." Indeed, Fiona's face registered no surprise. Yet the woman was listening intently. "I find," continued Deborah, "there's a great deal I don't yet know about him." Heavens, if that wasn't an understatement.

She'd caught the woman's attention.

"Might I ask your confidence, Fiona, in a delicate question?"

"I'll be of what help I can, ma'am."

Deborah toyed with one of the buttons on the gown. "I couldn't help but feel at dinner tonight that . . . well . . . that there is something unique about Patrick's family. Something everyone feels I ought to know. Yet no one wants to tell me. Something . . . how can I put this? Something people are wondering if I knew before I . . ." she started to say "consented to marry Patrick" but decided that was too much of a lie if she could confide the full story to Fiona at a later date. She opted for a simple ". . . married Patrick. I don't think it's complimentary, whatever it is."

Fiona's expression told Deborah her hunch had been right. It was clear there was something, and Fiona was debating whether or not it was her place to reveal it.

Deborah softened her voice as much as she could. "I don't want you to think I'm asking you to betray Mr. O'Connor. But I'm rather short of friends at the moment, and I would truly welcome your confidence."

Fiona hesitated. "Don't you think you'd be better asking that of Mr. O'Connor himself?"

"I have the feeling I'd get a far more honest answer from you."

Fiona licked her lips, deciding.

"Please, Fiona. I'd so much rather know. Please. You don't even have to tell me all of it now. Just as much as you feel you can."

Fiona began running her fingers along the carvings on the bedpost. It was a long moment before she began speaking. "It isn't so much about the O'Connor family as it is about Mrs. O'Connor's family. The Blacks. Her maiden name was Black. They've a bit of a history about them. There are certain family . . . traits . . . that have come down from generation to generation. And so people have come to expect . . . certain things of any Black. It isn't so bad here as it is in Ireland, but still, people know things. . . ." She stopped short of saying just what those things were.

In an effort at humor, Deborah replied, "Like talking to little men who aren't really there?"

Fiona's eyes shot up with such a start that Deborah's heart skipped. With a chill Deborah realized she hit frighteningly close to the mark.

"Tell me, Fiona, what is this family trait I should know about?"

Fiona simply looked at her, put a finger to her temple, and shook her head.

"They . . . madness?" questioned Deborah, wrapping her mind around the concept.

"Well, you've seen Mrs. O'Connor and her wee men. It's . . . it's not always the wee men, there's been . . . other things. With Mr. Patrick's grandda it was just going silent for days on end till he finally never spoke again. And with Michael—Duncan's uncle—Mr. Patrick's brother . . . heavens it's only been a year or so since he . . . well, he just became angry, like an animal. Mr. O'Connor had to send him away for fear he'd hurt himself or someone else. It's been . . ."

Deborah put the dress down slowly. "You're telling me that everyone in Patrick's family goes *mad*?"

"That's the thing of it. Not all." With almost a whimper Fiona added, "but many."

The pieces were falling together now. "And how old was Patrick's brother when he . . . well, when he began to . . ." she groped for a better word but couldn't find one and instead just gestured with her hand, ". . . go?"

"Just two years ago. 'Bout the age Mr. Patrick is . . ." her voice trailed off, as if suddenly realizing the rather harsh implications of her remark, ". . . now."

Deborah's brain raced in a thousand different directions. "So everyone is wondering if I knew I was marrying a potential madman," she said more to herself than to Fiona. Of course. And Patrick's outlandish behavior only served to intensify the matter. That was why no one seemed to think twice about Mrs. O'Connor's invisible companions or the fact that Patrick regularly hauled his wife around on his shoulder. Dear Lord, it gave the man license to act any way he pleased. And she could bet that Patrick regularly used that to his advantage. No wonder Archibald Morton needed to wait and see something before he approached Patrick as a partner—he needed to see if Patrick would live up to the family moniker. And Deborah could bet it wasn't just Patrick's character that made mothers far from eager to pair their daughters off with him. With Patrick's brother's history of violence, what did that predict for the possibilities of her future welfare?

"You didn't know. I knew it. It wasn't my place to tell you." There was something in Fiona's voice that didn't allow Deborah to quite believe her remorse.

"Well, Fiona," said Deborah, trying to keep the fear out of her voice as much as possible, "I won't say it eases my mind to know what you've told me. I'll not tell a soul that you revealed this to me. And you must understand I'm indebted to you for your honesty. You've done me a great service. I'm grateful."

Fiona nodded.

Something had to be done. She had to get word to someone, even in Austin. "So you'll forgive me," continued Deborah, "if I ask you yet another favor?"

The woman nodded again.

"Might I count on you to send a message for me, perhaps tomorrow night? And, you understand, I would need this message to be sent in the utmost confidence. It's vital that it stay between only us. May I ask this of you?"

"I'll be of any help I can, ma'am."

"I'm so very grateful. Thank you." Deborah's mind was leaping eight steps ahead.

"Good night now. You'll be all right now, won't you?" Fiona asked.

A very good question, thought Deborah as she mumbled out a "Fine."

As Fiona left the room, Deborah let her body sink back on the mattress. Well, if she had wondered how the situation could complicate itself, she had her answer. Deborah hadn't the vaguest idea how to make sense of all that had happened tonight. The flattery, the nearly shameless display of affection, the extravagant gifts. His controlling nature. The sideways glances of the dinner guests. The kiss. Oh, Lord, that kiss. The man was baffling enough before; now his very sanity seemed to be in question.

Deborah pulled her hands up to cover her face and let out a small whimper. "Deborah darlin'," she heard her old protector Senator Maxwell say, "You're in it up to your bootstraps." She rolled onto her side and pulled her legs up to hug her knees. She was in it so much deeper than bootstraps. If she wasn't careful, she'd drown. She crawled under the coverlets, not even bothering to change her shift for a nightdress.

Sleep had eluded Patrick most of the night. Each time he would doze off, Moira's voice would come softly in his ear, asking him what he'd done, mocking the plans he'd made, reminding him how very differently things had turned out. She sounded bemused.

He stared at the larger-than-usual pile of knotted rope coiled on the floor beside his bed. Even his nightly ritual of the rope had brought him no ease this evening.

Patrick pulled his shirt over his shoulders, wincing at the soreness of exhaustion lingering there. Letting out a breath, he leaned on the bureau and examined his face in the glass. Duncan's countenance stared back at him. Usually it was a comforting thing to see his son in his face, to know the similarities, and be reminded of the little piece of immortality every son gave his father.

This morning Patrick saw his mother's features in his face. Her strong brow, the color of her eyes that gave every Black an undeniable brand. Patrick had enjoyed the irony of it—that one of the most outstanding physical characteristics of the Black family was unusually *brown* eyes. Like a poor joke. There seemed to be so little of his father left in his face today. Where was the immortality Patrick was to have given his own father? Why could he not see any of James O'Connor in his face this morning?

Were fathers so easily erased from a man's life? James O'Connor had been a good man. A good father. How often Patrick's mother had praised James, told Patrick how lucky he was to have such a fine father. Each time she said it, Patrick saw the pained look in her eyes for the poor father she'd had herself. Patrick's own memories of his grandfather were not good ones. Patricia's pained look returned tenfold as she watched Michael fade from reality. Even as Patricia lost her own grip on the world.

They weren't good memories. The watching. The waiting. The comparing to all the awful family stories, all the bad memories.

It was why the plan had occurred to him in the first place. Who wanted a wife who would be looking at you sideways—comparing your every move to their own nasty memories? Measuring your character against the long list of other Blacks whose minds they had watched soften? *"Oh yes, I remember when Michael started out that way." "Don't you remember? Cousin Ian did that just before he lost his mind." "I can tell you this surely reminds me of the time . . ."*?

It was better to find someone who wasn't steeped in the family history, to get someone from off the Island. Someone who, even if she someday learned of the family trait, at least hadn't personally watched his brother Michael fall from humanity one angry day at a time. Or his grandfather. Or his mother.

And . . . someone whose sheer method of betrothal prevented her from ever becoming emotionally attached to you.

Patrick had loved enough for a lifetime. Love like that would not come to him again, so it was better to not even try and go through the motions. Moira was still with him in so many ways. She looked at him every time Duncan cocked his head a certain way. Her laugh echoed in the boy's. He could feel her hair just by closing his eyes and touching Duncan's.

Without warning, the feeling of Deborah's hair invaded his thoughts. So different from Moira's. Soft and wavy, delicate between his fingers. He'd thought it conveniently mousy when he first saw it. Yet, last night he'd noticed the spectrum of colors hiding in the waves. Tiny hints of gold coming out from under the ordinary, wheaty color. The way the hairs at the nape of her neck and the top of her forehead took on an extra curl. How fragile tendrils spilled out when she took off her spectacles. And when he kissed her . . .

The door burst open and Duncan flung himself into the bedroom, knocking Patrick backward onto the bed. They tousled for a time, pinching and poking in a gale of laughter and hollow threats.

"Pa?" Duncan asked as he settled in on Patrick's chest, planting his chin on crossed arms.

"Son?" Patrick snatched a pillow and stuffed it behind his head so he could look up easily into the boy's face.

"Why doesn't she stay in here with you like Ma did?"

Whoa.

You've your own self to blame, Trick. He learned his directness from you.

Patrick pulled a feather from the boy's hair. They'd gone through more bed linens tussling like this than he could count. "That's a mighty grown-up question for a lad."

"I'm six now." Evidently Duncan felt that entitled him to new levels of information. And inquisition.

"You are. And a fine six at that. But I'm thinking that's a question for *sixteen*, not six. Mighty grown-up questions tend to have mighty grown-up answers."

"Okay. Why?"

Patrick folded his hands behind his head, concocting an answer simple enough for a six-year-old. It wasn't easy. "Well," he began, "you know Deborah's sort of a magical Ma, right?"

"Uh-huh." Duncan's head bobbed in agreement.

"A magical Ma comes quickly. I didn't have the time to become good friends with her like I did with your Ma. We're still getting acquainted." Patrick was pleased to see the simplistic answer seemed to satisfy the boy. Until he watched the gears turning in his son's mind, forming more questions.

Duncan scrunched up his eyebrows. "But I heard you tell Mrs. Doyle you loved her."

"Uh-huh . . ." Patrick felt a trickle of guilt. But only a trickle. A boy needs to think his father loves his mother.

"But . . . I don't . . . how . . ." He eyed his father suspiciously. "You gonna tell me this is one of those com-pi-cut-ed things?"

"*Complicated.*" And blast it, if that wasn't exactly the word for the whole damn situation. "And yes, it's complicated. Mighty." He poked Duncan gently on the nose. "You have to figure these magical things are going to be complicated, right? If they were simple, everybody would have magical ma's. It's a very tricky business."

Duncan sat up on Patrick, crossing his arms. "I don't think it's compi . . ."

"Complicated . . ." Patrick assisted.

"Com-pu-cat-ed," Duncan sounded out. "It's easy. I like her. She's pretty."

"I agree."

"I like the color of her eyes. Like flowers."

"Me too, Dunc."

"But she doesn't laugh, Pa. Not much."

Patrick sighed in spite of himself. "We'll have to work on that, won't we lad?" He toppled Duncan over and tickled him soundly until they were both breathless.

"Go get some breakfast, Dunc, I'll be down soon. You know how Mrs. Doyle gets if we let breakfast get cold." With a swat he sent the boy scurrying from the room.

Patrick's thoughts left him pinned to the bed. What was it that had sparked between them, he and Deborah, last night? Why had it panicked him so? Was a purely physical attraction dangerous? Strategically speaking, it might be advantageous to simply bed her. Come now, he'd thought this thing through. He knew exactly where he would draw the line.

So why wasn't he drawing it? Why not just bed her and be done with it?

Because, came Moira's voice inside of him, *ye know that wouldn't be the way of it. Ye saw it yourself last night. Ye won't just be done with it. It will be just the beginning . . .*

Patrick sat up in defiance. What was so blasted awful about liking one's wife? The woman he'd seen on the balcony last night was sharp as a tack. An asset, even. If he grew fond of the feisty lady, what was lost?

He refused to even let himself consider the answer.

Even though he already knew it.

"How are they coming along, Mother?" Patrick asked at breakfast.

"Fine, son," replied Mrs. O'Connor with pride. "Just dandy. Shamus and I are of the mind these are some of me best." She held the socks out for inspection.

My Lord, thought Deborah, *he doesn't even have*

*to say what 'they' are. The woman's world consists
of socks and leprechauns.* And then, with a chilling
thought, her mind added, *and now it's your world.
Unless . . .*

"When do you think you can start a new pair?"
Patrick looked straight at Deborah. *Socks? What did
socks have to do with her?*

"Around tea time today, I'd be guessing. Wouldn't
you say, Shamus?" the old woman evaluated the remaining sock.

"I've a new project for you, Mother."

"Do you now?"

Patrick leaned back in his chair. "I'm of the mind
that Deborah will be needing a pair of red stockings.
Several pairs, as a matter of fact." He twirled his fork
between his thumb and fingers. It suddenly clicked.
Patrick and Duncan wore red socks. Now, so should
she. Deborah felt her toast sticking in her throat.

Mrs. O'Connor's wrinkled face erupted in a
worldly smile. "Now, I should have thought of that.
It's right you are, Patrick my boy. If she's an
O'Connor now, she must have the socks for it,
hmm?"

Oh, Lord.

Duncan looked at her like she'd just been given the
secret password into his world. "You got to," he
agreed with a captivating smile and wide eyes. Again
she was reminded of the boy's uncanny resemblance
to his father.

"Do I?" she replied, arching an eyebrow at
Patrick.

"Uh-huh," said Duncan, tugging her sleeve until she looked back at him.

After breakfast, Duncan peeled out the door, nearly knocking Mrs. Doyle over as she brought the day's post over to Patrick. Then she wheeled Mrs. O'Connor out to the parlor. Deborah eyed the stack of envelopes with gratitude. Patrick's daily business might buy her time alone in her room. She could draft the necessary note in ten minutes, maybe even less. Fiona could easily be given some errand that would allow her to deliver it. She'd get help and could be out of this mess by tomorrow, even if it meant crawling home to Austin.

Expectantly, Deborah watched Patrick rifling through the correspondence, waiting for him to become engrossed in the papers. He was absently rattling off a list of his intended activities when he stopped dead in his conversation. He stared at one particular envelope. Silence filled the room. Deborah watched his whole body change as he tore it open and read the contents. Whatever it was, it was tremendously important. She watched him read, looking for some clue to this new development. Perhaps a crisis that would draw him away, urgent business that might call him out of town. His eyes scanned the length of the document.

"Holy Goddamned Mary Mother of God!" Patrick's voice was awestruck.

"Finally," he said, not even aware she was in the room with him. "Jesus God Almighty, finally." He spread the letter out flat, admiring it, treasuring it.

Then he ran his hands down his face as if to stop his mind from spinning. He muttered something in what Deborah could only guess was Gaelic, and then proceeded to let out a triumphant whoop worthy of a five-year-old.

Deborah found her tongue. "News?" He hardly needed the question—the man looked like he was going to explode any second.

His gaze shot to her, suddenly pulled back into the current world. His eyes sparkled with excitement. "News like the world may never know." He jumped up from the table and began a lumbering jig around the room, ending square in front of her. With another string of Gaelic exclamations—which sounded mostly happy but had the unmistakable ring of something profane—he plucked her from the chair by the shoulders. Nearly holding her off the ground, he planted a hard, swift kiss on her mouth before pulling her back, proclaiming, "Duncan's right. You must be magic. You're the prettiest, most obstinate, fascinating goddamned talisman of good fortune I've ever seen."

He stood for a moment, looking at her. Deborah was again amazed at how easily you could watch the man think. His mind's gears were nearly audible. Yet you only knew that a storm was brewing in there; his face never gave a hint of the kind of thoughts whirling inside. Only the unmistakable evidence that they were there and on the move.

"Duncan!" he called over his shoulder without taking his eyes off Deborah. He didn't wait for an answer, but instead took Deborah's hands and nearly spun her about the room. "Pack your bags, Mrs. O'Connor. We're going on the adventure of your lifetime!"

Deborah's heart turned to ice water and puddled about her feet. "*We're? Going?*"

"*Sweet potatoes,*" he exclaimed nearly into her face, "but this has been too damn long in coming. Duncan! Son, get back in here!"

⊰ Chapter Nine ⊱

"Venezuela?!"

"Precisely. Actually, the island of Margarita to be exact. Off the coast."

Deborah fought a surge of panic. "Venezuela *South America*?" She forced herself to swallow hard. "Will you tell me if I ask you why?"

Patrick eyed her. "Well, I'll give you an answer, but I doubt you'll find it satisfactory."

"I'll take my chances," replied Deborah with narrowed eyes.

"We're going to find something. Something I've been looking for for a very long time. And someone may have just found it for me." This secretive information plastered an adventurous look on Duncan's face worthy of folklore. Deborah imagined it sounded to him like a treasure hunt. It sounded to her much more like a wild goose chase. One she was going to make good and sure she did not get pulled into.

"And I'm guessing," she countered, "you aren't going to tell me what it is you're hurtling across the ocean for?"

"*We*, my dear. We're—what did you call it—*hurtling* across the ocean. And no."

Although she was sure the answer wouldn't be good, Deborah couldn't help asking, "How soon are we leaving?" Long voyages such as this surely couldn't be organized on short notice. She'd have enough time to find sanctuary and slip away before this man carted her off to parts unknown.

"Well, that's the beauty of it, my dear. And the most advantageous part of being in the export business. It enables one to export oneself on rather short notice. I can't say for sure yet, but I expect we'll be on our way by tomorrow."

"Tomorrow!" Duncan yelled with joy.

Tomorrow. It thrust through Deborah's heart like a spear. A gasp left her throat, and she didn't care if Patrick heard it. *Oh Lord, how on earth was she going to get out of this?*

"Good thing we haven't completely unpacked you yet, Deborah. You'll be more comfortable with some different traveling clothes, but that can be done in Havana. I'm a seasoned adventurer, wife," he added, responding to the blatant shock she was sure plastered her face. "There's little cause for concern." A wide smile spread across his face. "Why don't we think of it as a honeymoon. With a treasure hunt thrown in for good measure." He grabbed her hand and gave it a swashbuckling kiss.

Deborah wondered what Patrick's response would be if she were sick onto his shoes for the second time in their short, odd marriage.

"I'm obliged, Luther." Patrick watched the sea-birds swoop and dive as the fish boats were coming in from their morning hauls. The air was thick with them and their cries.

"You're out of your mind, Trick. But then, I always thought you were. We'll make 'em as comfortable as we can."

"I know you will. I know it's daft, but I want them with me."

Luther raised a bushy eyebrow.

"I can't explain it. I've the feeling I'll . . . I'll need her there. With me. Hell, I want her there."

Luther spat into the harbor. "That wouldn't be the 'want' inside your britches talking now, lad, would it?"

Patrick glowered at him. "Pull your mind out of the bilge, Luther."

"Under your skin already, is she? Ah well, that's as it should be. But honestly, Trick, if you want 'em with you, why the hell ain't you taking a steamship?" He waved away a fly. "Ain't no way to treat a wife. 'Specially a new bride, no matter how much yer stuck on 'er. A boy's gonna have the time of his life on a rig like this, but this ain't much of a place for a lady, Trick."

"Delilah likes it enough on board."

"Well," said Luther with a twinkle in his eye. "Delilah's *Delilah*. She ain't some hot-house lily from—where is it you said your lady came from?"

"Austin. And Deborah's no hot-house lily." Patrick smiled as he recalled the picture of her snarling his wagon wheel with her parasol. Yet Luther had a fine point; she deserved certain comforts. "I'll pay you triple passage if you give us the first mate's cabin and the spare next to it. The lady deserves a bit of pampering."

Luther extended a hand. "I'll only take double. Consider it a weddin' present. And why the hell ain't you on a steamer for this, Trick? What's goin' on?"

Patrick shook the hand. "Let's just say I want to be quiet about this." He shot a look to Luther out of the corner of his eye. "And I want to keep my wife to myself. I don't want to share her with a gaggle of hen-pecking steamship ladies."

Luther laughed, his wide smile showing a missing tooth next to a gold one. He was the cleanest, most civilized captain Patrick could trust, but he still was a rather salty fellow. "You're lyin', Trick. You ain't never let a gaggle of skirts keep you from anything."

Patrick simply arched an eyebrow, letting the old man know he wasn't going to get more information than that. When Luther simply grunted in reply, Patrick changed the subject. "You signed on a crew yet?"

"Later this afternoon."

"Try to keep 'em the upstanding type for me, would you?"

Luther turned to stare at Patrick with narrow eyes, his hands on his hips. "Trick O'Connor, when a blue norther blows through here and tries to turn my ship into timber, you want some fancy pants pulling on the lines or you want a seasoned hand gettin' your lady to shore?"

"I want both, Luther. And I'll throw in a bonus in port if you can get it. Besides, you can't tell me Delilah wouldn't mind having a little *culture* on board for a change."

"Culture my ass, Trick. You'll get what I think can get us to Havana and you'll be happy for it."

Patrick settled his hat down over his head. "It's a pleasure doin' business, Luther."

Luther just chuckled and spat again. "Pleasure my ass."

" 'Pleasure my *potatoes*,' Luther," he corrected.

"Huh?"

Deborah's stomach sank clean through Madge's Persian carpet.

Patrick had deposited her there while he went to arrange passage. Desperate for escape from the impending trip, Deborah had spilled the entire story seeking help. Everything from pearls to parasols, kicks to kisses. Anxiety and isolation had the words tumbling out of her faster than she could stop them. To Deborah's shock, Madge showed little surprise nor concern.

"You knew?"

"Well, no," Madge replied, "not until today. But I suspected it went somethin' like that. 'Course, it is a bit more dramatic than I pictured, but as we're talkin' 'bout Trick I cain't say I'm really all that surprised."

"Oh, dear Lord." Deborah fought back tears. It was so clear Madge wasn't going to help her out of this that she thought she'd dissolve right there on the settee.

"I cain't say I approve. Men can be brutes when they get something into their heads. And I'm not one to trust 'em with much of anything."

Deborah's composure failed. "Then why won't you help me get out of this?"

"I'm gonna tell you why, Deborah honey, but I ain't so sure you're gonna like what you hear."

Resigned, all but defeated, Deborah fell silent to listen.

"I have traveled many places, sugar, and seen things you wouldn't believe. I have learned that things have a way of happening, that there are forces at work that we just don't understand. Sometimes life gives you a turn you wouldn't have planned in a million years, but it's just what needs doin'. You've got to figure fate knows what she's doing. Now listen, Deborah honey, the night before you came I had a dream."

Deborah rolled her eyes. *Dreams. Fate. I'm ruined.* Instead of being insulted at Deborah's blatant scorn, Madge just laughed softly.

"Now I had a feeling you'd see it that way, but I'm here to tell you that you need to listen to this. I've lived a lot longer and harder than you, and been in far worse scrapes than you fancy yourself to be in right now." She pointed a finger at Deborah. "Now are you gonna sit here and *hear* what I have to say or are you gonna just stare at me like I'm one of Patricia's invisible men? Listen up, child."

Deborah didn't see how she had any choice but to listen. The last thing she needed right now was one less ally.

For God's sake, she had no blessed allies at all.

"I had a dream," continued Madge. "Saw you clear as day even before I met you. I was just playing along the other day because it gives people the willies when I know who they are before I've met them. I saw you then, and I saw you in the future." Deborah's response must have shown on her face because the woman said, "Don't you look at me that way, dear, it's happened before and I've grown to trust it. I saw you *happy*, darlin'. And most importantly I saw Trick happy. Not just that devil-may-care thing he puts on for the world but happy in *here*." She tapped a jeweled finger to her heart. "Duncan, too.

"I'm guessin' you already know those boys are mighty important to me. Their happiness is, too. Couldn't you entertain the notion for one single moment that you might be part of that, no matter what it looks like now?"

"He married me at gunpoint!" countered Deborah, unbelieving.

"Not my Trick, honey. He'd never do that."

Deborah was growing angry. The whole Island seemed to be ganging up against her. "Well, all right then, it wasn't really a gun. But he poked me with a pipe and made me think it was a gun. It was just as cruel and I don't see the difference."

Madge erupted in laughter. "A pipe? Now that I'd believe. That man has the strangest moral code I believe I've ev-uh seen."

"How can you condone this? You! Of all people! How can you sit here with your independence and let him . . . let him *kidnap* me!" Deborah was letting her panic get the best of her.

"Because I am no stranger to unorthodox behavior, sugar. Trick does things in his own special way. I believe you are meant to be here, even if you don't see it now."

Deborah stood up. "I won't ever see it."

"I'm bettin' you'll change your tune, honey."

"Never."

After a short silence, Madge spoke again. "Well, I'll tell you what, then. I'll make you a deal."

Another deal. What I surely don't need is another deal, Deborah's heart moaned in her chest.

"Where is it y'all are goin'?"

"Venezuela." The word choked out of Deborah's throat.

"When y'all get back from Ve-ye-ne-zu-e-la"—the word had six syllables the way she drew it out—"if you still want to end this, shall we say *unusual* marriage, I'll lend you a hand."

Deborah turned to face her. "And what if I don't come back from Venezuela alive?"

Madge looked like the answer to this seemed all too obvious. "Why of course you will, hon, I've seen your future."

"You'll forgive me if I take no comfort in that."

"I'll forgive you for bein' young. And trapped. And scared."

"What's to stop me from running out of here this minute to the Ursuline sisters' convent up the street to plead sanctuary?"

Madge seemed amused by the thought, clearly

thinking it the most drastic of options. "Mainly that your husband is coming up the walk now."

The front door bell chimed just as Madge finished her speech. The floor spun around Deborah's feet and she clung to the mantle for dear life.

She couldn't even turn around when Patrick entered the room.

"Trick, honey. Deborah and I have had such a lovely visit. Sit down here, sugar, I've a need to talk to you."

Deborah could see their reflection in the mirror as Madge pulled Patrick down on the couch beside her.

"Your wife here," said Madge, her enjoyment of Patrick's newly married status coloring her words, "is so scared out of her wits she plum told me the whole tale. Everything. Trick O'Connor, you should know better than to bamboozle a lady like that."

Patrick started to rise. Madge yanked him back down. "Don't you go anywhere until I'm finished with you. And don't you worry, I'm not going to cart your lady off behind your back. Believe it or not, young man, I'm on your side. But fate or no fate, you owe this lady one king-sized apology for goin' about it the way you did. You're lucky she hasn't shot you in your sleep."

"She might still," countered Patrick, clearly taken aback by Madge's evaluation of the situation. Deborah guessed Madge Clooney was probably the only person in Galveston who could take Patrick by surprise.

"Well, good for her. I'd do no less. All right now, what's done is done. Fate's been kind enough to bring you together. Despite your ridiculous methods. Now, both of you, get it through your young thick skulls how to *behave* toward one another. Turn around, Deborah honey, and look at me."

Deborah turned. She felt the room closing in on her.

"Patrick Delaney O'Connor, I want you to get down on your knees in front of this here lady and beg her forgiveness for the—well, the just plain *stupid* way you went about this."

Patrick glared at Madge but did not move.

"You know how stubborn I am, Trick. Now I imagine y'all have got a lot to do today other than have a stand-off in my front parlor. Git down there, boy!" With that she fairly shoved Patrick off the couch.

"God blasted bloody damn . . ."

"Don't you go mouthing off at me, Trick. I've heard far worse than you can even think of. Down on one knee!" she ordered, craning her neck up at him.

With a look that turned him into six-year-old begrudgingly obedient Duncan, Patrick walked over and heaved himself down on one knee. Deborah could barely hide her surprise; she even felt a faint shred of amusement.

Madge came up behind him. "Take her hand. The one with the ring on it. You did have the decency to give her a ring, didn't you?"

"Yes, ma'am," growled Patrick. He took her hand. Deborah noticed it was a bit sweaty.

"Out with it!"

"Deborah," he began.

"No, you fool, look at *her* while you say it. And you'll say it a hundred times until I think it sounds like you mean it, so choose your words with care, Trick honey."

Patrick glared at her, grunted, then shut his eyes and licked his lips, composing. "I suppose this was an . . . inconsiderate way to wed you, but . . ."

"No buts, no justification, just buck up and apologize," interjected Madge, winking at Deborah.

After a long moment, Patrick pronounced, "I'm sorry."

"Good," said Madge, steepling her hands, her tone of voice implying that she expected him to elaborate.

"And Duncan really likes you, so thank you for being so kind to him despite what a . . ." he searched for a suitably dramatic word ". . . *Visigoth* I've been."

"My stars, Trick, that was excellent. Visigoth, hmm? I'm betting you have a fine vocabulary, Deborah hon."

"You'd be amazed," countered Patrick. "Can I let go of her hand now?"

"No. We're far from finished." Madge turned to Deborah. "I want you to forgive him."

Deborah stared, gasping at Madge in utter disbelief. "Absolutely not!"

"Now don't you give me none of that. If I won't take it from Trick, I surely won't take it from you."

The three of them stood there for a moment while Deborah wondered if the world hadn't just turned upside down.

Patrick pinched her hand. "Just do it," he muttered under his breath until Madge kicked his shoe.

"Well," began Deborah, "I suppose your motives were . . ."

Madge let out a barking sound. "Honey, were you listening to anything I just said to him? Now cut out the justifications and forgive the man. I ain't of the mind to stand here all day."

Now it was Deborah's turn to close her eyes. She didn't think she could do it. Her brain was in tangles. So much had happened. She wouldn't lie no matter what Madge said. With her eyes still closed, she said, "I will *endeavor* to forgive you."

Madge was silent for a moment. "Well, now that I consider it, I do believe that's probably the most we can hope for now."

"Now wait just one minute . . ." Patrick objected, rising.

Madge whacked his shoulder back down onto the floor. "Now *you* wait just one minute. She's being truthful, and that's a good thing. A marriage needs to be standin' on truth."

Both Deborah and Patrick let out a *hrrummph* on that note. It suddenly occurred to Deborah that Madge might be trying to unite her and Patrick against a common foe. She hated to admit that it was working. Deborah was sure that Patrick was as eager to get out from under Madge's thumb as she was.

"If y'all aren't the most bullheaded . . ." She didn't even finish the sentence. Instead she walked out from behind Patrick to stand next to the both of them.

"Fine, truth is good. Are we done yet?" groaned Patrick.

"No, Trick hon. We're just gettin to the good part."

Deborah couldn't even begin to imagine what the good part was. It surely couldn't be good. With Madge, who knew what to expect?

"Trick, you're gonna kiss her. Nice and sweet, like there might be a shred of feeling in that devious heart of yours."

Patrick snapped his head around at her with his eyebrows nearly knit together. Deborah just glared, wide eyed. They both started to object strenuously until Madge shot her finger up between them.

"And," she nearly yelled over their objections, "Deborah, you are going to let him. No fighting. Once, just once, I want you to *let* the man kiss you."

Deborah thought Patrick would find this part entertaining.

Just the opposite.

"That's it!" he howled, standing up and making for the door, nearly knocking Madge over in the process. "I've had enough . . ."

Madge was nonplussed. "What's the matter, Trick honey?" she called in a sharp voice. "You afraid I might see something you ain't ready to show me?"

Patrick stopped dead in his tracks.

Deborah thought about the kiss on Madge's balcony bench, and felt her heart turn inside out.

Madge sauntered up next to her. "Remember our little talk, dear? I'll see what I need to see. And if I don't, well, things still stand as I said. So now you

just stay put, don't go puttin' up a fight, and let's see
if he knows how to be gentle."

Deborah thought of his finger wandering gently
down her shoulder when he'd unlaced the corset. Of
the way his lips had just barely brushed hers before
something like lightning had shot through the both
of them.

When Patrick turned around to face her, she read
identical emotions in his face. Neither one was ready
to kiss the other again. The anticipation of whatever
would happen—and she knew something would happen—hummed though her body. She remembered the
look in his eyes as he hovered over her last night, his
breath spilling down across her neck. It became troublesome to breathe. She found her fingers fisting in
her skirts.

Patrick walked slowly, thoughtfully up to her.
Whatever would happen would be impossible to hide
or ignore. Every inch of her body knew it. He knew
it. She blinked in an effort to dispel the intensity that
kept building around her.

"Oh, that's a fine idea," came Madge's voice, suddenly soft now by her side. "Close your eyes, honey.
Just close 'em."

She closed her eyes thinking it might be easier not
to see him coming. It was a long, vulnerable moment
before she felt the startling touch of Patrick's finger
on her cheek. First just one, the way he'd touched her
shoulder with just one fingertip, then broadening his
touch to all four fingers and the heat of his palm. She
smelled the wool of his jacket sleeves and the salt air
of the harbor. Felt the tentativeness of his hands as

they moved to hold her face. He tilted it carefully up toward his mouth. That realization that he was genuinely, even affectionately, gentle flashed though her. This was no display.

Her eyes flew open in surprise only to meet his, looking at her with the same wash of astonishment that was pouring through her chest. It was there. The lightning was there. And neither she nor Patrick was pulling away from it this time. The gentleness of his touch compounded with Madge's staunch prediction that they could make each other happy dizzied her. Suddenly, it felt as if Patrick's fingers were the only thing holding her upright.

Patrick unconsciously licked his lips. He swallowed hard.

Deborah held her breath.

He kissed her. Softly, gently, with something almost like . . . surrender.

She let him.

Oh, Lord. What a powerful, frightening, indulgent thing it was to let him.

She held still while his lips grazed hers like a whisper. A soft, sizzling brush at first, but when he moved in and lay his mouth across hers, she drew in a breath. His thumb played across her cheek, sending tingles throughout her body. She felt his fingers gain urgency and push into her hair. Drowning, it felt like drowning. When he deepened the kiss just a bit more, a sharp, sweet taste came to her. She felt the gentle friction wrought by the pressure of his mouth, the prick of his rougher skin, and the angle of his face above hers.

Just this once. Let him.

His hand strayed down her neck to grasp her shoulder, as if wanting to pull her closer but resisting. After a moment he pulled her toward him. *"Let him"* chimed again, quelling her resistance—she wasn't at all sure if Madge had even said the words aloud.

She leaned in.

Deborah realized her fingers had let go of the skirts, flexing and spreading in the tide of sensations. His lips kept sliding across hers, lavishing her with soft caresses that seemed to melt everything in their path. She couldn't tell if the kiss had lasted three seconds or three hours. Her hands came up to touch his arms.

She touched him.

She'd never touched him before. Contact, but never *touch*.

His whole body responded. He sucked in a breath in almost a surprised way, then pulled away. The flash of near panic on his face told her he was trying to put the pieces together as furiously as she was. And she was guessing it made no sense to either of them.

Then the wall came up, just as it had done on the balcony. Before her eyes, his body transformed itself back into the theatrical showman. He arched an eyebrow at Madge. "Madame Cooney's parlor of forgiveness and fortune-telling is officially closed. You've been a fine sport, Deborah. Madge is a bit off her rocker, but she means well. Come now, wife, we've some supplies to get up on The Strand."

Madge's face registered satisfaction. She'd seen

whatever it was she was looking for and everyone in the room knew it. Deborah couldn't think of a single thing to say. Madge didn't seem to think words were needed. The whole thing just pushed this surreal experience that much farther away from reality.

Patrick guided her out the door and down the front steps, as if nothing had happened. Deborah was scrambling for any shred of composure. How could he be so callous after what just happened? A sharp, rejected hurt shot through her, erasing any of that silly magic she thought she felt. Make each other happy indeed. It was all just insane nonsense.

At the end of the sidewalk, she yanked her arm from Patrick's grasp and squared off at him. She used the only weapon she had. "I know about the family trait. The madness." She watched a hint of—no, it couldn't be regret, it was only surprise—flash across his face. "The whole Island's just waiting for you to follow in your brother's footsteps." It was a cruel thing to say. She knew it.

"Yes, they are," he said slowly, eyeing her. When he added, "I know," the edge in his voice told her she'd wounded him. It took much longer for the devil-may-care mask to return to his face. "Am I?"

⊰ Chapter Ten ⊱

The Thorn looked entirely too small.

Too small to be thrashing about on the Gulf of Mexico, much less the vast Atlantic Ocean. Too small to share with the colorful—and that was putting it kindly—crew. Far too small to share with Patrick O'Connor despite the other occupants. Deborah was infinitely grateful for the presence of another female.

Compared to the other ships moored in the harbor, *The Thorn* was actually large. Still, Deborah guessed even the massive steamship off to her left would feel too small for the voyage she was about to undergo.

Standing on the dock, surrounded by barking seagulls, mounds upon mounds of cartons, crates, and cases, bustling dock workers, and mean-looking sailors, Deborah felt totally alone. She wondered if the bizarre, resigned sense of calm she felt was what enabled men to walk into battle with dignity. This was so much more complicated than fear. Fright, trepidation, an anxious wonder, all of it made her feel as if her life wasn't even hers anymore, that she was just walking around in someone else's melodramatic circumstances.

"I felt the same way when I first saw her, hon."

Deborah looked up to find a clean, stalwart-looking lady standing next to her on the dock. The woman had a head full of dark-brown curls barely under control. She wore a loudly striped skirt, with a bodice fairly groaning to constrain her ample figure. She looked every ounce the captain's wife, even if she was much cleaner and better groomed than Deborah was imagining.

"Excuse me?" Deborah bumbled out.

"Looks tiny, don't she? You're thinking she could never get you to where you're goin'. Safely, that is. You're standin' here, thinkin' you're lookin' at your death. And this ain't at all what you had in mind when you walked down the dock. Am I right, sugar?" She said it with such compassion that Deborah didn't mind being caught doubting.

"You are. Yes, you are."

"I'm guessin' you're the new Mrs. O'Connor. I'm Delilah. The old Mrs. Davis. The Captain calls me Sweet, the crew calls me Ma'am, but I'd sure like it if you called me Delilah. We'll be far too cozy to be formal on this ship." A crewman walked by dragging a burlap sack and she jabbed him with her elbow. "Poke, you treat Obie's onions like that n' he'll have your hide, son. They ain't rocks, you know. Treat 'em *gentle-like.*"

As she saw her trunk being loaded into the hold, Deborah panicked. This was it. There'd be no escaping after they pulled up that gangplank and pushed off the dock. The finality of it, the irreversible nature of this voyage choked in her throat and thundered in her pulse. The power she'd felt in Patrick's kiss. The impossible wonder of all Madge had predicted. How he'd cut her into ribbons with his remark. How she'd fought back with a cruel slice of her own. Too much attraction and so much hurt.

She scanned the dock to see Patrick far away on the back deck of the ship consulting some map. At that moment, she was absolutely, positively sure she could not do this. *Run*, her brain screamed at her. *Just run*.

"Delilah, where might I . . ." She lifted her skirts a bit.

"On a ship, it's called a head, honey. And I wouldn't use the ship's right now if I was you. I'll walk you down to the Washington Hotel if you like. The ladies' parlor there will suit you far more."

Anywhere not crawling with men of any kind seemed ideal. "I'd appreciate it."

Deborah made an attempt at small talk as the women sauntered down the dock toward the hotel, calling orders and greetings to half a dozen earthy men on the way. Deborah's resolve doubled as she spied the caliber of men heading toward *The Thorn*.

The hotel was small but clean and well appointed. Recognizing that the ladies' parlor had only one door, Deborah crafted a quick plan. She steadied herself as she put a hand on the parlor door. In a burst of deception, she whispered to Delilah, "I've some tricky skirts on. Don't mind if it takes me a bit. I'm feeling a bit warm. Could you see if you could find

me a glass of water somewhere?" *"Go find water?"*
When you're standing with one foot in a powder
room? How convincing might that be?

"Need some help, sugar?" offered Delilah, looking
amused.

She backpedaled. "No, really, I'll be fine. It'll just
take me a while, that's all." She hesitated before
adding, "I don't want to keep you. . . ."

"They'll manage up at the dock just fine without
me. Take your time. Might be the last nice parlor you
see in a while. I'll go fetch you a drink, hon."

Deborah shut the door and exhaled. She shut her
eyes in a quick prayer, counting to twenty. Slowly,
she cracked open the parlor door to see Delilah turning the corner toward the hotel's dining room.
Holding her breath, she rushed from the room in the
other direction. Surely a building as large as this had
more than one door. A quick scan revealed a small
side door to her left. She fled toward it, fumbling
with the handle until it swung open onto a side
street. She pushed outside and shut the door, falling
against the hotel wall with her eyes closed in relief.

Freedom.

Act fast. Stay calm. Look ordinary.

Thud.

A large hand planted itself firmly on the wall in
front of her face.

"I considered running myself this morning. If that
makes you feel any better."

She knew the voice in the first syllable.

Deborah slumped against the wall.

"At Madge's . . . it wasn't . . . I'm . . . I'm sorry, Deborah."

They both fell silent a long moment.

"Would it help to admit I'm impressed? I'd figured on you bribing someone, but this is a far more intelligent choice." A faint hint of all the wonder-filled intimacy she'd seen at Madge's returned to his face. "You're not going to die on this voyage, you know," he said softly. "I'll take care of you. I happen to think you're well suited for adventure."

Deborah thought she didn't look like the kind of woman trained for high adventure. She had filing cabinet and ledger written all over her in meek, ordinary letters.

Patrick moved closer to her, not taking his hand from above her shoulder on the wall. In fact, he planted his other hand above her other shoulder, effectively pinning her to the wall. "I think we ought to try *getting along*." And in those two words the tangle of attraction pulled in around her.

"I don't want to go," she admitted.

"I *will* take care of you. You are not going to die. In fact, you might very well live for the first time."

"Do you believe in Madge's dream?" As soon as she asked the question, Deborah became quite sure she didn't want to hear the answer.

"I find myself quite willing to test the possibility." His eyes traveled down the curve of her throat and back up to her face. "There is something about the way your neck curves," the tone of his voice was bewildered, "just *there*," his finger brushed under her ear, sending a ripple out across her chest. "Who'd have thought . . ." He didn't finish the sentence. She wasn't even sure he knew he'd said it aloud, for an instant later, the thoughtful expression disappeared. "Come now." His gallantry returned. "Duncan's nearly inside-out with excitement. He's itching to show you his cabin."

His eyes sparkled at her. He wrapped his huge hand around hers and pulled it into the crook of his arm. "Come, wife," he said, his voice soft and poetic. "Let's go live us an adventure."

They turned the corner to find a frantic-looking Delilah, spinning around and stamping her foot.

"Now how in blazes did you . . . ? Did she . . . ? Oh *hell*." It took her no time at all to guess the sequence of events. And then she burst out laughing.

"I don't even want to know. But it sure as hell is pleasant to think you done met your match, Trick O'Connor." She winked at Deborah. "I'm a'growin' fonder of you by the minute, hon," she cooed, and then sauntered up the street.

"Do you know why I'm so fond of pearls, Delilah?" Patrick called after her.

"No," she called wearily back over her shoulder. "I sure don't."

"They start out as an irritation," he answered, staring at Deborah. "The more irritating, the better. The best pearls come from oysters that started out mighty annoyed."

"I knew that," Delilah replied, a smile tinting her voice.

Patrick took a long look at Deborah. One that

spun sparks through her before she could stop it. He smiled. "I'm gaining a high regard for the idea."

Patrick spread his hands on the bow rail. The varnish had lost its battle to the age of the wood, making it oddly smooth and scratchy under his fingers. A heroic surge of adventure coursed through Patrick's bloodstream, as it had since they shoved off that afternoon. His life had turned itself inside out in the last week. His carefully laid plan had exploded, but exploded into something wonderfully larger. He inhaled. The air seemed to seep down to the soles of his feet.

With a start he realized that the thing coursing through his veins was *life*. Being alive. It wasn't the offshore breeze, it was *him*. He'd been playing at being alive, displaying lifelike symptoms for everyone else, convincing himself he was still thriving. And it had gone on for too long. He was so good at it that he hadn't even realized the truth until the last rope was cast off. In that potent second, that last slow moment before the ship gave itself to the push of the wind, Patrick felt that same wind thrust him into life. Into wakefulness. Into his future which had been swallowed for too long in his grief for the past.

He'd told himself he'd brought Duncan and Deborah along to keep an eye on her. He knew, though, that he'd brought his family with him, taken the risks of bringing them along, because of the overwhelming ache to have them near.

I like her. He allowed himself for a moment to admit it openly. Patrick let the thought swim around in his head a minute. He watched the current swirl off the bow in a cyclone of bubbles. The weight of Madge's prophecy and his instant need not to let her stay behind tugged at his resistance. Finally, as the magic of the wind, waves, and sunset seeped through him, he let his curiosity venture one inch further. *I wonder if . . .*

She fascinates me. She did. He thought about the sensation that had broken open in his chest when she let him kiss her. She ignited long-dormant corners of his spirit. Pieces of him that had stayed conveniently dark and unattended.

At that very moment, as if cued by his thoughts, he heard the cabin door open. Deborah and Duncan came up on deck. The boy was in constant, wide-eyed motion, pointing at something new every second. He clung to Deborah's hand as they both struggled to find their balance against the ship's gentle motion. Together they marveled at a seagull's ability to fly seemingly motionless. The gull barked and swooped low over their heads. The antic sent Duncan into a frenzy of giggles, barking back at the bird in an amusing imitation.

Patrick heard Deborah laugh. Tentative, pressured, but there just the same. He liked the laugh. He wanted to hear it more often. He wanted to be the one to make her laugh. He suddenly envied Duncan.

He took a step toward them, and then stopped himself. There'd be time enough. Let them have this moment with each other. He eased himself back a bit out of view behind a barrel and watched. He hadn't ever had the chance to just watch her with Duncan.

Right now he wanted to just look at her, at the two of them together. At the picture they made together, enjoying the world.

The setting sun had pulled out from behind a cloud, throwing a rosy tone over the sky and the water. Flecks of light played off her face and arms as the two of them peered out carefully over the rail to view the wake. A gossamer curtain of stray hairs played across her cheeks and neck. Across that particular curve that kept intruding into Patrick's thoughts. The spot behind her jaw, just under her ear. The spot where a woman might put perfume. The spot where a man might kiss his wife awake in the morning. Or touch her gently as she lay sleeping.

Or lay dying.

His heart suddenly replayed the merciless agony of shutting Moira's eyes. Of looking for a pulse, and finding only terrible stillness. How quietly, how dreadfully easily she had left him alone. It was a vicious thing to stand by helplessly and watch your reason for being slide silently from your life. The burn, the pain of the memories that made it easy to stay distant and go through the motions flared back to life. And it was so much easier to stay burned than to stare the scar in the face.

"Damn lantern." Patrick struck his head against it for the third time.

"Potatoes, Pa, potatoes. Remember?"

"*Potatoes* sharp-edged, low-hung, scalawag of a lantern." Patrick rubbed the sore spot and tried unsuccessfully to shift farther down on the tiny bunk.

"Reckon sailors are smaller than you, Pa."

"What? Who ever said you had to be short to be a sailor? I bet all the pirates were as big as me. Bigger, even." Patrick managed a salty sneer for effect. "Argh, mateys." He squinted one eye shut and scanned an imaginary horizon. "It be takin' a large man to captain a black vessel and scourge the seas."

Duncan giggled.

Patrick sighed.

If there had been any hope for a quiet night where Trick O'Connor could contemplate his new adventure, this wasn't it. Spectacular as they were, the strange new surroundings aboard ship were keeping Duncan awake. He was tired and cantankerous and all too exhausted to sleep. It was well after ten, and Patrick was near the end of his patience.

Yet if the truth were really told, Patrick wasn't entirely disturbed by it. Duncan's endless popping out of bed and complaints of lethal shadows had kept Patrick from dealing with the real issue of sleeping in the same room with his wife. By the fourth episode, Patrick had simply resigned himself to spending the night hunched up next to Duncan in the tiny adjoining cabin. If anyone on the vessel was going to get any sleep at all, it seemed the only way. It felt only human to let Deborah have the cabin to herself tonight, in any case. So much—good and bad—had passed between them in the last twenty-four hours, it was overwhelming to be near her. She looked as if she felt the same way. They were both scrambling for a foothold, a place to start making sense of it all.

After no less than seven bedtime stories, Duncan's

eyelids gave in to the pull of fatigue and the boy fell asleep. Patrick dared not move. He simply angled his head out of range of the damnable lantern, hunched down an inch farther—which put his feet propped nearly halfway up the opposing wall—and let his own eyes shut. With a small laugh he thought that here—surrounded by unending coils of rope to knot—he had no need to relax. He was absolutely exhausted.

Patrick woke with a start several hours later, bumping his head on the lantern again. It was still night, and the ship was surrounded with a velvety, quiet blackness. As he gained his bearings, remembering where he was in the strange surroundings, he marveled at the sense of peace that enveloped him. He'd sailed more times than he remembered, spent more nights on ships than he could count, but never felt the strange sensation he felt now.

He couldn't have slept for more than three hours, and in a damned uncomfortable position for that matter, but he felt as if he'd slept a month. He was wide awake. Through the porthole's meager light he could see stars. They spilled enough glow into the cabin to outline Duncan's face. There was just something about the way that boy looked when he slept that made Patrick willing to take on the whole world to secure Duncan's happiness. The lushness of his lashes against that downy cheek. The trusting way his mouth fell open, breathing slow and easy. The open, upturned curve of his hand laying on the pillow. His son.

Patrick picked up the small toy turtle that was Duncan's constant nighttime companion and perched it on the blanket, taking care to place it on the side next to the wall so it wouldn't fall again. Dunc needed familiar things around him tonight. Thinking a moment, Patrick unbuttoned his shirt and folded it up into a small bundle, tucking it next to Duncan. Moira had done that with her dressing gown when Duncan was a small child whenever they went out for the night. She claimed the scent would let Duncan know he was never alone. Even though he was rather sure that, at the moment, he smelled nothing close to the talcum and roses of his former wife's dressing gown, he pulled off his shirt and tucked it in next to the boy.

He ducked under the tiny doorframe out into the dining area that joined all four officer's quarters. The hatch overhead was propped open a bit, letting the cool night air fill the cabin. A shiver told him that taking off his shirt wasn't the most sensible of ideas. And wandering about the ship half naked in the moonlight wouldn't exactly dispute the family reputation, would it? He tugged quietly on the latch to his quarters, taking care not to wake Deborah.

She is my wife now. He watched her sleep, noting how her lashes lay against her cheeks, how her mouth fell open in peaceful breaths. *I like her. She fascinates me.* His brain kept saying that over and over.

Patrick watched her for a long moment before he pulled his shirt on. Then, as quietly as he could, he rummaged through his trunk for a small package.

He slid open the department-store wrapping and pulled out three pairs of ladies' stockings.

In rose.

Not red, not shocking-odd-family red, but a softer, more genteel hue. Rose.

Patrick laid them on the chair next to the bed and silently left the room.

⚜ Chapter Eleven ⚜

"Good afternoon," Deborah announced as she pulled herself up on deck after a long morning of hiding in the cabin. She simply couldn't stand being cooped up anymore, and thought she'd best get on with things anyhow. Big as it was, it wasn't a huge vessel. She and Patrick would have to face each other no matter how long she hunkered below decks. She couldn't hide in the cabin forever.

The sun and breeze felt spectacular. The day was near picture perfect, pleasantly cool, yet clear and bright. It felt as if she could see forever, scanning the horizon in every direction. Deborah felt silly for keeping herself from this marvelous weather.

"Hello." Patrick looked up from the jumble of rope he was splicing as Duncan sat at his feet. Evidently he was teaching knots to the boy. Deborah remembered the loops of rope at his feet when he fell asleep her first night in the house, his odd evening ritual. It brought on a strange collection of feelings. His eyes were warm as they held her gaze, yet there was still the uncertainty that had sprung up in Madge's parlor. He looked different somehow, changed in a way she couldn't quite name. Heavens, didn't she feel the same way herself?

"Glad to see you up and about," he ventured. "I was hoping you weren't seasick."

"I'm not queasy," she replied, grateful for a safe topic, "I just keep bumping into things. It's rather aggravating."

"Me, too," chimed in Duncan.

"It'll come to you. By the time we dock it'll feel odd to be walking on land that doesn't move."

"C'mon, Pa, help me finish." Duncan tugged on his father's shirt and drew back his attention. Patrick looked so at home, leaning against the mast with his enormous legs angled out, his elbow parked casually on one jutted knee. He'd left his shirt open and rolled up his sleeves, and she watched the sinews of his arms flex as he worked the knots. The precise way his hands wove the line.

The rugged appearance suited him. His warm, tousled look made Deborah suddenly wonder where he had slept last night. With Duncan? On deck? Did it matter? What mattered was where he was going to bed down tonight. And with whom . . .

"I should ask you how you caught him, but I ain't so sure I want t'hear the story," Delilah teased as she appeared at Deborah's side with a cup of tea. "Trick said you drank tea. I've a private stash of my own that's off limits to the men. But you're welcome to it anytime."

Deborah took the cup gladly.

"Careful, hon, there's an art to drinkin' this standing on a ship. I've burned myself and my skirts too many a time."

Deborah leaned against the nearby wall for support and sipped the welcome hot brew.

"Hungry?"

Deborah nodded. She'd skipped breakfast even though she could smell it strongly enough to taste it on the air that seeped mercilessly under the cabin door.

"Lunch is soon, but I've a notion there's a bun or two back down in the cabins. You come with me."

Delilah was evidently rather starved for female companionship, for she kept company with Deborah for what seemed like hours. Deborah was glad of the diversion, not knowing what to make of the silky rose-colored stockings spread across her chair when she woke this morning. She knew what they were, could make a dozen guesses as to what they meant, but didn't know how to treat Patrick as a result of their offering. Was he branding her as an O'Connor or offering a peaceable compromise? Olive branch or shackle? The man was growing more complicated with every passing day.

Finally, an hour after lunch, Patrick came clunking down the cabin stairs to the dining table. Deborah only had to duck her head an inch or so, but Patrick had to nearly fold himself over to fit his considerable frame through the doorway. "Delilah," he groaned, rubbing an obviously sore back, "I want my wife back."

Delilah giggled knowingly and picked up Deborah's teacup. "I'd be a fool to stand in your way, Trick."

"Bless a woman who knows her adversaries. Say," he drawled, eyes glinting at Deborah, "there's a word worthy of your vocabulary, my dear."

"I imagine you've considerable opportunity to use the word," Deborah teased. "You count your adversaries in the high numbers I gather, Mr. O'Connor." It occurred to her that she'd never teased him before. Taunted certainly, but never teased.

It seemed to please him to no end. "In the thousands, Mrs. O'Connor. In the thousands."

Delilah knew her cue to exit. With barely a word, she bustled up the steps, her confounded chuckling echoing through the tiny hallway.

Deborah watched her go, if only to keep her eyes from Patrick.

"And you?" came his silky voice. "Are you among my hordes of adversaries?"

Unsure of which was the safer reply, Deborah remained silent.

"Ah," sighed Patrick. "The lady knows when an answer is important. And when not answering may be the best answer of all." He reached up to the cabin ceiling and pushed the overhead hatch open farther to let more light and breeze into the room. He rounded the corner of the table until he sat directly opposite her.

He rested his chin on his hand, staring at her. The slice of sunlight washed over him, setting off the flecks of gold in his eyes. There was something in those eyes. Fascination? No, it was more intimate than fascination. Whatever it was, it made Deborah's skin tingle. Had she not been a woman so deceived by men in her past, she might have even called it attraction. But Deborah no longer had confidence in her ability to judge the sincerity of a man's affections. There had been attraction with William's father. Warm, flattering affection from the reporter, Samuel Hasten. Both had been the farthest thing from love.

After an uncomfortable pause, Patrick straightened in his chair. "I've an idea," he began. "Wife, I'll strike a bargain with you."

"A bargain?" Deborah could only imagine what kind of deal was in the offing.

"Ask me whatever question you wish. Any question at all. I know you've a dozen buzzing around in that head of yours."

"And?"

"And what?"

"Surely any deal of yours has a catch."

"Indeed. This one does, as well." His eyes seemed to double their glow. It poured right into Deborah's stomach.

"And?" she said, not quite sure she wanted to hear it.

"And I will give you an honest answer."

Deborah balked. "Honest? From you? Are you sure you know the meaning of the word?"

She expected him to retort. To defend himself with some justification. He did not. Instead, he locked her eyes for a long moment, and said softly, "Yes."

Those eyes. They melted her composure. Trying to stare back, Deborah straightened her spine, put both hands flat on the table, and said, "I want *three* questions."

The corner of his mouth crept up. He folded his elbows on the table. "Two."

"Two, then."

Patrick stayed still, leaning in at the table, his eyes never leaving her. The sunlight guilded the tips of his eyelashes to a shimmering gold. With the exception of one thumb running absentmindedly around the other, he sat motionless.

It only took Deborah about a minute to decide which two questions. They had been setting fire to her mind for days. "Why," then she thought to add, "in *detail*, please, are we going to Venezuela?"

Patrick pursed his lips a moment before answering. "To find a pearl. A very particular, very valuable pearl." He reached into his pocket and, to her surprise, produced the bracelet he'd given her at Madge's dinner party. As he spoke, he pulled her hand across the table and began to gently refasten the piece. The tingle in her skin grew into something much deeper. "You see all the different colors of these? Pink, green-like, yellow, violet. Pearls come in a dozen soft colors like this. Water temperature, whatever got inside the shell, the oyster itself, these things make for the different tints. But all of them are light, soft colors." Patrick's eyes took on a faraway, adventurous look as he continued to play with the bracelet on her wrist. His fingers were fluttering over her skin, stroking, spinning the pearls, fingering the strands, doing things that made Deborah's head spin.

"But oysters aren't the only animals that make

pearls. Conchs do as well. You've seen conchs, those overlarge pointed snail kinds of shells? There's a kind of conch from near here that makes pearls in a bright red. They're small and rare, but you come across one occasionally. There's been a legend—around for centuries—about a different conch pearl. One with a dark, vibrant red. And very large." He circled his fingers to make an image about the size of a grape.

"Imagine: a scarlet, shimmering whopper of a pearl. La Roja, they called it—the red pearl. Found in the gulf way, way back. But, like most great treasures, stolen and never recovered. Most don't even know the legend, and those who do consider it pretty much imaginary folklore."

There was a fire in his eyes she'd not seen before. "But it isn't. La Roja is real. I've learned it's in the hands of an Indian tribe near the mouth of the Amazon River. They consider it sacred, and they've guarded it very well. Only now the tribe is dying out, and someone I trust has told me the pearl may be surfacing soon. On Margarita Island."

His eyes shifted from the bracelet to gaze into hers. "You are now one of only three people on earth who know." The heat in his eyes ran through her down to her fingertips. "I am going to be the man to find La Roja and bring her back." His tone challenged the world to prove otherwise.

Such a larger-than-life, exotic, adventurous dream. A *quest*. The romance of it all tugged at Deborah's ordinary, invisible life. To be one of only three people in the world to know such a secret. She couldn't help but be drawn in by the impossibility of it. The conviction in his eyes pulled her in. He looked eager to share it with her.

She couldn't refute it anymore; this was a powerful attraction. The way he was touching her now. The cadence of his breath and the inescapable lock of his eyes. Oh, Lord, she had been so easily fooled before. She, Deborah, the astounding judge of character, so blinded by Samuel's carefully crafted wooing. But the pounding in her chest refused to cease.

She knew what question number two had to be. It came out almost as a whisper. She could barely believe herself bold enough to ask it, but she had to know, now that she had his pledge of honesty.

"What are your feelings . . . for me?"

She'd caught him by surprise. His fingers stopped.

"I remind you of your promise of honesty," she added suddenly, feeling vulnerable. Every ounce of breath seemed to flee her body.

He took ages to answer. His eyes told her he was choosing his words carefully, holding himself to the honesty he'd pledged.

"I had not expected," he said finally, "to like you . . . so much." He said it without any hint of teasing or pretense. It was an admission. Something she guessed Patrick O'Connor didn't do very often. His thumb began to make gentle circles on her wrist. Then he did something Deborah had never seen him do: he looked away. She knew, instantly, that it was not because he chose to, but because he needed to. A rare hint of his own vulnerability.

Deborah's mouth formed "Oh," and she thought she said the word softly, but she wasn't exactly sure any sound came out. They both sat there, completely still except for Patrick's wandering thumb, thinking. Gaping at the nakedness of the moment, drawn to what was growing between them.

Patrick had regained his composure when he looked up again. "Might I have the same bargain of you? An honest answer?"

She looked at him, fully aware of what question he intended to ask, but wanting to make him say it. Not at all sure what her answer would be.

Patrick reached to her other hand across the table. He now held both her hands in his, his thumbs and fingers playing havoc with her sensibilities.

"May I ask," he began formally, "what are your feelings . . . for me?"

It was again a long, careful moment before she replied, very quietly, "Not yet."

There was just a moment when she saw the disappointment in his eyes, but it was quickly followed by an understanding, a compassion. A recognition that this, however exotic, was no fairy tale.

Patrick brought her hand up to his lips and left a tender kiss there. He started to say something, then stopped himself. He started again, but stopped himself again. In truth, Deborah had no bloody idea what to say either. Until . . .

"Potatoes," she whispered.

The afternoon dragged by. It was filled with details, small conversations, sights and sounds, but all of these floated above the undercurrent Patrick felt between him and Deborah. He couldn't even remember the last time he felt so unnerved in the presence of a woman. Goddamn it all, she'd undone him in two questions. The exact two questions—the *only* two questions—that would have unraveled him. How had she known? He needed time alone to think, to come to grips with this growing attraction, but it was nearly impossible on the small ship with Duncan tugging at his pant legs every two minutes.

Worst of all, he could tell that Deborah was feeling the same. Both of them were slightly short with the boy's endless requests. Even though he was trying to look anywhere but at her, they kept catching each other's glance across the ship. She was watching him as much as he was watching her.

The coming sunset was beginning to work its magic on his bloodstream. With a potent shock he remembered that after sunset came night. And with night came . . . came what? What he needed right now was about a dozen miles between him and the new Mrs. O'Connor, not the confines of a tiny cabin. Then again, maybe what he needed was to be right next to the new Mrs. O'Connor. Touching her.

No, he decided, what he really needed was to know what the hell was going on. And where to go from here. But—and this got under his skin most of all—he had no damned idea.

With a grunt he went down to the fore deck hull, thrashing around until he found a spool of rope. He slashed off a length. He made for the deck, hauling himself up the mast to the small lookout's bucket. It seemed the farthest away he could get, and the sea was calm enough. Patrick slowed his breath and closed his eyes. He ran the rope across his fingers, lacing them through it until the calm began to come. One knot . . . tight and hard. Two knots . . . a bit easier. Three . . . looped and smooth . . . four . . . *you like her*. Patrick undid that one and tied it again. Five . . . tight. Six . . . *you more than like her*. Seven . . . tighter. Eight . . . *you want her*. Nine . . . *tonight*. Ten . . . *tonight* . . . eleven . . .

Forty-three knots later, the cold gulf waters were looking like an excellent option. His body was humming with desire. Every time he closed his eyes he saw her face. His fingers slid over the rope and he thought about her corset laces. The act of releasing her body from that hard encasing to flow soft and smooth under his fingers. Patrick grunted in frustration and flung the coil into the gold-flecked trail of the sun on the waves.

Duncan shouted something to him from below, having watched the rope fly overboard. Deborah craned her head up from her conversation with Delilah, the arch of her neck burning into his chest. The sun caught on her bracelet—it pleased him that she hadn't removed it like she did the other night. It slid slowly down her upstretched arm as she shielded her eyes from the slanting sun to look at him. Patrick shook himself, the slow slide of the bracelet doubling his arousal.

It was bloody hopeless. *You might as well try to hold back the tide,* he thought to himself.

Patrick put on a clean shirt and trousers for dinner, taking care to wash the salt off his body. He combed his hair and shaved. He stared at Deborah throughout dinner, taking no care to fend off the comments Delilah made about his distraction. He chased Duncan around the deck seven times, tiring the boy out. It felt good to run, to exert himself, but it felt even better to know the boy would go to sleep. Patrick was in no mood to sit up and play the good papa with his son tonight.

Either Duncan sensed his father's determination, or God was kind, for the boy practically fell asleep on Patrick's lap as they made ready for bed. Patrick slid the boy under the covers, perching the turtle again on the wall side of the bunk. "Good night, son."

"G'night, Pa. Tell Ma I love her."

"She can hear you in heaven, Dunc." It was something they said to each other nearly every night.

"Yeah, but I mean t'other one, too."

The other one.

Deborah. Duncan loved Deborah. Patrick closed his eyes and let the boy's words seep into him.

Evidently God *was* kind.

ᐳ Chapter Twelve ᐸ

Deborah stood on the fore deck, watching the ship slice through the moonlit waves. The sea spread out calmly before her, coated in mist that moved, lifelike, about the ship, ebbing and flowing across the rhythm of the water. The moon looked distant, veiled by the mist. Only one or two stars could be seen. It was still early in the evening, and behind her Deborah could hear the bustle of the ship settling in for the night. Dishes clanging, the low muttering tones of the crew as they played cards in the hold below her.

From here it looked as if the ship could turn in a dozen different directions. Choose from a hundred different courses and find a thousand different ports. She, who had so few options in life, found herself awash in possibilities.

Madge's dreams and prophecies came to mind. Her life had been too much a product of hard reality to allow that kind of nonsense. Parents gone before she was ten, scooped up by the loving yet obligated Maxwell family into the status of a marginal family member. Surrounded, yet still very much on her own.

And yet the lure of some kind of destiny would not go away. Too many unbelievable circumstances had conspired to bring her to this point. And then there was Patrick. . . .

The thin thread strung between them this afternoon pulled at her continually. It was as if she knew where he was on the ship at every second. Her eyes kept straying to him. Patrick was certainly right about pearls having mystical powers, for the bracelet on her wrist seemed to melt into her skin, sending constant reminders of what his fingers had done. It rolled and slid in a distracting, hinting way that made her crazy all afternoon.

Yet she didn't take it off. She didn't want to.

He was going to come on deck any minute.

She knew it. Her skin seemed to expect it. And Deborah had no idea what she was going to do about it.

She inched farther toward the bow, in a futile attempt to put some distance between them.

There was nowhere to go. She knew it. He knew it. The whole universe seemed to know it.

Deborah shut her eyes when she heard the footsteps she knew were his come across the deck. He didn't say anything. He just came up to stand beside her—not too near, but close enough—against the railing.

"Hello," he said finally in a voice as smooth as the mist.

"Hello." Deborah replanted her hands on the rail. She forced her fingers not to grip, wiggling them instead.

"Duncan asked me to deliver a message to you. He said it just before he fell asleep."

"I'm glad he's asleep. Last night was hard on him."

Patrick waited a moment before continuing. She watched his fingers run along the railing. It made her think of the way they'd run along the inside of her wrist. *Oh, my.* "He told me to tell you he loves his Ma."

Deborah's chest cinched in, aching at the words. "He shouldn't ever forget her. It's good that he still loves her." The sharp irony of wanting such to be true of her own son, the boy who would probably never know her, might not even know she existed, drew a lump up in her throat she could hardly bear.

Her words must have shown it, for Patrick turned to her with an astounding tenderness in his eyes. "He said 'both of them'."

Deborah felt her heart both expand and contract at the same time. It was a painful, lovely sensation. She couldn't even attempt a response.

His face nearly glowed in the golden light of the ship's lamp. He worked to say something, and she realized speech eluded him as much as it did her at the moment. Finally, placing his hand atop hers on the rail, he whispered, "Thank you." The words were weighted with a grateful father's love.

Patrick's fingers clasped around hers. A breeze pulled some of her hair loose from its knot, and he reached up and brushed it aside. His hand stayed on her face, lingering against her cheek. Patrick's fingers found the corner of her spectacles and tugged a bit, arching an eyebrow in a request for permission to remove them.

She knew what it meant. And she let him. Everything fell out of focus with them gone. Everything except his face, which had come decidedly nearer.

"They hide a certain color in your eyes," he said. "I can't decide if I mind having it hidden all the time, or if I like the fact that I'm the only one who gets to see it." He smiled, and it flashed like lightning through the dark night. Deborah felt him slip one hand around her waist and turn her toward him. Her skin registered every inch of his fingers' progression around her bodice. She looked up into his eyes. There was no fear about his size now. It was something to surrender to. Something to hide in. His other hand wandered up her arm, and the unsteadiness of her feet had nothing to do with the ship's rocking.

Very slowly, looking into her eyes until the last possible moment, he drew his head down and kissed her. A soft, velvety kiss, as powerful as the one he'd given her in Madge's parlor. An embrace that swirled around her like the gulf mist. Despite all the anxieties clamoring within her, she pulled her hand from the bow rail and placed it on his chest. It was like touching a tornado.

And then she let him.

She dropped her defenses and let them step together across that imaginary line they'd drawn. She breathed in his nearness, letting the warmth from his chest seep through her hand until it seemed to pour straight into her stomach. It was wonderful. Deeply, incomprehensibly wonderful. Slowly, she returned his kiss. Then not so slowly.

His body responded, the recognition of her kissing him shooting through him with a force she could feel. His back stiffened, his breath came deeper, and his muscles flexed against her. Patrick made a low, urgent sound and pulled her in tighter, folding her completely in his arms. He slid one arm up around her neck and pressed his kiss down upon her until her lips parted and her head fell back. Curved against the solidity of his arm, her weight came out from underneath her. Letting her tongue wander over his, she gave herself over to the dizziness that seemed to seep outward from the friction.

His other hand tightened around her, holding her up. And when his tongue left her lips to wander down the curve of her neck, she was quite sure it would be a week before she could stand again. And she wanted not to stand. She wanted to fall, to tumble just like this felt, to let him lay her across some sweet and lush place and succumb to it all. His breath spilled across her bosom as his hands spread across her back.

Deborah let her hand roam up to his neck, and then into the thickness of his hair. It was just like she imagined—and she hadn't even realized she'd imagined what his hair felt like. Strong, soft, and full of life. With a small cry she pulled him closer, stroking his chin as his face came back up against hers. With a gulp of air, she pressed her mouth up against his, seeking his tongue with hers. There was nothing charming about this kiss—it was hungry and seeking and very quickly dissolved the willpower she had left. She could feel his hips press against hers, his own hesitation falling away under the pull of her touch. The knowledge that he was giving in to it as much as she was more compelling than the fire in his eyes.

It was she who pulled away first, needing to breathe. He kept his eyes closed for just a moment, lingering, his lips brushing the curve of her ear. Deborah scrambled for a mental foothold against the storm in her body.

His hands slid up her back to stroke beguiling circles over her neck and shoulders. One finger traced a steamy path just barely under her neckline. "It's late," he murmured in a husky voice.

"No, it's not," she countered, recognizing his insinuation.

"Perhaps, but let's pretend that it is." His fingers found their way up the nape of her neck, and tugged a hairpin free.

She shook her head out of his grasp. "I'm not much good at pretending. And I can't pretend that this is . . . is . . ." She couldn't think of a word.

"Isn't mighty appealing?" he finished for her.

"Of course it's appealing. You know it is. But . . ." Patrick's response was to continue tugging at the hairpins and give her ear an altogether exotic nip.

"It's late." He murmured right into her ear, sending vibrations down her spine.

"It's not," Deborah argued, panting. "Patrick, I won't deny what's . . . what's happening here . . . but it doesn't erase . . . it can't erase . . . what's gone on in the past. You've not courted me, Patrick, you've captured me. I'm not the type of woman who can just swoon onto the coverlets simply because I . . . because you're . . ." She didn't want to go any further. She'd said too much already.

Patrick's frustration colored his voice. "Deborah, we *are* married."

Deborah turned on him. "No, we're not married. *You* married *me*."

He did not reply.

"Do you know who you married?"

"I married Deborah Marie Edgerton. A damned surprising woman."

"I'm no blushing bride, Patrick. I'm not going to stand here and dissolve."

That look, that thoughtful look that was a mix of admiration and amusement, came back to his face. "I'd enjoy it if you did." It was an admission, not a retort.

"I imagine you would. Immensely. And perhaps it might even be easier for all concerned, but it still won't happen. I ask you again, do you have any idea who you married?"

Patrick leaned back against the railings and folded his arms. *And you're about to tell me,* his posture teased.

"I've a past, Patrick. I've not led the most attractive life. I'm no innocent. And . . ." she hesitated only a moment before revealing, "I know enough of a man's bed to know I'm in no hurry to get there."

She watched for some sign of surprise in Patrick's eyes, but found none. Instead he pushed himself up off the railing and pulled her toward him again. "Then I'd say you didn't know nearly enough about the right man's bed." He pressed up against her, and drew one finger slowly over the curve of her bosom. "Can you honestly say you don't want me?"

She thought about denying it. But it was so self-evident. Now who'd be pretending?

He smothered her in a long, powerful kiss. Her eyes fell closed as her brain clouded over with desire. Yes, she wanted him. In ways she couldn't have begun to expect. In ways she could neither deny nor hide. She fought her way to the surface, forcing out a "No." It was a sigh rather than a statement.

"Then I say it's late."

She wanted to. The temptation was so strong.

But she couldn't. She opened her eyes and gave him the strongest look her smoldering body could muster. "No."

He held her face in his hands. "Are you certain?" *Oh, it was the wrong question.* Of course she wasn't certain. She was growing less certain every second. His fingers pushed back to tunnel through her hair. She put her hands up on his chest to push him away, but touching him was a mistake. Instead, he pulled her in close, his eyes devouring her. "Let me," he said in a husky whisper reminiscent of Madge's soft command.

Oh, don't say those words. "Patrick . . ." It was getting harder to resist.

"Let me." The words were seeping with need, with request this time rather than demand, like an exquisite invitation. He began to cover her jaw in small fluttering kisses. To give in, to indulge in "happily every after," to *let him* became overpoweringly tempting. She took a deep breath.

"I know you," he said silkily into her neck. "I know who you are and all about you. I chose you. *Let me.*"

I want to.

He knows. He chose me. He . . .

Chose?

Deborah's spine suddenly turned to ice. "What?"

He pulled away, the desire still in his eyes.

"What do you mean, you *chose* me?" She said it slowly, her mind whirring.

"There's no deep, damning secret to reveal, Deborah. I know everything about your past in Austin. The newspapers. The scandal. I know all about it."

Her breath choked in her throat. *If that's true, then he . . .* "You know . . . all those things?"

"I know who I married, Deborah. You can't scare me away now."

Suddenly the whirling pieces snapped together in her brain. He knew about her past.

Oh, dear God.

He had sought her out.

He wasn't just looking for an unfamiliar woman for a wife, he was looking for a desperate one. Deborah pulled herself out of Patrick's arms. It all came hurling at her, a tidal wave of recognition. He'd wanted a woman who had no other options.

She'd been *hunted.*

Her hands began to shake. The mist suddenly became thick and menacing around her. With a fierce cry, she pulled back and slapped him.

"How could you *do* such a thing?" she cried, sorry she wasn't powerful enough to hurt him more. "You stalked me. Like an *animal*. Picked me out as prey like a wounded animal." She hissed the word out. She'd been deceived. By a smooth-tongued man. *Again*. The recognition of her folly stabbed into her like a knife. "*My God* . . ." She ran for the cabin, feeling as though she'd collapse into a thousand pieces at any moment. And no one would care in the slightest.

"Deborah, wait . . ." But she was gone.

Patrick slammed his fist into the mast. He stormed around the deck, seething. One of the crew poked his head out of the hold to see the commotion, but Patrick gave him such a dangerous glare that he retreated immediately. Finally Patrick came to rest against the bow rail, gripping it in fury.

It stung to have his actions painted in that kind of light. Predatory.

She was right.

Hadn't he gone into this only as a means to an end, the methods needed to reach a goal? Yes, it was a damned important goal, and yes, things were much different now, but in the beginning he *had* singled her out for her assumed weakness. Preyed upon her just as she said.

Patrick bent over and rested his head on his forearms. He was disgusted with himself. She was right.

Nothing he felt for her now changed the hard fact that his first intentions had been just as she said.

What you did was unforgivable, Trick. Unforgivable. What you feel now won't change that.

Patrick pulled his hands down across his face. His life was both falling into place and falling into pieces. He was on his way to find The Pearl. Duncan loved his new mother.

But his wife was sobbing in his cabin. He'd hurt her—mercilessly—and it mattered. Not just because she was Duncan's mother, or because she was his wife of necessity, but because she was Deborah.

And Deborah mattered. More than he ever could have imagined.

᛭ Chapter Thirteen ᛭

Sweet heaven, it was hard to avoid someone on so small a ship.

Patrick was exhausted after nearly three days of careful maneuvering to avoid Deborah. And three nights tangled like a pretzel in Duncan's cabin enduring the boy's endless questions about why he and Deborah seemed angry at each other. Not one of the many simplistic, placating answers he'd crafted for the boy worked. And then there were the glaring looks from Luther and Delilah every time he dodged Deborah's company. It was obvious from their conversations that Deborah had not revealed the questionable nature of their courtship—evidently they thought it some newlywed spat.

Meals were excruciatingly polite. Cool and perfunctory. Deborah spent most of the time in the cabin, coming out for carefully timed stretches to allow Patrick access to clothes and such. Everyone on the ship knew something was amiss, but no one spoke of it.

He watched Deborah when she wasn't looking. Watched the defeated set of her shoulders as she read

to Duncan. The slow pace of her walk as they played
games or scanned the horizon. Heard the strain in
her laughter.

He knew she was watching him. He could feel her
movement about the deck, staying almost out of
sight. He could hear her padding about the tiny
cabin late at night. Feel her on the other side of the
wall. He imagined her writing stacks of scathing letters, condemning him for his actions, berating herself
for the kisses they'd shared. Worst of all, he imagined
her swallowing her pride and writing to implore help
from the very people he knew she'd fled in Austin.

To distract himself, Patrick had fashioned a sort of
swing for Duncan. He'd woven together several
ropes to make a kind of upright hammock that he'd
fastened to one of the stable booms on the middle
deck. He'd spent endless hours designing it, fitting it,
rigging it, and then pushing Duncan back and forth.
Duncan was, of course, beside himself with pleasure.
But when back and forth weren't amusing enough
anymore, Patrick pulled it down and re-rigged it with
several pulleys so that with a tug on a rope, the
swing could move up and down just underneath the
sails as well. He told himself he'd rigged the pulleys
so that he wouldn't tire himself, but he had really
fashioned the pulleys so that Deborah could hoist
Duncan's weight easily. It gave both him and
Deborah something to do that didn't require much
thought and kept them from having to go near each
other.

On the day before they were to make port in
Havana, even up and down wasn't entertaining

enough for Duncan, so Patrick strung the swing up from a higher boom. It gave the swing a larger arc, with more room to maneuver. It was just the right combination of wonderful and daring—sending Duncan up into the air over their heads—to make Duncan thrilled. Even Deborah could make the swing whirl and swoop easily with today's good wind and frolicking waves. Duncan's squeals of delight brought a smile to Patrick's face as he made his way down to the cabin to find a clean shirt and shave.

He took pleasure in being amongst her things, even though they were always neatly packed away. This morning, though, he found a book left out on her bed. An old, worn Bible. It was stuffed with mementos, small cards, flowers, ribbons and such until it nearly couldn't close. Just tiny pieces of the things were visible outside the pages—a corner here, a petal tip there. He touched the cover, surprised by the emotion it held for him. Patrick realized that despite knowing the facts, he knew so very little about the woman. He wanted to know more. A strong temptation rose to look through the book, to see inside her life. And yet he couldn't bring himself to betray her in yet another way. He lay a hand on the book, fingering the binding, thinking of her and how she had come to invade his thoughts. He heard her voice echo as she called out to Duncan on the swing.

Suddenly, there was a cry from way overhead. A man's yelp of alarm and fear. Then a nasty, slow, splintering sound, followed by ripping noises and cries fraught with danger.

And then came Duncan's wail. Then a scream from Deborah. A dread-filled, straining scream atop Duncan's now panicked screeches.

A torrent of other noises—more yells, the groaning of wood giving way, panicked shouts among crew members—filled his ears as he flung himself out of the cabin and up the stairs.

Patrick's chest exploded when he came up on deck. One of the jibs flapped wildly. Ropes and wood were everywhere. A man had fallen from his high lookout post, and he lay in an unnatural tangle on the deck. But the huge boom was what sent Patrick running. The man's fall had knocked the boom out of position so that it lurched to one side, hanging like a broken wing over the edge of the boat.

And from its far end dangled Duncan.

The boy was screaming, flailing low over the water.

Deborah was flat on the deck, tangled in the ropes that were attached to Duncan's swing. She'd been pulled hard against the side rail by the weight of the lurching boom. She was shouting, pulling and fighting the ropes to try and bring the boy in closer to the deck. She cried for Duncan to hang on.

Patrick scanned the entire scene in a fraction of a second, and then sent his body flying across the deck. He threw himself down behind Deborah, wrapped his arms around hers and twisted the taut end of the rope around his own wrists. He heaved. Deborah cried out, the tension on the rope and Patrick's pull evidently cutting further into her hands and arms, but then she gritted her teeth against the pain and pulled with him. She seemed tiny against the huge bulk of his straining body, feet scrambling for a hold, struggling for Duncan. Other crew members came alongside, pulling from on top of the rail. Slowly—entirely too slowly—Duncan began to rise away from the water. Patrick gained more rope by winding it further around his arms, and he and Deborah pulled harder, begging Duncan to hold still.

Deborah was crying under her breath beneath him. He noticed the hemp around her arms and wrists was growing pink, and watched small trickles of blood seep between her fingers. His own palms were burning. The force of holding Duncan on her own must have shredded hers. Together, shouting and thrashing, angling their two bodies around to brace their feet against the rail, Patrick and Deborah began to hoist Duncan back toward the ship.

Delilah ran over to the railing, leaning, her hands grasping for any part of Duncan she could reach as he swung wildly. The boy's face was near white, his hands blue from their grip on the swing, his body shaking as he looked down at the hungry waves.

Catch him. Catch him, damn it. Catch any part of him. Patrick's own hands seemed to reach beyond the rope to try and grasp his son. Delilah caught hold of Duncan's pant leg.

With a yell of his own, Patrick doubled his pull to keep the boy from swinging away from Delilah's grasp. The force of his lunge pulled him and Deborah over backward. The rope drew hard against their hands. Pain shot through his shoulders and flooded his palms. Deborah cried out. The crew shouted and gave a mighty heave on the boom to bring it in.

For one heart-stopping moment Duncan lurched sideways, and then fell with the swing into Delilah's and Luther's scrambling arms. The crew pulled the boom farther in, and Duncan lurched again, sending him, Luther, and Delilah tumbling to the ground.

For two or three seconds a silence fell over the ship, an exhale of relief and exhaustion. Duncan was aboard.

"Pa!" came Duncan's crying moan. It was frail and heart-wrenching.

"Oh, God, Dunc. Son, are you all right?" Patrick was trying to disentangle himself from the twisted ropes that now laced Deborah and him together. For a split second he caught her gaze, red and tearful.

He didn't have words or time for the moment. But his world had shifted in a second.

Duncan was sobbing now.

Patrick wrapped his son in his arms with a ragged sigh. "Dunc. My God, Dunc. You're all right. It'll be all right. Duncan. Oh, Duncan." He kept murmuring to the boy as he worked the knots to free him from the tangle. Duncan's tiny arms were like vices around his neck, tight and frozen with fear.

"Lord sakes," came Delilah's breathless cry from over Patrick's shoulder. "You O'Connor men seem to make a habit of scaring the life out of me."

Patrick pulled Duncan free from the last of the

ropes. The boy plastered himself to Patrick's chest. He couldn't pull his son near enough, get him close enough to his hammering heart to slow it down.

There was a great, gaping lurch in his chest when he heard Deborah's voice behind him.

"Are you all right, Duncan?" Her voice was thin with pain.

Duncan pulled his head up from Patrick's neck. He wiped his nose on his sleeve. "Uh-huh," he responded, putting on a brave face for her.

Patrick couldn't even look at Deborah. There was too much pummeling through his chest to meet her eyes.

"You were a very brave boy, Duncan." Her voice was kind and gentle. Her hand came over Patrick's shoulder to touch the boy's cheek. It left a small, red smudge where she touched him with one finger. Her palm was torn to bloodied ribbons, and angry blisters had sprung up between red-pink flesh. Such ugly wounds on such a delicate hand. And Patrick guessed that she had used her better hand to touch Duncan.

The small fissure in his heart—the one so carefully kept in check—fell wide open.

"You were brave," Patrick managed to get out.

"I was." The quiver in Duncan's voice faded a bit.

Even though he was quite sure it would be his undoing, Patrick turned to look up into Deborah's face. Her hair was pulled from its pins and the top button of her blouse had been torn loose. There were two rips in her shirt sleeve. She held her hands away from anything, her fingers spread in pain. He made himself hold her gaze. Made them look at each other. Forced himself not to back off from what had just happened. What they had done together.

"Thank you." Two pitiful words. It was so very far from enough, but he couldn't say more. Her eyes shimmered with a tear. He pulled one hand from Duncan's chest and placed it gently on her elbow. "Thank you."

⇥ Chapter Fourteen ⇤

"Ow. Ow-ow-*Ouch!* Do you realize how much that hurts?" Deborah winced as Patrick insisted on scouring her wounds to a pulp.

He kept his head bent over her hands. "As a matter of fact, I expect it hurts a lot."

"It's bad enough—*ouch!*—that Delilah felt called upon to snip off half my palms—*ow*, please, not there—must you baste the remainder in soap?"

"An infection would hurt more." Patrick wrung out the cloth.

"I cannot imagine what would hurt more." Deborah sucked her breath in through her teeth as she tried to wiggle her fingers. Her heart sunk as Patrick dunked the cloth back in the tub for another round.

"There are small caterpillars in the Amazon jungle that crawl in through your ears while you're sleeping. They slip down your throat and into your stomach. Then they eat you very slowly from the inside out. They say you feel every single bite."

Well, yes, that certainly qualifies as hurting more.

Deborah felt the room starting to spin. She leaned back against the chair, but her shoulders hurt, too.

A slow grin spread across Patrick's face. "I'm just teasing you. I made that up. To take your mind off the pain."

"A very poor diversion." She eyed Patrick's expression. "How *much* of that did you make up?"

"The part about eating you from the inside out. The Amazon has its share of nasty critters, but the ear-loving caterpillars are in Africa. And they're beetles."

"How relieving." Deborah tried not to look so repulsed.

"And those only eat your ears," he teased her further. "But I hear it's very unpleasant—hearing the crunching and all."

"Unpleasant? Such as having someone scrub off the last remaining layer of your skin? With—OUCH!—alcohol?" She flinched for the hundredth time as Patrick soaped yet another finger.

"It's only soap."

Deborah made a face. "It's exceedingly strong soap."

Patrick swept his eyes over her. "You're exceedingly filthy." He reached the cloth up to wipe something off her forehead. As he let the cloth linger beside her brow for a moment, almost intimately, they both fell silent. They'd not talked about it yet. Delilah had spirited Deborah off to tend her wounds while Patrick calmed Duncan. It was near sunset, and this was the first they'd been alone together. Both of them were grasping at ways to cope with the situation. To pretend that things were still the same when the truth was they had become very much different.

Flustered, Patrick dropped the cloth to the cabin floor. In the small confines he had to angle down on his knees to retrieve it. The movement put him at Deborah's feet. He straightened up very slowly. When he finally raised his head to look at her, fear, uncertainty, and gratitude played across his features. The golden brown of his eyes rippled in the lamplight. She felt their intensity down to her toes.

After a moment, he broke away, and began to busy himself bandaging her hands. There was something wildly powerful in the way he touched her now. It had both a gentle and a dangerous quality.

"It was a damn fool thing to rig that swing," he cursed, almost under his breath, as he worked the bandages. "What kind of father hoists his son up on a ship mast like a blasted sail?" Deborah didn't reply. Yes, she supposed there was some element of risk to it, but it had been getting harder and harder to keep Duncan amused over the trip, and the swing had made him deliriously happy. Who could have foreseen such an accident?

Patrick's fingers were still gentle, but the tension in his neck and shoulders showed the gathering storm. He was torturing himself for putting Duncan in danger. She'd known it had to come out sooner or later. "He's a boy," Patrick cursed, still not looking up. "A tiny boy. And what do I do? I take him halfway across the world toward some godforsaken jungle, just because I can't bear to be away from him!" He

took a large strip of cloth and yanked it in half.
"What kind of selfish man puts his own damn son in
such danger? After all I promised to Moira. . . ." The
name of his lost wife opened the floodgates. "He's
my . . ." His control dissolved right in front of her as
the terror of the afternoon took its toll. "What if . . .
oh, Sweet Jesus, what if . . . ?"

Patrick's head fell into her lap. His hands groped
up about his head and she heard him moan another
tortured question into her skirts. It broke her heart
to watch him come unstrung. He drew in a few
ragged breaths. Then she saw his shoulders give a
great, silent shake as the guilt and fear wracked
through him. A single, unspoken sob.

Something uncurled in Deborah's chest. A powerful compassion and respect for this man who loved
so fiercely. Gently, she lay her bandaged hand on his
head. She held it there, unmoving, uncertain. He
stilled in her lap. Deborah made a small, careful
stroke through his hair. She closed her eyes, frightened of the moment, of the depth of feeling welling
up within her. Oh, to be loved so fiercely. To be the
object of a loyalty so strong that it would transcend
every other objective or code. She wanted that.

She wanted this man's kind of love. She allowed
herself to wonder if, in spite of everything, they
might be the ones to bring happiness to each other.

Deborah felt Patrick drop his hands to her lap.
Eyes still closed, she placed the other hand on his
head. She could not move her hands much—they still
stung ferociously—but she let them wander in short

strokes. The steam from the tub next to them hung in the air. She could hear his breathing, feel his hands begin to move, feel him raise his head off her lap. He was looking at her. She knew it. And she knew when she opened her eyes that there would be no going back.

Deborah opened her eyes.

Patrick's gaze was a warm wash of power—soft and pulling.

He held one bandaged hand. "What you did . . . for Duncan . . . I can't . . ." And it didn't matter that it stung when he placed a soft kiss on her palm. No flash, no control, just a pure gesture of gratitude.

Without a word, Patrick reached for the damp cloth. He rose up on his knees and began to gently wash her face. He stared into her eyes as he wiped the warm cloth across her forehead. Slowly, he brought the cloth down the side of her face and followed her jaw line. A long, lush stroke that made her inhale a jagged breath. He reached up and wiped the other side with as much care, stopping at her jaw to venture slightly down her neck.

Deborah felt a trickle of warm water drip from the rag and run down to her shoulder. It felt like his fingers had wandered there. She gulped in another breath.

"You're a mess," he whispered. He pushed a strand of hair back from her forehead, the touch of his bare hand shooting through her. He pushed back the torn collar of her blouse and wiped her collarbone. She could feel his eyes on her neck, feel him pressed up against her knees. It was overwhelming, this thing between them. Her hands came up in a useless defense.

"Please," he said softly, unbelievably softly.

Deborah swallowed and closed her eyes. She leaned back in the chair and let down her resistance inch by inch. Patrick rewet the cloth, and when it returned to the side of her neck it was warm and distractingly smooth with soap. He moved to the button on her blouse, and she flinched.

His hand came up to graze her cheek, imploring her to open her eyes. When she did, the tenderness that flooded his eyes took her breath away. "Let me," he whispered, cupping her face. His hand slid down her face and came to the button. He pulled the blouse open and pushed it back, exposing her shift and corset. Delicately, he wiped her chest, the water trickling down her bosom, dampening her shift and the edge of her blouse. She watched his hand move across her body, captivated by the movement, the servitude of it, the tender seduction of the act.

When he pulled the blouse off her shoulder, she did not flinch. To her own surprise, she let her head fall almost lazily to the side, exposing her shoulder further. The warmth of the cloth and the softness of the lather mesmerized her. Patrick was making slow arcs over the curve of her shoulder. The sensitivity of her cleaned, wet skin was astounding. Even the air that touched her seemed to have a texture.

She didn't want to fight it any longer. She knew that now. The power of Patrick's gentle request lay siege to any resistance that was left in her.

Patrick eased her wet blouse sleeve over the cumbersome bandages and dabbed carefully at the red slashes left by the ropes. There was a bit of pain, but the astounding friction of his hands and the cloth on the inside of her wrist was wonderful. And when Patrick lay a flurry of soft kisses on the inside of her elbow she felt she might melt and trickle right off the chair like the water down her arm.

Suddenly there was no cloth, just the exquisite movement of his bare hand sliding on the soap. Deborah felt her shoulders relax into the chair. All her anxiety seemed to slide off her body with the second sleeve of her blouse. He washed the other arm in tender silence, but she could hear his breathing. Deborah didn't want to open her eyes. She wanted to just feel.

She felt a soapy hand feather a touch across her neck, leaving a soft curve of the suds that slid down onto her chest and ignited her skin. Her spine arched instinctively. Patrick's hand began tracing dazzling circles just below her collarbone. It became harder to breathe.

When Deborah's eyes began to flutter open under his touch, Patrick found himself whispering, "Shhh." He wanted her to stay as she was, receptive, feeling.

His pulse began to pound as he watched the slow arc of soapsuds sink toward the curve of her bosom. His skin singed as he watched the creamy bubbles slide and disappear under the shift. The wet fabric took on delightful textures as it clung to her skin. With a deep breath he splayed his hands across her chest and let his thumbs wander ever so slowly down to where the soap had gone. Enticing curls of wet hair clung to her neck. She breathed deeply, her chest rising up to meet his fingers as they touched the upper curve of her breast.

Dear God, she felt exquisite. A low, silky growl came from deep in his throat. He'd not even kissed her and yet the power of his desire astounded him. What would happen when she touched him? In a flash he realized that she could not touch him, not with those wounded hands. The idea that he was just hers to touch, that this would be his touching of her, his giving to her, roared through his veins.

Patrick glided his hands back up to her shoulders to gently nudge them forward. He wanted to do this in silence, hoping she'd understand. When he inched his fingers down toward her lacings, he could practically watch her body recognize his intentions. And it was a damn attractive sight.

His breath came harder as he felt the laces give under his fingers and the corset finally fell away. The sight of her inhaling against the transparent wet shift, the cling of the garment to her supple curves, sent him over the edge. Sliding his hands down her arms, he leaned in and kissed that sweet, calling spot just under her ear. The taste of her wet skin was satisfying beyond his imagination. The instant, ancient flex of her body pounded through his loins. And before he could stop himself, he covered her neck and breasts in deep, inviting kisses.

"Patrick . . ."

"Shhhh."

He wanted to take her and show her he could be gentle. It scared him beyond sense how much he wanted her. How he wanted to bury his face in her hair and feel her ripple underneath him and hear her sigh his name. Patrick didn't want her because it fit the scheme of things, because of Duncan or the accident, he just plain *wanted* her. *Her*. With an intensity that left reason miles behind.

He put his face close to hers, letting his thumb stroke her cheek. Every bone in his body cried in refusal when he said quietly, "If you want me to stop, I will. But I don't want to—not for every pearl in South America. But if you need me to stop, Deborah, tell me now. In another minute I won't be able to."

He could see her wrestle with it. There was no question her desire had been lit, for her skin was flush and her breaths quick and shallow. But he knew her. She'd not go further without trust. Without respect. Without some proof that this was not just lust, but a venture into the kind of marriage neither of them had planned.

He wasn't sure himself. What was it he was feeling? The desire was there, to be sure, but he was certain there was more. He touched his forehead to hers.

"Patrick?"

"Yes?"

"I need to know what you're feeling." What other woman would be so direct? She was so blasted practical. He found it delightful.

He groped for the words, his physical urge giving way to the suddenly more powerful desire to give her what she needed. What he realized he *wanted* to give her.

"You fascinate me," he said, tracing the path of her eyebrow with his finger. "I don't know what to do with you." Patrick knew that wasn't what she was looking for. Passion clouded his thinking and he cursed under his breath in frustration.

"Try again, Patrick."

He shook his head, pulling his hand down across his face. *Come on now, Trick, fire up that silver tongue of yours and find the words. It's now or never, man.*

"You . . . you said it yourself: you didn't marry me, I married you. I used you, sought you out as a means to an end. I'm . . . sorry. It was a terrible thing to do. Then again . . . I can't make sense of an inch of it, but I . . . Deborah . . . I'm *glad* I stole you . . . and not just on Duncan's account. I want . . . hell, I can't explain it."

"Try." Her voice told him she wanted him to find the words. Wanted him to give her what she needed. So she could give herself to him. She wanted it as badly as he. Patrick took a deep breath.

"Lately I wonder if I've gotten it backward. If you didn't find *me*. I want . . . I want you with me. I want to be a . . . *husband* to you. I . . . God damn it, this is hard . . . I think we really are . . . something to each other." He couldn't spit the words out. "I never thought we could, but now . . . you . . ." his voice fell off, convinced he'd muddled it.

With her bandaged hand, she touched his chin.

And then she kissed him softly. "What if we really are?" she said quietly, her eyes wide.

"What if," he repeated. It was more an exclamation of amazement than a question. His hands began to roam down her sides.

"What if you were a husband to me?" Her eyes fluttered as his hands found her hips.

"What if I did everything I was thinking?" Patrick was thinking of running his hand across her thigh at the moment. It made it a trifle difficult to talk.

Her eyes took on a lush tint of passion he'd not seen before. "What if I wanted you to?"

Oh, Lord.

Patrick moved in against her, beginning a long, deep kiss. He tongue swept across hers, calling, inviting, until her arms came up around his neck, and she began to curl and arch under his hands again.

As he undid the buttons on her shift, he let his kisses wander until she almost pushed up out of her chair. What a thing it was to give her this marvelous pleasure. To watch her unfold before him. To be the one to please her. To be a husband to her.

Patrick's mouth was weaving a head-spinning magic over Deborah. She couldn't pull enough air into her lungs to fight the fire curling up from her stomach. The unfulfilled ache to touch him back only fed her craving to be touched all the more. There was no pain now, only fierce, hungry pleasure.

Every time she moved to embrace him as best she could, he gently placed her arms back down. This

was another of Patrick's extravagant gifts—but one
of an entirely different kind. This, she knew, cost him
his distance. It would cost her her own. Here, now,
not in that dusty charade outside Galveston, would
be their wedding.

She barely heard his voice when he said,
"Deborah, can you stand?"

"Mmm?" she said, fighting to clear a thought.
"I'm sure my knees wouldn't hold me."

Patrick shot out a breath. "Well," he said in a low
rumble, "I can't get these blasted skirts off unless you
do."

"For God sakes, Patrick, stand me up then."

His laugh was rich and delicious when he did,
amazed at her blatant desire. And she found herself
wishing she could fumble with his shirt buttons with
the same urgency he went at her skirt waist. After a
couple of tuggings and soft cursings, the heavy skirt
fell to the floor. Then the petticoat, leaving only the
wet, half-undone shift. Patrick tried to bend down to
gather them, but it was nearly impossible with both
of them, and the tub, in the tiny cabin. Instead he
picked her up and slid the skirts over to the corner
with one swift kick.

It felt wonderful—weightless and delicate—to be
held against him like that. With a groan of pleasure
he let her slide down his body, leaving slow kisses in
a dozen wicked places as she descended. She wanted
to stay there, pressed against him, but he eased her
back into the chair. When he dipped the cloth in the
tub again she thought she would melt on the spot.

Patrick began with one foot, then the other. It was without a doubt the most sensual thing Deborah had ever experienced. The man did things to the curve of her ankle that made breathing impossible. There was soap and water and hands and the tantalizing cling of wet cotton everywhere. And when he worked up her calf and over her knees, all hope was lost.

She wanted him everywhere. She wanted him in her life, in her carefully guarded heart, his body in hers. It was torture not to be able to touch him, to explore his chest as he shed his shirt. She welcomed it when he peeled the wet shift from her body and she lay against the chair, naked before him.

Patrick kneeled down in front of her and doused her with soap and warm water again. The water rippled and singed against her exposed skin. His wet, soapy hands caressed her breasts, slid across her belly, spread across her hips. Then, as his fingers wandered up her thighs, it was as if the chair could barely contain her. His fingers found that singular and welcome place where every slow, intimate stroke filled her with desperate need. There was no more "let" him. Now was about "want." Hunger. *Craving*. Patrick gave her touch after luxurious touch, climbing, calling, his fingers creating and quenching and fueling the need. Giving, seeking, building to a breathtaking, lightburst of a moment where she felt the chair had tumbled off the end of the earth and she with it.

When she caught her breath and opened her eyes, Patrick was staring at her with a potent mix of grati-

fication and hunger. It wasn't about the giving any
more. Her husband's need to take pleasure of his
own practically filled the air.

"Come, wife," he said huskily. "It's high time we
made a marriage bed." In a single move he plucked
Deborah from her chair, water still dripping from delightful spots everywhere, and lay her across the bed.

Patrick was so taut with need after watching
Deborah come to her release under his hands that he
had no idea how he could be gentle with her. He
needed her now, this second, right here. He tried
slowing his hands down as they slid across her hips
but they wouldn't. He was leery of this hunger he
could no longer leash, but it was too late. As carefully as he could, he lay down next to her, groaning
deep in his throat as he felt the length of her body
touching his. Dear God, he wanted his hands and
mouth on every part of her all at once. In the midst
of his raging passion, he suddenly realized that she
knew it. She knew his need was beyond his control,
and she welcomed the chance to fill it. Openly gave
herself to the power of it. He was free to take his
pleasure in her, but only—and somehow this made it
all the more potent—because he had given hers so
freely.

Patrick let go the last shred of his control. His
mouth groped hungrily at the sweet curves of her
breasts, tasting the traces of soap left in that delicate
hollow just below her ribs. Burying himself in the
waves of her hair, Patrick sent his hands urgently
down the warm, wet side of her body. Her muscles

pulsed and flexed as he pulled her thigh up against him, and he pressed his hips to hers. Patrick gave himself over to the fantastic pleasure of bedding his wife.

His wife. He kissed her with deep and powerful urges, taking and tasting, delighting in the friction, craving the contact.

When he could wait no longer, he entered her slowly, reveling in that pure, perfect instant when she sighed and opened her eyes and body to receive him. The rhythm began. And built. Hard and fast. Before he could think another moment, he crashed toward the light and hit it at blinding speed. She followed in the next moment with a shudder he felt to the depth of his soul. His heart broke open in a thousand pieces and Patrick O'Connor came to the realization that he could love again. That he would love again. And that it would be this woman, this ill-begotten godsend of a bride, who would give it to him.

⊰ Chapter Fifteen ⊱

"He's asleep." Patrick shucked his shirt off for the third time and eased himself back into the bunk beside Deborah. She watched him fold his large body into the tiny bed, newly amazed at the flexing of muscles and the delightful warmth that flooded the cabin when he came through the door. It didn't matter that Duncan had been tormented by nightmares most of the night—the boy had been through so much it was a miracle he slept at all. And despite the interruptions, each of his trips to Duncan's cabin gave her another chance to wonder at this man. His brief absence gave her a respite to think it all through, marvel at its impossibility, only to watch him come back through the door and remind her it was all real. She could barely sleep anyway; her astonishment fueled too much energy.

"Poor Duncan. He's a strong boy. He'll be alright." Deborah angled up on her elbows, sore but eager to soothe his spirit.

"That he is. But I'd prefer a sleepy boy this evening. I'm of no mind to be interrupted again. It's mighty hard to pull your arms away from a naked woman." The glint returned to Patrick's eyes. "Naked, and glowing. Those things tend to bolster a man's spirits, you know."

Deborah rolled her eyes. "You *are* a Visigoth." The sparkle in his eyes gave her hope for their future together.

"Oh, lass, do you not know how many ladies *yearrrn*"—he rolled the 'r' for effect until he sounded nearly Scottish—"for such a man?"

"I've done a weeks worth of 'yearn'ing"— Deborah tried to roll the 'r', with disastrous results— "in the last few hours." She suddenly blushed. "Dear God, do you think anyone heard us?"

Patrick gave a healthy laugh. The brogue continued, "Potatoes, woman, do you think I care? Did you know, m'dear, that ye' make the most *intrrriguing* sound when properly pleased?"

Deborah's eyes popped wide in shock. "Patrick!"

"Aye, 'tis true." He folded his hands behind his head and gave a grunt worthy of a Visigoth. "Gives a man a fine satisfaction to hear it."

Deborah was scarlet down to her toes, she was sure of it. "Must you?" She tried to put a scolding tone in her voice but found it impossible. Not with the way he was looking at her.

"I believe I must." With that growled into her neck so fiercely, the vibration made her laugh. He clasped his hand over her mouth, and in an entirely-too-accurate imitation of her said, "Dear God, do you want the whole ship to hear you?"

This, of course, only sent her into further gales of laughter, so she bit his finger in self-defense.

"Ah, so it's biting we've come to, is it?" Patrick pounced on her, pinning her in a split second. "Are you sure you're ready to travel down that path, lass?" He let his gaze wash across her body. His face transformed as he looked at her. Then, still holding her hands above her head, he stared deep into her eyes. His foot found her ankle under the covers and began exploring. His hand wandered down her arm, down her neck, down to make entrancing circles over her heart. That's all it took to send the sweet hunger flaring up again. Amazing.

The man's eyes lit. "How are you?"

"Are you asking me if I'm sleepy?"

"No."

"In pain?"

"No."

"If I need my dressings changed?" She waved her hands at him.

"I've changed enough of your dressing for one evening, don't you think?" His foot had moved up to her calf, holding her still in a way that made her skin tingle.

"I might need to consider this a moment."

Patrick's hand made a languid circle up the curve of her left thigh. "I'll allow eight seconds."

Deborah reached up and kissed the base of his neck. "I'll only need five."

Patrick leaned in "Four . . . three . . . two . . ."

"Pa!"

The Thorn pulled into port about an hour after sunrise. It had been a long night. Deborah's body hurt nearly everywhere. From the stiff way Patrick bumped around the cabin, the same could be said of him. He'd gotten up so many times last night to tend to Duncan, Deborah wondered if he had slept at all. He looked exhausted, and yet changed. As if weight had lifted from his face. The man had a twinkle in his eye to rival Duncan's cheerful expression.

And Duncan *was* cheerful. Awake painfully early, seemingly recovered, making noises in the adjoining cabin. Whining at why Patrick wouldn't let him in the larger cabin. After twenty minutes or so, Patrick came to the end of his temper. Trousers barely on, shirt still open, he threw open the cabin door and bellowed for Delilah.

She came sauntering over, already dressed, wiping her hand on an apron. Deborah slid down under the coverlet when she saw Delilah craning her head to see past Patrick into the cabin. From the look on the woman's face, she didn't need to see anything, she'd guessed it all before the moon even rose.

"For the love of God, Delilah," groaned Patrick, "would you take the boy somewhere for me?"

Delilah's answer was merely a worldly chuckle. "Duncan," she called, still looking straight at Patrick, "I can't seem to find that bit of chocolate I hid way down in the hold. Would you come help me find it, sugar?"

"Oh, yes!" came Duncan's voice. He flew from the other cabin past Patrick. "Bye, Pa!"

"You're a godsend, Delilah." Deborah could tell even by the angle of his shoulders that he was grinning.

"Ain't I now, though?" replied Delilah over her shoulder. "You tell that pretty little wife of yours that I'll hold breakfast one hour for you two, and not a moment longer. I've got a list of supplies to get that'd stretch a mile long today. And sugar, you'd best remember you've got only six hours to make your steamship."

Patrick merely shut the door and put his head against it. He swore softly in Gaelic.

Deborah stifled her laugh. It was amusing to see him frustrated. It offered a glimpse of the all-too-human man carefully hidden under the wild pirate caricature. She pushed herself upright—with some difficulty, considering how much her hands hurt—and sat against the wall, pulling the bedclothes around her. The weight of yesterday's events settled down around her shoulders and sobered her.

"He seems fine," she offered.

Patrick sat down on the bunk next to her. For the first time she noticed the red marks circling his own arms. New noises and the scents of a busy harbor came in through the porthole above them. He flexed a wrist, rubbing it. "He's a strong lad. He'll be all right, I'm sure."

Deborah paused. She pushed the hair out of her eyes with a bandaged mitten of a hand. "And what of us?"

Patrick showed no surprise, only careful thought. "What of us?" he finally asked in reply.

Deborah took a deep breath. "Last night changed many things."

"Mm-mm." Patrick leaned back and pulled up his

knees, resting his elbows on them. He leaned his head to look at her as they sat side by side on the bunk. His manner told her he wasn't about to trivialize the bridge they'd crossed. He looked ready to listen. "It did," he agreed.

"It did not *erase* anything, Patrick." Deborah thought about what it felt like to hit him when she'd learned of his pursuit.

He thought for a moment before replying, "True."

"I'm at a loss. You've still done something I consider cruel. And yet again . . ." she flailed her hands in frustration. "Oh, Patrick, I'm . . . I'm not at all sure last night was wise."

Patrick reached out to still her hands. "Last night was very likely the wisest thing I've done in a long time."

Deborah blushed in spite of herself. She needed to talk through this, to think it out—together, if they could manage it. "But there are still things between us, Patrick. However wonderful last night was . . ."

"Glad to hear you consider it wonderful," interrupted Patrick, smiling.

". . . it doesn't change some things," continued Deborah. "You used me, Patrick. I don't know how to forgive that—yet. I'm not certain what I should do until I can. Patrick, I don't know if I can put all this together in a way that makes sense to me."

Patrick blew out a breath. "Mighty deep questions for before breakfast."

"A vat of coffee wouldn't make it any clearer and you know it."

He pulled his hand across his stubble and looked

at her. "Has anyone ever told you you're a damned
sensible woman? I expect any other woman would
just lie lazily on the sheets, wearing a dreamy smile
or some such thing, but you sit up and *analyze* the
situation. You have a go at the serious questions before you've even got a petticoat on. Potatoes,
woman, is it always going to be like this?" She very
much liked the twinkle in his eye when he said "always."

"I imagine it is." She leaned her head against the
wall. He had a way of making her heart run miles
ahead of her brain when he looked at her like that.

"Remind me to tell the ship steward to have a vat
of strong coffee brought to our room—at sunrise—
every morning. I'll need three or four cups before you
even wake up, if you keep on like this."

Deborah shot him a "you're evading the issue"
look.

Patrick exhaled. He fingered a large blister on his
left thumb. "You're asking my opinion?" he said.

Deborah nodded.

"Well, Mrs. O'Connor, I don't think this is ever
gonna make much sense. You'll find I don't deal
much in sense. I don't do things in ordinary ways."
He turned to her. "Look, Deborah, I can't change
what I did. It was wrong. I regret hurting you. But
that plan brought me to you, and you to me. No
matter how I look at it, I can't see that as a bad
thing. Reprehensible method, yes, but . . . I . . . God
damn it woman, what I'm trying to say is that things
are *different* now. I know you see that. You'd

never . . ." he made a gesture around the room to their clothes from last night lying in piles on the floor, ". . . if you didn't." He made a frustrated sound and bumped his head up against the wall.

There was something between them. Something amazing and incomprehensible and growing. What if that was enough? Enough to build on? Enough to heal the wounds? Her voice stammered a bit when she asked, "Do you care for me, Patrick?" She knew he would be truthful with her.

Patrick was silent a long moment before he turned to her. "More than I know what to do with," he said, his voice soft and low. He put a hand up to cup her face. He hesitated a moment before he asked, "And what about you? What do you feel?"

Deborah squinted her eyes shut a moment. "More. More than makes sense. More than I think I want to." She opened her eyes and looked at him. She could see into him, see the remnants of the wall he'd torn down last night. See tiny flecks of vulnerability inside all that bravado. See enough to pull so strongly at her heart it nearly stung. "But it's enough. To start."

"I'll take it," he whispered, pulling his forehead in to touch hers. "Deborah." They held still a long, solemn moment. "It's different now, you know that."

"I do."

A grin spread across his face. "This'll spoil my reputation."

"A worthy cause," Deborah laughed.

"I may have to hoist you over my shoulder now and then," he added, a glint in his eye, "just for effect."

She squared off at him. "Visigoth." She smiled.

"Troublesome wench." He loomed over her.

"Lawless pirate cowboy." She pushed at him with her shoulder.

"Don't *ever* you call me cowboy . . ." and his entire face changed when he added "Wife." The word came out of him in a deep breath. It was a promise.

"Husband."

There wasn't a bone in her body that hurt enough to stop him from laying her back down. *Husband.*

Havana was a humid, noisy beehive. People scurried everywhere, yelling, arguing, and kissing each other in boisterous hellos and goodbyes. Patrick led them through the maze of crates and crowds, keeping a careful hand on Duncan and a protective arm around Deborah. To her it was all incredibly foreign. The loud peaks and spikes of their language punctuated the air wherever she turned. She gaped in surprise when Patrick spoke with someone in Spanish. At least she guessed it was Spanish. She had no idea what they spoke in Cuba.

On the one hand it looked very intriguing, on the other hand part of her was glad she would only spend a handful of hours in the place. Everything looked so very different from Texas. She was amazed at how comfortable she had come to feel with Delilah and everyone on *The Thorn,* amazed at how she now longed for that once hostile-looking vessel. Her life had changed on that ship, as had Patrick's and Duncan's. Perhaps forever.

Their cabin on the steamship, modest as it was, felt luxurious next to the tiny confines from *The Thorn*. Patrick sighed in satisfaction when he tested the bed and found it big enough. Duncan came flying in from his adjoining room, throwing himself on the bed to tussle with his father. It was a delightful sight, watching the two of them laugh and hurl themselves across the bed. She sat down on a chair, enjoying the moment.

Suddenly, Duncan's head popped out from under a pillow to point at Deborah. "Damn, Pa, look!"

"*Potatoes* . . ." corrected Patrick in a mock threat.

"Yeah, Pa, but look!"

It took Deborah only a second to realize what the boy saw. She waited with delight for Patrick to see it, too. His face practically glowed when he did.

"She's got 'em, Pa. Don't she?"

"Aye," Patrick smiled, his eyes dancing as he looked at Deborah. "That she does, boy."

Deborah poked her feet out from under her skirts, showing off the rose-colored stockings that labeled her a member of this strange, delightful family.

"They're not red though, Pa. I mean, not really. Pink-like."

"Rose," replied Patrick. The word rolled of his tongue in a silky tone. Deborah smiled and wiggled her feet playfully.

"Rose," repeated Duncan, trying the word out for size. "It's not red, though, like ours."

"It's close enough," said Patrick, the warmth of his gaze rushing through Deborah's blood.

"It's a place to start," Deborah agreed.

"Here." Patrick directed Deborah's gaze across the map to the tiny island off the Venezuelan coast. "Isla de Margarita. It's still the dry season there, so we'll have a better time of it traveling."

Deborah picked up his finger, which practically covered the entire island on the map. "It seems small. How difficult will it be to find the pearl in so small a place?"

"Mighty. You'd be amazed. The mountains and jungle seem to grow up right out of the water next to the beaches." He rolled up the map. "You might guess not everyone's in a hurry to have this thing found, you know. I reckon I might not be that popular when this is over. The island's still got a strong influence from the Caribe Indians. Pirates, too. You think the beetles sound mean. . . ." It was entertaining to watch her squirm.

"Sounds as if you'll fit right in," Deborah teased.

Patrick applied an expression of mock indignation. "On an island filled with pirate fortresses? With mountains named after a woman's breasts? How could you say such a thing?"

Deborah flushed. It was sinful how much he enjoyed shocking her. She got a look on her face that just sent his blood singing. "A woman's breasts?" she repeated.

"Well, it seems there are two of them. Right next to each other like so." He drew a picture in the air with his hands just for the sport of it. "Pirates have considerable imaginations."

Her eyes took on that indignant look as they peered out from above the spectacles. "Narrowly focused, it seems."

Patrick laughed. Her wit delighted him so. He grabbed her by the waist. "A well-crafted pair do tend to linger on a man's mind, I expect."

"And I suppose you're going to tell me that pearl is nestled in her bosom?"

"Well," he murmured, focusing his gaze on the anatomy in question, "If I had to pick a place . . ."

". . . Where every man would look first?" she interrupted, pushing his forehead back up with her hand.

"A fine point," he laughed. "A fine point."

⊰ Chapter Sixteen ⊱

They didn't know a soul on the steamship.
Deborah found this to her liking. It gave her and
Patrick a chance to immerse themselves in this new
relationship. She found she could make herself forget
their stormy beginnings and enjoy the process of getting to know the man. He seemed to enjoy the
anonymity as well, for he slipped into the pirate per-
sona again, only this time with a dashing warmth instead of the domineering tone she had seen before.

At dinner, Patrick—Patrick *her* husband, she reminded herself with pleasure—commanded the table
and the conversation. He told fabulous stories, filled
with details and drama. People were drawn to him
instantly. They found his grandiose nature wonderfully entertaining. The women eyed him. The men
shook hands with him and clasped his shoulders,
laughing. It wasn't hard to be swept up by the current of all the attention.

As a matter of fact, it was incredibly attractive to
someone who'd spent most of her life on the social
fringe of things. Patrick would tell a story or make a
comment, catching everyone's attention, and then he

would look at her. A lush, unhurried look that seemed to broadcast he couldn't get alone with her fast enough.

The bandages still on her hands ensured the matter of her injury would come up sooner or later. Deborah wasn't sure she was ready to hear Patrick's sure-to-be-oversized version of their adventure aboard *The Thorn*. It was unavoidable, though, the way she kept having trouble managing the silverware. The others couldn't help but notice. Without a friend yet on the ship, Deborah had been forced to rely on Patrick to brush her hair. It had been a wonderful sensation, to be sure, but it also made putting it up unrealistic. Of course, Patrick was all too willing to leave it down, and he kept playing with it, running his fingers through the ends and sending shivers up her spine. If nothing else, his telling of the story would explain to the curious eyes of the other women as to why Deborah wore her hair down instead of put up properly. And yet she worried. He was so given to dramatics. She somehow didn't want to be the subject of his tales.

A kind young woman across the table—Catherine, Deborah thought she said her name was—set things in motion when Deborah dropped her fork for the third time. "Do they pain you much? Your hands?"

"A bit," Deborah replied, trying not to let her anxiety come through in her voice. "Mostly they're just clumsy. I'm afraid I've taken my fingers very much for granted before now." She made herself smile, feeling better when the woman smiled warmly back.

"I can imagine. Did you injure them recently?"

"Yes." She scrambled to find a polite, brief way to describe what had happened. She hoped it might prevent Patrick from telling the story, but she knew that wasn't likely. And yet, it had been such a painful experience for him, she almost hoped he wouldn't tell it. "There was an accident aboard ship. But everything is all right now, and I'm sure I'll heal quickly."

Deborah felt Patrick's gaze on her. His hand wandered languidly up her back to play under her hair at the nape of her neck. "Deborah injured her hands saving my son," he said with more emotion than she guessed he planned.

"Extraordinary," Catherine remarked. And Deborah knew it was lost.

Patrick launched into a passionate retelling of Duncan's accident. He made it sound as if Deborah had single-handedly pulled Duncan from under the waves, dismissing his own part even when Catherine remarked about red marks on his own hands. Weaving the tale, he hoisted Deborah so far up on a heroine's pedestal that the height began to make her ill. It seemed a very long way to fall from grace. And so very far from the truth.

His embellishments began to dredge up old fears, of Patrick's ability to bend and shape events to his liking. The attention was too glaring, the growing admiration of those at the table too stifling. Deborah tried to disclaim the story once or twice, but her meager attempts disappeared behind Patrick's fantastically spun tale. The air around her grew too thin. When she nearly knocked over a wineglass grappling with her fork, it became too much. With a pathetic attempt at excusing herself, she fled from the dining room.

"No, I don't know where they are now, sir." Mrs. Doyle began to shut the door. "I'd not be giving out the master's whereabouts to every face on the street even if I did. He'll be coming back soon enough and you can pester him then instead of meself."

"But I've . . ." the man insisted.

"It's no business of mine what you've a need for. You've left your card twice now, I've no more information to give ye. Good day to you, now." With a tumble of Gaelic under her breath, she shut the door. "Mother of God, Fiona, I grow tired of this." She fairly snapped her dust rag at an offending tabletop. "I can't fathom which of him bothers me more."

"Which of who?" Fiona put the last of the candlesticks back in the cabinet and shut the door.

"Which Patrick. The sullen one or the besotted one. Both of them are mad as hatters, that's what they are." She bustled into the kitchen, sure the bread dough had dried out with the constant interruptions this morning.

Fiona's voice came in through the doorway. "He's not mad, Mum."

She lifted the cloth off the bowl, relieved to find the bread rising nicely. "Not yet anyways. Ah well, can't say as the quiet around here bothers me none. It's Patricia I'm worried about, it is. She's looking so lonely."

"He shouldn't have left," Fiona said sharply.

"And who are you to say a man can't have a honeymoon? He left a mite quickly, I'll grant you that, but I don't know a man on earth doesn't behave like a schoolboy when his heart's got the best of 'im." Mrs. Doyle chuckled, remembering the look on Patrick's face when he told her of his travel plans. You could have lit a fire off his eyes, for heaven's sake.

Fiona shut a drawer loudly. "He's not besotted, Mum. Amused, perhaps, but not besotted."

"And where do you come off saying such things, darlin'?" She didn't care for the edge in her daughter's voice.

"Nowhere. It's nothing."

"And I'm made of biscuits." She stopped kneading the bread. "What's eatin' at you, child?"

"There's nothing eating at me, Mama." Fiona shut a second drawer more carefully.

"Fiona, dear . . ."

"It's nothing, I tell you. Mrs. O'Connor's just being especially difficult today, that's all. It gets tiresome when she has no one else to talk to but me, that's all."

To be sure. Mrs. O'Connor was a handful when she had a full house of family, but the woman was too much to handle when she focused all that wild energy on one young lass. Fiona needed a respite from the old woman. "Makin' ye daft today, is she?"

"Very nearly."

Mrs. Doyle gave the bread dough a last final punch and returned it to the bowl. "I've no more to do here for an hour or two, Fiona. Why don't you go find a book in the master's study and sit for a while? I can tend to Herself while I finish the mending. You look wasted, child. Rest yourself a bit." She touched her daughter's shoulder. It was tense.

"She *is* a bit much today. And I could use a chance to put my feet up, even for an hour or so."

"Well, alright then. Fetch yourself a cup of tea while you're at it. And I've left a few cookies in the far cupboard if you fancy a treat. The old ladies will tend to themselves for the afternoon, hmm?"

"Thanks, Mum!"

Fiona pulled the study door shut behind her, glad to be alone in the quiet. Lord Almighty, but Mrs. O'Connor could talk a soul's ears off. It was bad enough to be in one conversation, but to have to sit and listen to her constant chatter to her invisible men was more than a soul could bear. The whining lilt in the old woman's voice and the tick-tick of her knitting needles had grated at Fiona mercilessly this morning. She breathed in the smells of the study with relief. The leather of the chairs and books. The paper. The ink. Impulsively she threw the door latch.

Fiona moved slowly to the desk, running her fingers along its corners. She ran her hand up the back of the chair, leaning against it. There were worn spots on the leather, impressions in the cushions from where he sat. He spent so much time at that desk. The wood on the arm spindles had the stain worn off where his hands would rub them. Carefully she touched one.

His place. His things.

A noise from the street startled her, and she backed

away from the desk toward the bookshelves. The man had an impressive collection of fiction, stories from everywhere around the world. She knew which one she wanted to read this afternoon. Running her fingers across the rows of spines, her hand came to rest on the volume. *1001 Arabian Nights*. Exotic tales. Wild men who loved fiercely and lived on adventure. That's where she wanted to lose herself this afternoon. As far away from old Irish biddies as she could possibly get.

The tales spun their magic, and air melted into the pungent warmth of a desert evening. Her tea became an exotic Arabian drink, her cookies sweet figs and dates from the silver bowl of a handsome sultan. She became the clever young maiden, spinning tales to win her freedom and fascinate her dark, brooding captor. It was wonderful.

Something dropped into her lap as she turned a page. A small brass key on a red ribbon. The impression in the pages told her the key had been there a long time. The book was too high up on the shelves to be reached by either Patricia or Duncan, so it had to be Patrick's. What was the key? What did it unlock? What was so secretively hidden behind the lock?

A gate to a secret part of Patrick O'Connor's life. The lure was irresistible. With a quick glance to the window, reminding herself she'd locked the door and the house was nearly empty save for the two older women, she fingered the key. She lay the book down, taking care to keep the correct page open, and stood up to survey the room. The desk seemed a likely start. There was a lock on the top drawer, but it obviously required a much larger key. This one was small. *Like a chest or box.* Her eyes darted around the room but saw nothing that looked like a likely match for the key. *It's hidden. Of course it's hidden.* Fiona poked around the room, testing shelves, moving things, until she came upon a wooden statue. It was a broad, squat figure, an elf-like man sitting on a bench. With a quick intake of breath she noticed a cleverly hidden hinge on the elf's knee. She turned the figure. There was a leaf nailed loosely over the middle of the bench. She pushed it to one side and it swung easily on the nail. There, staring out at her from the side of the bench, was a small round keyhole. Fiona inserted the key and closed her eyes. With a good twist she heard the tumblers fall. Using both hands, she pushed the lid back until the little man rested upside down, his head on the shelf.

It was a small box, lined in red velvet. Inside were several papers—letters from the looks of them, a velvet pouch, an old-looking pen, and three more keys on another red lace. The keys were ornate—female looking. She guessed they opened chests of Moira's things. Fiona picked up the pouch. It was heavy, and its contents rolled like stones or marbles in her palm. She pulled open the string to view a small collection of pearls and other gemstones. None of them astounding in size, but all very beautiful. This really didn't surprise her—she knew Patrick collected gemstones as part of his exporting ventures. In fact, she'd always wondered where in the house he kept them. It gave her a delicious pleasure to now know Patrick's secret hiding place.

Fiona turned her attention next to the letters. Two had Moira's handwriting—she guessed them love letters. She didn't want to see those. The other two had strange handwriting, one a man's hand, the other a woman's. Noting what order they were stacked, she pulled the one with a woman's writing.

"Blessed Mother!" Fiona gasped under her breath as she read the letter. It was a short, businesslike letter. It was from a Miss Deborah Edgerton.

Confirming an employment.

As a secretary.

"The devil!" She read further to see Deborah give the date of her arrival. It was the same day that Patrick had brought his new "wife" home. What had he said they'd had, "a few surprises at the train station"? The letter made no reference whatsoever to marriage. Why the devil had Patrick brought this woman here under false pretenses?

Her mind spun to the night the new Mrs. O'Connor had asked all those questions about Patrick. She'd mentioned they didn't know each other well. That they'd had some kind of unusual courtship. "Unusual to be certain!" she remarked to herself. Had Patrick O'Connor gotten himself a wife by fraud?

But why the silence? Why would any woman agree to such a charade? Why hadn't Deborah told Fiona the whole story when she confided in her the first time? It didn't make sense. But one fact became crystal clear. Patrick's marriage was no love match. Saints, it could hardly be called a match at all!

He doesn't love her. I knew it. I'm betting all we see is the satisfaction of some well-done plan. He's not happy to be married, he's happy to have pulled off such a stunt! This was a far bigger, far more delectable secret than knowing where Patrick kept his private things.

Fiona made a small circle around the room, tapping the letter against her palm, thinking. What to do? What to make of this secret?

Her eyes returned to the box. The other letter—the one with the strange male handwriting. Slipping that woman's letter back carefully in its place, she pulled out the other document.

It was from an Alejandro Torres. The man had a scrawling, uneven hand. Young looking. As if he wrote too infrequently to gain much skill at it. It told of a gem, a pearl called La Roja, that he seemed to have located. From his words, Patrick had been seeking the pearl for some time, and had given Torres orders to keep a lookout for it. Torres urged Patrick to make all due haste to Isla de Margarita in Venezuela.

So that's where they were headed. And why. And why Patrick told no one where he was going and touted the trip as an impulsive honeymoon. She bet he'd taken Duncan so that he wouldn't have to keep anyone in Galveston informed of his location. Fiona felt insulted that Patrick didn't trust her with either his son or his secrets. They'd spent so much time talking together. And now she knew he kept so much from her. The realization stung her sharply.

Fiona thrust the letter back into the box and

snapped the lid shut. "Aye, well, Mr. Patrick, sir, we'll see how long your little secret holds out now, won't we?" She turned the key and crossed the room, replacing it in the page. She clamped the book shut and replaced the volume on the upper shelf. "You canna keep it up forever, man." Fiona paced the room in growing anger. "Can you now?"

After two more laps her gaze landed on the tray of silver calling cards on the table just inside the door. Thumbing through them, she saw that two of them were from the same man, Archibald Morton. Of Morton and Napson Cotton and Export. They were a rival of Patrick's, weren't they? Wasn't Morton the one Patrick was always grumbling about—shady business practices and all?

She stared at the card for a moment, running her thumb along the edge. She tucked the card neatly into her shirtwaist. Patrick would turn to her in a crisis. She knew he would. She'd been beside him all through his grieving of Moira. They'd practically raised Duncan together. When trouble hit, it wouldn't be this practical joke of a bride he'd turn to, it'd be her. He'd realize what she meant to him. How she could handle the dark side of the Black family. No prim, spectacled lily of a woman could handle what would eventually come over Patrick. But she could. She was no stranger to the unseen side of a life, to the constant war of dark and light forces that gentlefolk liked to think never existed. Things a woman like herself knew to be all too real. If she couldn't win over his heart, she'd have to start by winning over his soul.

• • •

Patrick found her near the rear of the ship, pacing across the deck. He knew she heard him coming, for she stopped her pacing and simply stared out to sea with her back to him. The rise and fall of her shoulders told him she was not crying, but breathing hard. Struggling for control against something. Something he evidently sent crashing down upon her. For the life of him, he didn't know what it was.

"I don't know," he said, keeping a distance between them. He was grateful most of the ship was at dinner and they were alone on the corner of the deck. They needed to talk about this but he surely wasn't going to get her back into the cabin anytime soon from the set of her spine. She didn't respond. "You're going to have to tell me, Deborah. I'm mighty poor at guessing games."

She still made no answer, save for stiffening up when he took a step or two closer.

Well all right then, I'll just stand here.

After about a minute, she spoke. Her voice was soft but sharp.

"You lie so *easily.*"

He didn't like her tone. "I told no lies. All of those things really happened."

"Not the way you tell it. You twist the facts around to mean a dozen other things that were never there." Her bandaged hands wound around each other clumsily.

"I spin a good yarn. It's an Irish trait."

"You and I both know what kind of 'yarn' you are capable of. You puff up the facts so easily. Everyone is so very entertained." She still wasn't looking at him.

"Deborah, are you going to tell me what this is about? Somehow I reckon my conversational abilities aren't the issue here."

"Do you even want to know?" She turned to him. "Can you handle the plain truth, Patrick? Not the dramatic version?"

The look in her eyes cut through him. He tamped down his anger, trying to tread carefully. He walked toward her and said, "Yes," as simply as he could.

"I am no heroine."

"You are. You saved Duncan."

"No, *you* saved Duncan. I merely got tangled up in the rope. I was no more than a well-placed knot. Why must you make that into some heroic exploit?"

Patrick shifted. "For one thing, my son was on the other end of that 'well-placed knot'." She rolled her eyes in exasperation as he continued. "What? Do you think I didn't see you straining against the bow rail? You were holding on, pulling, calling to him to keep him calm. You were in pain. I was right behind you, pulling, do you remember?"

"I didn't save him."

Patrick twisted away. "Now who's bending the facts, Deborah? I don't understand. Why is it so awful that you did something important? Why can't I show my gratitude in how I tell the damn story?"

"Because you tell it so well I don't know what you really believe! If you can be so convincing in your oversized version of things, how could I know what the truth is?" He heard her words choke in her throat, bringing him back around to stare at her. "How do I know what to believe, Patrick? How can I trust you to be honest to me when you tell such lies at a simple meal? With people we barely know?"

"They weren't lies! You saved him!"

"You made it seem more than it was." She squared off at him, angry.

"It *was everything* to me! Lord, woman, how can you not know that?" Patrick stomped around the deck, annoyed that she'd taken such a tiny thing and turned it into some kind of calamity. "Fine! Have it your way. I *exaggerate!*" Why couldn't she see herself for the heroine she was? Why couldn't she hear his admiration in the way he told the story?

But he had lied to her in Galveston, hadn't he?

"What do you want?" It was not a retort; it was a genuine question. In truth, he had no idea.

"I want to know you're telling the truth."

Well, there was something really useful. He *was* telling the truth, now, only she couldn't see it. *How the hell do you fix that?* In frustration, Patrick replied, "What? You'd prefer a signal of some kind? Should I tell you I'll rub the side of my neck when I'm lying so you'll know?"

That made her really angry. "Must everything be a game to you? Why is the truth between us such an awful thing?"

"It's not."

"Then why do you avoid it so?"

"I *don't.*"

"You do."

"I do not, woman."

"Prove it to me, Patrick."

Now he was getting truly angry. "How do I goddamn prove it to you? Never tell a story again in my
life?" He stalked in circles, waving his arms. "How
foolish is that? Sweet Jesus, Deborah, I've no blasted
idea what to do about you!"

She leaned against the rail and eyed him. That
damnable, immovable, sensible expression that made
him want to swat her and kiss her at the same time.

"Tell me something true, Patrick. Something plain
and true and important."

*Oh, Lord, off we go with the quizzes again. Tell
me what you feel, Patrick. Tell me the truth, Patrick.*
The woman was infuriating. "I hate this!"

"I'm well aware of that."

"I can't see what this will accomplish."

"I'm not backing down, Patrick. You ought to
know that by now."

He stuck a finger at her, pointing. "I will *not* promise you I'll never tell wild stories again. I won't stop
being who I am just because it disturbs you."

"Accepted."

She wanted truth? Well, all right then. "You irri-
tate me, woman."

She was looking at him, analyzing his face. That
made him furious. "I can see that."

Patrick let out a frustrated groan and turned away
from her. He indulged in a long string of Gaelic.
"Goddamn it! You are so annoying. I can't see how I
could *possibly* be coming to love you when you are
such a . . ."

He stopped, frozen.

Oh, hell. Had he just said what he thought he'd just said? He squinted his eyes shut. How had that come out? The last thing he wanted to do was turn around and look at her, look at those analyzing lavender eyes, let her see his heart cracked wide open. It had erupted out of him before he even knew it himself. God bloody damn it. Now what?

She was silent behind him.

"I didn't intend to say that," he admitted, then cringed. *Oh, good, Patrick. That was a blasted lousy thing to say.*

"I know." There was no insult in her voice. She'd understood his meaning, thank God. This would have been a very poor moment to insult his wife. Now he couldn't help but turn around and look at her. She stood just behind him, her hands folded across her chest, a look of amazement and wonder on her face. "Well, what do you know?" she marveled. "I *can* recognize the truth when I hear it. And, when you're not thinking too hard about it, you can actually speak it."

Patrick was at a loss. "What do we do now?"

"Well, I'd suggest not rubbing your neck," she said, stepping closer to him. Patrick shook his head in amazement. This woman never ceased to surprise him. "I asked Luther to tell me what he knew about pearls just before we left *The Thorn*," she said. "He told me that in order to get a very perfect, round pearl, the irritation has to go quite deep inside the oyster."

"Did he now?" Patrick couldn't help but smile. "Did he also tell you that the only way to make a perfect pearl more valuable is to find its perfect match?" It suddenly became quite all right that she now knew. He was coming to love her. "What do you say to that, Mrs. O'Connor?" He closed the distance between them.

"I'd say we're looking at a mighty big pearl."

❧ Chapter Seventeen ❧

"Catherine says you ought to be a pirate." Deborah turned her back to Patrick and lifted her hair. He made that low, smooth noise deep in his throat that he always did when it came time to help her undress. The man enjoyed it far too much. For that matter, so did she.

He nuzzled her neck while his fingers worked the knot on her corset lacing. "I am, you know." Delicious tingles skipped up her neck and down her spine. "I may just bind your hands for the rest of our marriage—I'm rather enjoying this."

"They'll heal soon enough. For God's sake, you change the dressings often enough. But . . . they look . . ." She couldn't finish. The scarred skin looked ancient and battered every time the bandages came off.

Patrick's hands left the laces to slide down her arms. "They will heal." He applied the comic brogue he used when teasing Duncan. "And I'll not be carin' what they look like." His hands wrapped around hers. "Only be carin' about what they've done.

And," he added with a hinting laugh, "what they might do once we loosen them."

She wanted to touch him. To stroke her fingers through the tawny hair on his chest. To run her hands across the strong expanse of his back. Patrick had a beautiful back. The planes of his muscles spoke of strength and command. He carried his huge body with such control that one almost forgot the man's size. There were nights in the last ten days on this ship, with the luxury of space and privacy, when she thought she'd tear the bandages off with her teeth to let her hands touch him. But there was a part of her that feared unwrapping her hands only to find their feeling gone. Her sense of touch numbed by the scars. The very idea of it seemed unbearable.

"Tell me," said Patrick, now back at the laces, "which part of me will you have at first, once you can touch?"

Deborah laughed. "Have at? What a lurid way to put it."

"I flatter myself to think you'd be a mite eager once we free up those hands of yours."

Truth be told, she would be eager. It both embarrassed and excited her that he knew it. "Flatter indeed. How do you know I'll be in such a hurry?"

The bodice fell from her chest and his hands wandered around her waist. "I know." His voice sent warm ripples everywhere. In a quick motion, he loosened the waistband of her skirt and sent it to the floor. "We'll not have this much privacy once we dock on the island tomorrow. We'd best make good use of it." With that he swept her off her feet and deposited her on the bed. Staring at her, he kicked his boots off. He started with his shirt buttons. "I'd much rather it was you undoing these."

"The thought has occurred to me."

Shirt off, he leaned down beside her. He was so warm. Heat seeped out wherever they touched. "Any other thoughts you might like to share?"

"Of the wicked or the lofty variety?"

"Hmm." His fingers started at just under her ear and wound a silky path down her neck. "I'm not feeling very lofty at the moment."

"Astonishing." Just because she couldn't resist the urge, she put a hand up to his face. She frowned at the vague pressure that was the only result. And the coarse noise of her bandages catching on his beard.

As he slid her shift off one shoulder, a wicked grin came to his face. His eyes nearly glowed. "I've decided it's your turn."

"You know I can't touch you. It's awful, but . . ."

He stopped her with a finger to her lips. "I don't mean that. Don't fret, I'll make sure you get your chance at that, too, to be sure. But that's not what I mean. I mean . . ." he said, moving the other shoulder off and starting at the buttons, "it's my turn to ask you the questions and your turn to give me the truthful answers."

Oh my. She had an idea where this was going and she wasn't sure she was ready. There was a hungry look in his eye that made her skin smolder. The last button gave way and he pushed the shift aside with a soft exhale. He sent a cascade of silky caresses across her upper body until it became difficult to keep her eyes open. Deborah kept waiting for him to ask a question but he just caressed her instead. The combination of expectation and pleasure was breathtaking. As she let her eyes fall shut, his mouth started at her collarbone with unhurried, lush kisses. She gasped in shock and amazement as he teased her neck with soft bites. Bites that wandered lower to deliciously wicked places.

"Question one: Does this please you?"

Surprise sparked through her. Could she admit to how much pleasure this brought her? Now who wanted to flee from the truth? And it wasn't exactly as if she could hide her heaving breaths from his notice. As if sensing her resistance, Patrick nipped her just the slightest bit harder. *Oh my*. It was hopeless. She replied with a "yes" that was more a gasp than anything else.

His laugh hummed across her bosom. "Well, what do you know? I can recognize the truth when I hear it. And you, when you are not thinking too much about it, can speak it." Trapped by her own words. After a moment, she realized she didn't mind at all.

Patrick sat up a bit on the bed until he was straddled across her legs, gently pinning them. He clamped his knees on either side of her ankles so that she couldn't move. Then, with smoky eyes, he began by massaging her legs.

He asked question two as his fingers slid up the back of her calves. "How ma . . ." her speech fell off as he found a spot that made her skin sizzle, ". . . mm-many questions are there?"

"Eleven." The man practically purred the answer.
Deborah wasn't sure she'd even make it to four.

Deborah awoke to a trail of whisper-like kisses as
he nestled her in his arms. He was looking down into
her eyes as if he'd been watching her sleep. There
was an air of importance in them.

"Question twelve," he said softly, brushing a lock
of hair away from her cheek.

"There's more?" *I'm not sure I could take more.*

"Just one." Somehow she knew from his eyes that
this was a crucial question. Not about caresses.

Deborah nodded.

"Do you love me, Deborah?"

Heavens. She wasn't expecting that.

He didn't even try to make it sound casual or ordinary. Didn't pretend that it didn't matter. It mattered
a great deal. He let the vulnerability of it show
clearly on his face.

She trusted him with the most honest answer she
could give.

"Almost."

Green.

A shade of green Deborah was quite sure she'd
never seen before. Isla de Margarita was a rich, emer-
ald green that seemed to give off a glow of its own.
As if the plants and exotic-looking trees absorbed the
sun's glow to radiate it back again. Bouncing along
on a smaller boat that shuttled them over from the
ship port on the mainland, the island seem to erupt

out of the turquoise water. Glistening beaches filled
some parts of the coast while forests seemed to grow
right out of the waves in others. The island appeared
almost frighteningly foreign, all too close to the jungle of her imagination. The breeze carried a warm,
pungent odor as they neared shore. Thick with floral
scents, heavy with moisture and soil.

As they neared, signs of life emerged from the
blanket of green. A sudden flash of color turned out
to be a bird. The distinct sharp edge of a building
came into view. As they rounded a sharp outcropping
of land, a *"punta"* as Patrick had called it, civiliza-
tion appeared. Docks, streets, fortifications worthy
of the island's pirate heritage, churches, and a
bustling market sprung to life. A town carved out of
the jungle. As she leaned over the bow of the boat,
Deborah could make out two or three more such
towns farther down the coast.

The crystal-clear water gave Duncan a thrilling
view of the undersea plants and animals. Patrick had
to keep a firm hand on the lad's breeches for fear
he'd flip himself over the edge in his eagerness to see
the wonders. In truth, there were colors under the
waves Deborah had never seen before. Deep and brilliant to the point of fantasy. As if someone had
strewn a garden of fireworks under the bay. Magical.

There was nothing magical about hoisting the end-
less trunks and cases up the beach to the small inn.
Young children stared at her and Duncan while
Patrick directed half a dozen men in the transfer.
Somehow he managed to fit right in, sliding into the
scenery with a practiced charm. She and Duncan, on

the other hand, all but broadcast their foreign state as they clung together on the end of the dock.

"*Aqui! Una mas, a la derecha, Señor.*" Patrick came up to them, wiping his forehead. "We'll be settled in an hour or so. You'd best come in from the sun anyway. It's much stronger down here, we'll need to be careful for a day or so to keep you from burning."

"Aw, Pa . . ."

"Aw, nothing, Dunc. Unless you want your backside bandaged up like . . . *your Ma*'s hands there, you'll do as I say." His voice still caught every time he referred to Deborah as Duncan's 'Ma.' It wasn't discomfort that tripped his tongue, it was amazement. He said the words with affection. It caressed her as surely as his hands.

"You can't burn your bum, Pa," retorted Duncan with narrowed eyes and a jutted chin.

Patrick leaned down, eye to eye with the boy. "Maybe not from the sun, but then there is the matter of your Pa's hand . . ."

Patrick's huge hand evidently served as enough of a deterrent, for the boy turned to Deborah with a theatrical dignity. "Let's go see what my room looks like."

"A fine idea." Deborah suppressed a smile as she slid her hand through Patrick's elbow and they headed up the dock.

The inn was an odd-looking thing. A plantation-like house, ringed with a wide porch and huge shuttered windows. Though grand in its architecture, its small size and less-than-pristine upkeep spoke of richer days. Patrick had told her of the wild rush that had taken place decades before when the pearl beds were first discovered. The former grandeur peeked out from details around the island, but the lean of the recent years was plainly visible. The pearl rush had been a bright and brilliant star that had burned out quickly. Its afterglow had an obvious bite to it.

The room was simple and thankfully clean. Windows and beds were strung with white gauze against the insects. She imagined the pests of Margarita were a long sight meaner than the mosquitoes of Galveston. On Patrick's instructions, Deborah had packed three trunks for use in the inn—the rest stayed shut until the journey inland. Patrick worked the latches for her and flipped the trunks open.

"Why don't you get yourselves settled? I've got a few things to tend to in town. Stay up in the rooms until I come back. This isn't the kind of place to be roaming around." Patrick dug through his own trunk until he fished out a packet of documents.

"You're still short, Alejandro."

"*Sí,* and you are still too *grande* for your own good, Trick." The two men found a dark corner table and sat down. "You know, no one *here* dares to call me short. If you say it any more loudly, I may have to kill you." The last word came out "keel," almost a hiss through his teeth. The barkeep put down two shots of a potent-smelling clear liquor. "What is this Texan fascination with size?"

"You think too much for a little man on a tiny island." Patrick knocked back half the small glass in a single gulp. Just for fun he made a face as if the liquid burned his throat. It did—it was horrid stuff—but he liked to tease Alejandro Torres. "God, man, have you learned nothing about liquor in the last eight years? It's as bad as I remember it." He made a gasping sound.

"And you are as bad an actor as I remember. You've downed a dozen of these in my sight without flinching. Have you gone soft, *amigo?*"

"Well, I'm married. Is that soft?"

Alejandro smiled. He had the kind of smile that set women's hearts aflame. Teeth that glowed against the dark olive of his skin. When Patrick had met him as a boy of fourteen, he was already too handsome for his own good, and always the first person to extol his charm. He wasn't short at all—the man stood over six feet tall—but he took such offense when Patrick touted his own larger stature that it was too much fun not to call him short. "I am glad to hear it." Alejandro hoisted his glass. "It has been too long since Moira. Men of our great passion need a woman around, eh? How could you bear to leave her behind?"

"I didn't."

Alejandro choked a bit on his drink. "*Dios,* you brought her along?"

"She's upstairs." Patrick drained the glass.

"On a trip like this?"

"I had my reasons."

"They had best be damned good ones, my friend. It is the dry season, granted, but still . . . this is no honeymoon jaunt, Trick."

Patrick pulled the documents from his coat. "As a matter of fact, it is."

Alejandro swore emphatically in Spanish.

"I'll die before I see them harmed, Torres. I'll ask no different of you to protect my family. Why I brought them is my business, *si*?" Patrick leaned down lower over the table. "Have you found it?"

Alejandro leaned back, his head falling in a long, gloating nod. "I have indeed."

"And is it . . . ?"

"It is indeed. Such as you have never seen before." Alejandro narrowed one eye at his friend. "This is going to cost you a lot of money, *Gigante*. That is, if you can even persuade them to part with it."

"Come now, Torres, I'm a mighty persuasive man."

"You had best be a very rich one as well," countered Torres.

"I've enough." Patrick would sell everything if that's what it took. The red pearl had been found. La Roja would be his to bring home. Patrick O'Connor would make his mark on the world, and his family would be secure and comfortable for the rest of their lives. That meant more now than it ever did. "How much time do we have?"

"Not much. The tribe moves upland for the dry season in a few weeks. If we do not meet up with them before the move, it will be much harder. They have many places to hide farther up the mountains." Alejandro softened his voice. "And I am worried word will seep out if we do not move quickly."

"True enough," agreed Patrick. "When?"

"I am thinking tomorrow morning. The two of you can be ready?"

"Three. Duncan is with me."

Alejandro let out a longer string of expletives. "You brought *the boy* with you? *Jesús,* Trick, I know he's all you have but . . ."

"He's not all I have anymore. I want them with me. Both of them. I'll stand no argument on this, *comprende*?"

"Your mind has left you, *Gigante.*"

"And nearly so my patience. One of these days that rock-encrusted thing you call your heart might actually understand. It stands as it is. And you'll be well enough paid for it to have your mind leave *you* for a dozen women, so keep your worries to yourself." Patrick stood up. "Ten o'clock. North end of the market square."

"Ten it is. Get some sleep tonight, Trick. You will be on your guard for a long time after tomorrow, no?"

❧ Chapter Eighteen ❧

The circle of women and children stared at her as if she were a ghost. A host of black eyes, unblinking in their wonder. They tilted their heads in curiosity, murmuring in low tones amongst themselves. The women stared at her hair and eyes, amazed but frightened. The children pointed to her skirts, the lace edges of her blouse, and her shoes.

"What are they saying, Patrick?" she whispered, instinctively placing her hands on Duncan's shoulders and pulling him close.

"Bluntly put, they're wondering how you got so white. That one over there's a bit more poetic, she wants to know how you made the sun stay inside your hair. I'm not entirely sure, but I think that boy wants to know what made your eyes sick."

"Oh, my." Deborah swallowed, the pressure of being on such display tightening her ribs. "You're certain they're friendly?" she whispered.

"Certain. Just surprised. You have that effect on people, you know." How Patrick could be so calm as to wink astounded her. She'd seen things in the last six hours that made her feel as if she were on another planet. Jewel-colored lizards. Tiny frogs Alejandro said could kill you. Flowers that looked too extraordinary to be real. And things with more legs than any living creature ought to be allowed to have. Why should gawking natives pose any concern?

Finally, one older woman, obviously in some kind of leadership position, moved forward. She stood entirely too close to Deborah. Patrick had warned her of the customs as they traveled, how Venezuelans stood much closer to each other than Americans, and how it was considered rude to back away. She felt Patrick's hand come up against her back, reminding her to stay steady. After a long glance, the woman turned to Patrick and said something decidedly favorable. A toothy smile cracked across her ancient face. She said something to Deborah, then inclined her head in a slow, graceful gesture of welcome. She turned and motioned to a small common house.

Deborah nodded in reply. Patrick introduced her as "Cochara." She was wife of this tribe's late chief, and mother of the present chief. She was small and stout, and her skin had the leather of many years, but her bones and carriage spoke of a former beauty. There was a tremendous dignity in her bearing, a knowledge in the way her hands swept about the air as she talked. Her clothes and simple jewelry were studded with dozens of tiny pearls. One half of her left ring finger was gone.

Sitting on a simple chair made from a cut stump, Deborah listened as Cochara introduced Duncan to each of the four small boys. Alejandro and Patrick interpreted, and gradually the boys began to work out a tentative friendship. Once a game involving a big stick and several melon-sized fruits was introduced, all fears dissolved and the boys scrambled off into a nearby clearing to play. *Children are children everywhere,* Deborah thought. And when she found herself chuckling at the boys' antics alongside the other women, her anxiety lessened. *Perhaps women are as well.*

Cochara introduced each woman in the circle with the same care she had done for the boys. She gave each woman's name, cited their family, and a particular talent. "I am the healer," she said when she finally introduced her own family and herself. "My son is chief, as was his father. Great men. Good, strong spirits. Such as *Gigante* here." Cochara gestured to Patrick.

"Alejandro calls you that as well," whispered Deborah over Patrick's shoulder. "Is it Spanish for Patrick?"

"No," laughed Patrick. "It's Spanish for 'huge.' It is Alejandro's fault—the damnable nickname stuck with them and I've never been able to stop it."

"You could be known for many worse things," interjected Alejandro.

"I'd prefer to be known for a few better."

The men of the tribe were out fishing, and would be back in two or three hours. Deborah, Patrick, Duncan, and Alejandro would spend the night here before traveling on. Patrick kept the conversation light, purposely not revealing the nature of his visit. He'd instructed Deborah to do the same.

After an hour or so Alejandro and Patrick were

called over to join the boys' games. Alejandro joined in, but Patrick elected to stay by Deborah's side. She was grateful he wouldn't leave her alone. When Alejandro had left, Deborah noticed Cochara staring at her bandaged hands. She eyed them analytically, eventually asking a question of Patrick.

"She burned them," he replied. "Torn and burned by some ropes on the ship." With a knowing glance at Deborah, Patrick kept the story to that fact. No heroic exploits, no dramatic tale-telling. He'd done it for her sake; she knew that.

Cochara flicked her fingers, holding out her hands in a request to see Deborah's. Deborah complied. Cochara gave two quick orders to another younger woman and began to slowly undo the bandages. Patrick's hand came around Deborah's waist, comforting, supporting. Cochara looked up at Patrick when he did. She asked another question.

"Quite some time ago. No, well, I don't think so. Deborah, Cochara wants to know if they hurt all the time or only sometimes."

"Only sometimes," Deborah replied, then listened to Patrick relay the answer.

Cochara looked straight at Deborah now, asking a question.

"She says, 'do they frighten you?'" Patrick translated.

Deborah's eyes widened in surprise. Her hands? Did they frighten her? What an odd question. But yet, the look in Cochara's eyes was so deep, so wise. They did. They did frighten her. She was frightened of how they looked, how little they felt, how slowly they seemed to be healing. Her heart fairly pounded as Cochara reached the last layer of bandages. "Yes," Deborah said quietly, nodding her head. "They do."

There was no need for Patrick to translate her reply. She felt Cochara's hands tighten comfortingly on her own. Deborah thought of the missing fingertip, of how beautiful Cochara had obviously once been, and knew where the old woman's understanding came from.

The younger woman returned with a flask and a torch. She planted the torch next to Cochara. It was growing dark; more light seemed to be a good idea. Then Cochara unwrapped the last of the gauze. Deborah's skin felt thick and raw in the open air. Her hands were blotched pink and white, swollen and clumsy-looking. Scabs and scars slashed ugly lines across her palms and fingers. They looked pale and death-like, held inside Cochara's leathered, dark fingers.

Cochara spoke in soft, melodic phrases. Patrick translated quietly beside her, his own wonder seeping through his words. "She says . . . she says hands help—no, wait, heal. Hands *heal* the heart. She says your hands were torn because . . . because your heart was torn." Patrick spoke slowly. "That the hands are . . . are not healing because the heart is still hurt."

Deborah all but stopped breathing. Even Patrick's hand had tightened around her waist. His voice was low and pained. He knew as well as she who had done the tearing. She did feel torn. Ripped from one life into another. Shredded into tiny bits that were only now just coming back together. It felt awful to have one's soul bared by a total stranger. The moment was as awkward and painful as when the bandages were removed. Deborah was as naked and raw as her hands. In a way it all made perfect sense.

Cochara took Deborah's hands and held them up to the light. She spoke with strength. "She says you must . . . hunt—no, it's 'look,' not 'hunt.' Look at them. Hard and . . . straight . . . at them until you can see what they will be." Patrick translated.

Transfixed, Deborah stared at her hands. The torchlight lent them a warmer glow, hiding the blotches and scars. She could feel a little bit of the heat from the fire. Slowly she flexed her fingers, exploring, wondering. Cochara was nodding her head, smiling, saying something encouraging that needed no translation. She put her gnarled hand, the one with part of the finger missing, up to Deborah's. They were hands that had labored hard. Hands that had healed despite their own deformities. Hands with strength and dignity that went beyond beauty. Solid, sure hands. Deborah began to see the wisdom of Cochara's words.

As if she knew this, Cochara took the jar from the younger woman's hands. She held it over the torch, rolling the squat pottery jug between her hands, chanting something like an incantation. Deborah's fear crept back up. Patrick's hand began to make soft circles on her back. "Steady," he said softly.

Cochara placed the warmed pot on her lap, unwrapping the leather top. She dipped her hands in and pulled out a white, shimmering substance. Thick and gooey, like pudding, but it sparkled in the torchlight. *Like pearls.* Hadn't Patrick told her some native peoples held pearls to have healing powers? The mixture looked like some sort of poultice made from crushed pearls. A soft echo of acknowledgment went through the other women around her. The mixture oozed down Cochara's hand as she held it to the light, speaking to it. Patrick had forgotten to translate, fascinated by the moment as much as Deborah was. She didn't care that she didn't know the exact meaning of Cochara's words—she knew the purpose of them and that was potent enough.

The poultice was warm and fragrant on Deborah's hands. Cochara's strong fingers worked it slowly into Deborah's skin, flexing muscles, stretching tendons, soothing away the swollen tightness. It was an insistent, compelling grasp. The strong scent swirled around Deborah's head just as Patrick's hand kept swirling around her back. The rise and fall of Cochara's voice pulled her into the touch. Her hands began to feel more human than they had in weeks. As if life were seeping back into them.

Cochara dipped a finger into the jar. She held it up, speaking to Patrick. Patrick asked her a question, and she answered it with a sharp voice. They talked for a minute, then she motioned to him. To Deborah's amazement, Patrick leaned forward and stuck out his tongue. Cochara made some kind of declaration, then dropped a bit of the mixture on his tongue. He swallowed it.

Cochara turned to her. She spoke, then turned to Patrick, requesting a translation. "Cochara says you have to swallow your healing. She says it can't come from the outside alone."

The woman motioned for Deborah to open her mouth. Despite her reservations, Deborah did as she was told. The mixture was warm and sweet, gritty like sugar, but not unpleasant. It tasted, well, it tasted magical. Powerful. Deborah felt ridiculous for being so caught up in something so completely . . . completely what? Foreign? Barbarian? Superstitious? Yet she couldn't escape the deep-seated feeling that something important had happened. Something mysterious and unquestionable. The expression on Patrick's face told her he felt the same. They stared at each other for a long moment, wondering.

Cochara began to rewrap Deborah's hands—with only half as many bandages. Patrick told her Cochara's instructions were to remove one layer of bandages every day until all were gone, and "to keep looking at them so they'll know what they should be."

"I was intrigued by your message, Miss Doyle. Patrick is a hard man to find these days." Archibald Morton settled back into his chair. "Your concern for your employer is admirable, young lady. Please, tell me how I can help." His tone of voice somehow conveyed doubt and belief at the same time. It wasn't that surprising. The man's duplicity was known far and wide. Most exporters had to have a little bit of the pirate inside to be successful. Even Patrick had that.

"Well, Patrick's spoken of you often, sir," began Fiona, leaving out the fact that Patrick's words had never been complimentary, "and when you left your card last week I thought it might be best to ask your help." Fiona wrung her hands slightly for effect. "I can't help but think he's in great danger. If he was alone, I'd leave it—he's more than able to take care of himself, and it wouldn't be my place . . . but with the boy along . . . the lad's been through so much . . . I . . ."

"Of course," agreed Morton, leaning in. "You're obliged to share your concern. I share your concern for the delicacy of the situation, but rest assured, Miss Doyle, you did the right thing in coming to me."

Fiona smiled. "I knew it. Mr. O'Connor can be rather . . ."

"The man is rather given to extremes, isn't he, my dear? Must be a difficult task, keeping a line on a rambunctious boy in a household like that. You've done an admirable job. Then of course, there are such . . . *considerations* . . . in serving that family."

"Aye. That is true."

Morton stood up and walked to the window. "Miss Doyle, you've been honest in sharing your concern with me. I'd be obliged if you allow me a confidence."

"Anything to help Mr. O'Connor, sir."

Morton turned and looked at her. He was a round, greasy sort of man, given to smacking his lips and wearing odd-colored ties. He eyed her with a particular expression, showing he was going to be listening very carefully to how she answered the next question. "Tell me, my dear Miss Doyle, do you share my concern over your employer's recent choice of wife?" He slowly arched one eyebrow, testing.

Click. The small, silent sound of an alliance forged. The satisfaction of it curled up Fiona's spine and into her smile.

"Indeed I do, sir."

His own smile spread slowly. "I am so grateful to hear that, Miss Doyle. So very grateful indeed." He sat down again. "Come, let's you and I talk."

Deborah squinted and turned her head away. "Dear God, what *is* that?"

Patrick sucked his breath in and stuck his leg out toward Alejandro, who had a large knife between his teeth. Both of them were staring at the fiendish-looking red slug on Patrick's leg.

"You've never seen a leech before?" asked Patrick, rolling up his pant leg.

"That is not a leech. It's a monster." Deborah checked her ankles for the twelfth time.

"You should be glad it is only one, *Gigante*. Although I do admit it's a big one," sneered Alejandro, poking the end of it with the knife and watching the vile creature react.

"Aren't you glad I carried you across, dear wife?"

Deborah swallowed hard. "Infinitely."

"All right, Alejandro, I've had enough of being lunch for the little devil. Get the blasted thing off me before he drains me dry."

"Disgusting!" chimed in Duncan from over Deborah's shoulder, displaying a young boy's insatiable fascination for vile bugs.

Alejandro leaned in. "*Uno, dos . . .*"

Deborah shut her eyes and turned away. Whatever Alejandro was planning to do, she didn't want to witness it.

"*Tres.*"

"Wow!" exclaimed Duncan.

"*Potatoes,* Torrez, you're supposed to cut the *leech,* not the *man,*" cursed Patrick.

"Then you should be happy I did not choose to use my whip, eh, *Gigante*? That would have been more amusing, no?"

"No," groaned Patrick. "You can look now, Deborah. The carnage is over."

Deborah forced her eyes open. "I'd say the carnage has only just begun. Why is every insect intent on eating us down here?"

"Not every," countered Patrick, smiling as he held a cloth to the spot on his leg once occupied by the villain in question. "Just the big ones."

"You *did* tell her about the Indians, didn't you, Trick?" Alejandro smiled.

"No," Patrick replied, "I figured she had enough to cope with without worrying about people eating her as well."

Deborah shot the pair of them a nasty look. "You know, husband, I think you would have a much more enjoyable time carrying me the entire trip. Women are given to swooning under such circumstances, you know."

"I doubt if you've ever swooned." Patrick picked up the leech with a stick and flung it into the water beside him.

"I doubt if I've ever seen a leech the size of a catfish before." Deborah shook out her skirts just to ensure nothing occupied them but her legs.

"I've seen far bigger in Galveston," Patrick countered. "Only they come in suits and smiles and you don't notice them until they've sucked you clean dry. And I wouldn't be so much afraid of those kind, wife. You've already had dinner with some of the worst of them."

Alejandro had moved to the side of the clearing, where he was pointing to a strange mark carved into the tree trunk. "We are only an hour away, Trick. It's time."

"You're right." Patrick rolled his trouser leg back down and fished in his pocket. He brought out a small leather packet.

"What's in there, Pa?" Duncan peered over into his father's hand.

"Tribute, Duncan. We need to send our respects on ahead to the chief. Let him know we're coming on friendly business." Patrick's hand held a small collection of gold coins, small pearls, buttons, ribbons, and a mirror.

"Doesn't seem like much, Pa."

"It's not intended to be much. Just sort of a hello. Show them a few things they haven't seen in a long time to catch their interest."

"Oh."

Deborah looked up at Patrick. "How interested would they be if you showed them something they've never seen before?"

"Very," replied Patrick. "Why?"

With that Deborah took the knife from Alejandro's

hand—he'd cleaned it, thankfully. She hoisted up her skirt—enjoying the shocked look on Patrick's face when she did—and handed the knife to Patrick. "Cut a wide swatch of lace from my petticoat. I'd imagine not much lace finds its way up here," she said, straightening up with a smile.

"*Dios mio,*" Alejandro swore softly. "Where did you say you found her?"

Patrick just stood there, running his hand over his chin and shaking his head. "Right now, I'd have to say 'heaven,' Torres." He leaned down and cut off a piece, leaving a soft but promising kiss on her knee when he was done.

Deborah set her skirts to rights as Patrick handed Alejandro back his knife. "That's rather a bit north of Austin, Mr. Torres."

Patrick re-wrapped the package and handed it to Torres. "Find a man to take it on ahead, Alejandro." He stared straight at Deborah with fire in his eyes. "And take Duncan with you."

"Pa . . ."

"Go, son," commanded Patrick, his gaze still locked on Deborah. "Your mother and I will catch up in a minute. Or so."

"But, Pa . . ."

"Give it ten years, *niño,*" snickered Alejandro as he led Duncan from the clearing, "and you will understand. Let us go find a really big bug to scare your mother with, hmm?"

Patrick said nothing as they left, but let his eyes hold Deborah to the spot where she stood. There was something in his eyes that bloomed a deep satisfaction in Deborah's chest. It felt good, wonderfully, powerfully good, to be thought of as clever. To know that her intellect captivated him as strongly as the physical attraction. He moved in closer, sliding his hands around her waist. He could nearly encircle her waist, his hands were so large. A warm, urgent tingle spread out from his grasp.

"You amaze me," he said, pulling her tight against him.

"Good," she replied.

"I haven't been amazed in a very long time," he murmured into her neck as he left a burning line of kisses there. Deborah inhaled against him, his salty, spicy aroma sending sparks into her stomach. The kisses traveled down her shoulder as his hands spread against her bodice. He could arouse her in seconds, it seemed. Make her ache for him in an indecently short span of time.

"I'd say all of three days," she laughed, feeling his body tighten against hers.

"Too long . . ." he groaned into her chest, nipping at her through the fabric of her blouse in a way that made it hard to remain standing. "Too long." To be desired. To have someone so openly, honestly hungry for her. Her skin sparkled under his touch. She fought for her breath.

"Patrick, I don't think . . ."

"No, don't think. No thinking right now."

"You're making it difficult, believe me." He already had the first four buttons of her blouse undone. "It's just that . . ." She lost her train of thought as he pulled the blouse from her waistband and skimmed his hand up under the fabric. The slow curve of his fingers, the pressure of his palm. "We're in the . . ." The exotic friction of his tongue against hers. "All those . . . I . . ." Patrick began to ease her down against a rock. "I don't want to lie down in this!" she squealed, finally able to get a sentence out.

He pulled her back up against him. "Not enamored of the jungle floor, are you?"

"It's rather . . . populated," she complained, catching her breath.

"Well," Patrick purred, lifting her up. *Oh, Lord, there was that look again.* She was undone for certain. "There are alternatives." With a wicked grin he deposited her up against a tree.

Her eyes shot wide with the realization of his intent. "No," she gasped, "it's not . . ."

"It's quite possible. Rather nice even." His hand found her thigh. An indecent moan escaped her lips as she felt him sliding the stocking over her knee.

He pressed up against her, urgent yet slow and deliberate. Patrick held her to the tree with insistent hips while his hands destroyed the last shreds of her inhibitions. "Here?" She attempted a resistance, but the arousal in her voice betrayed her. "In front . . ." —she felt her blouse fall off her shoulders—". . . in front of all the insects?" It seemed so very appallingly, deliciously, indecent.

"Well," said Patrick with a liquid, silky laugh as her corset fell, "it *is* always more effective if you show them something they've never seen before."

"Oh, my."

⊰ Chapter Nineteen ⊱

He was in love with her.

The realization had dumped itself into his chest, right there in the jungle, like a bucket of cold water. When she had hoisted her skirts and handed him the knife, he knew—damn, who was he fooling? He had already come to know—that she was so much more than an acquired wife. She was a partner, an asset, a mate. Someone who brought out parts of him he'd kept neatly under wraps. The strength of his feelings refused to be denied.

He was in love with her.

It had churned through him when he took her there, sweating, coupling up against the tree, listening to her own passion overtake her embarrassment. He watched her for a moment as she repinned her hair, and marveled at the power of this affection. How, as they made love, he had felt her body call out to his until he wasn't sure where his body stopped and hers started anymore.

I love her.

When Deborah looked up at him a moment later, the certainty of it rang in his bones: he loved her.

Fiercely. Parts of him he thought dead for certain were springing back to life. It was a gift. A marvel.

A gift he might very well ruin in less than a day's time.

Patrick could not escape the aching fact that he was about to tell the biggest lie of his life in front of a woman who lived on truth. Patrick was about to spin the most unbelievable tale, the most exaggerated story he'd ever crafted, in order to win a pearl from this tribe of Indians. Was the financial gain, and the stability it'd give to his family, worth what it would do to Deborah?

He knew, as he took her hand and they walked silently through the soft, green forest, that it would drive a wedge between them if he did it. He'd torn her heart once. Cochara had seen it, known it, pinned the sin on him with brutal honesty. And, damn her, recognized that in harming her he had wounded himself.

The past couldn't be helped, he tried to tell himself. It wasn't as if he didn't already know what he had done. Hadn't planned it down to the last detail.

It was just never supposed to matter.

If she hated when he put her on a pedestal, what would she think when he made himself a legend right in front of her, inserted himself into a centuries-old folktale purely for his own gain? He knew, now, that it would cost him part of his soul if he did it.

More than that, it would rip Deborah's heart in half. And no amount of Cochara's magical potions would put it back together.

That night on the ship, when he had dared to ask

her if she loved him, she had said "almost." Pure honesty. He had adored her for it and been terrified by it at the same time. Had she, like him, gone beyond "almost" in the days since that question? Had her doubts peeled off like the layers of bandages? The answer underneath lay as raw and naked as her hands. There were only two layers of bandages left. He couldn't bring himself to ask her again. Like her fear of what her hands would be, he feared the consequences of her answer. If she loved him, Patrick knew he'd never be able to live with the knowledge that he had shredded that love before her very eyes. Yet Patrick knew of no other way to gain the pearl. He'd be in debt over his head if he returned from this trip without it.

That first day, in the surrey after the wedding, he had promised he would never lay a hand on her.

He wouldn't have to.

He had a far more lethal weapon at his disposal.

If he could bring himself to use it.

Deborah put her head on his shoulder as they walked. A tender, affectionate touch. Patrick wrapped his arm around her waist, certain he heard the sound of his own heart tearing.

"This is madness. You were right in bringing this to me." Archibald Morton held the letter from Alejandro Torres in his hand. "I must confess I had my doubts when last we met, but I assure you I share your concerns now."

"I'm glad to see it, sir."

He ran his fingers over the sharp edge of a letter

opener. "It takes no small amount of spine to do what you did, Miss Doyle. I respect that." He looked up at her with small, dark eyes. "So I won't ask you how you came into possession of this letter. And no one need ever know. It will simply be enough that we both have the family's best interest at heart."

"It's an island in the middle of nowhere, sir. I fear for the boy."

"It's remote, that's certain. But Venezuela is far from uncivilized. I have some associates in Jamaica who may be able to help us. Do you know anything about this Torres character?"

"I'm afraid not, Mr. Morton. Mr. O'Connor's not spoken of him before. He's not even spoken of this . . . this pearl before."

Morton snapped the document shut. "I can assure you, Miss Doyle, that there is no such pearl. I am not without expertise in this field, and I can tell you that red pearls are exceedingly rare. Exceedingly. They're not even native to that part of the world. And as for one of the size this letter claims, well . . . I fear to say, your employer is chasing an ancient legend. One that may very well get him killed. Venezuela may be civilized, but there are tribes of local savages that might not think twice about hacking him up for his efforts." He raised an eyebrow, as if asking to keep the letter in his possession, before placing the letter in his top desk drawer. Fiona nodded her approval. The more people who saw that tall tale, the quicker she could get Patrick and Duncan home.

Morton continued his questions. "When did you say this letter arrived?"

"Shortly after he brought *her* home." Fiona didn't like referring to her as "Mrs. O'Connor."

Morton tapped the letter opener end-up on his desk. His eyes gazed far off over her shoulder in thought. "Does she know?" he finally asked, slowly.

"Know what, sir?"

Morton's eyes returned to her. "Do you think Mrs. O'Connor knows of her new husband's *unusual* family history?" His use of her title made her cringe.

"She didn't. Not before. One night she asked me directly what it was that everyone was wondering if she knew about Mr. O'Connor. She'd picked up on odd looks folks were giving her, and she begged me to tell her what I knew. So I did." It had been satisfying to be the one to tell her. The woman had to realize how deep she was into a dark and dangerous place. Her reaction had been predictable. This woman wasn't the one who should handle Patrick's dark side. She hadn't the spine.

"What was her reaction?"

"She was afraid. Disturbed."

"Who wouldn't be?" He pulled out a clean sheet of paper from a drawer and filled a pen. "Can you tell me what you know about this woman?"

"He's not told me much. Nor has she. All I know is from the letter. Her name is Deborah Marie Edgerton. Or it was . . . before. She came from Austin. She took most of her belongings with her on the trip so I don't know anymore than that."

Fiona watched Morton make a few notations. He put the pen down and steepled his fingers, tapping them together slowly. "We'll bring them home to

safety, Miss Doyle. And we'll see to it that the
O'Connor family is spared any *significant* and *lasting*
financial ruin." His fingers stilled. "However, I feel I
have to say it might take . . . shall we say, *unconventional* measures. There may be some unpleasantness.
Can I count on your confidence, my dear?"

"Aye, sir. That you can."

"Well all right then. You just leave everything to
me." He stood up and took her elbow. "I'll get word
to you when it's needed. But be certain, Miss Doyle,
the boy's life is at stake. Now is no time for meek-
ness. We must stay strong and sure in our duty."

"Indeed."

Something awful was about to happen. Patrick
had been up all night, pacing the camp like a jaguar.
He'd been distant most of the afternoon. Yet, when
he looked at her, there was a turbulent longing in his
eyes. The strain in his shoulders told her he was
weighed down with a heavy decision. The hard edge
of his features told her it was a decision he would not
share with her. And so she did not try to follow when
he walked away from camp at sundown to stare at
some weather-beaten document Alejandro had given
him. She wasn't surprised when she woke up alone.

Her concern turned to fear when he kissed her
long and hard just before they left for the Indian
camp. "Stay calm, stay out of sight, no matter what
happens," he had said, with a new clarity in his eyes.

Deborah's heart pounded in her chest as she
watched Patrick walk off into the clearing. She,

Duncan, and Alejandro were up on a ridge, watching unseen from a safe distance.

This native people were dark and lush in their coloring, but with none of the grace of Cochara's tribe. No rich culture showed in their huts or their clothing. Deborah felt as if someone had plucked her out of the nineteenth century and thrust her back ten thousand years to some prehistoric jungle. In an odd flash of humor, Deborah thought it would not have been hard to find things these people had not seen before.

They were a short and solid people, compact and strong-looking. Odd shades of mud and strange ornaments decorated their hair. The men wore little clothing. Deborah had to wonder what the women wore, but there were no women in sight. She saw some huts farther behind the two common house structures they stood in front of now, a circle of smaller houses she guessed to be family homes. The women were no doubt in them now, peering at her through the cracks in the stick walls.

One man stood out clearly as their leader. He bore ornaments of bone and stone that no other man wore, and his bearing had authority.

Patrick walked toward him. He looked like a giant next to these men. She could tell, by the way he carried himself, that he knew it. That he was using it.

It evidently had the desired effect, for she could see a mixture of fear and awe come across the men's faces as Patrick asserted his height. Patrick said two or three sentences that produced gasps of reaction

from the Indian men. Then he released the gun from
his waist and dropped his knife to the ground.

At the sight, Alejandro's jaw dropped. He swore
profusely and angrily in Spanish. Patrick's actions
were evidently a surprise to Alejandro—and not a
pleasant one. Alejandro pushed Duncan behind him.
Deborah knew instinctively that this was bad. Very
bad.

"What the devil is going on?" Deborah demanded
in a whisper to Alejandro.

"*Dios mio*, Señora, do not speak!" Alejandro shot
back. For the first time in the entire journey, Deborah
saw fear in his eyes as Alejandro strained to hear the
conversation.

It wasn't that hard to hear. Patrick was talking
loudly. The men behind the chief were downright angry now. A few even backed away, murmuring. The
chief stood squarely in front of Patrick's display, eyeing him. At the conclusion of his strange declaration,
Patrick thrust one hand, palm up, in front of the
chief. He kicked his knife toward the chief.

"Dear God!" said Deborah. "What is he . . ."

"For the love of God, Señora," snapped Alejandro,
"be silent no matter what happens!"

Deborah shot him a fearful glance, but Alejandro's
eyes were locked on Patrick's hands. To her horror,
she watched the chief pick up the knife and cut a
large "X" on Patrick's palm. It turned red, but hardly
bled at all. In fact Patrick's entire hand and arm were
pale. He held it up over his head, showing the wound
to the group, who shouted in alarm. With a huge bel-
low, he turned and walked away from the group,

holding his hand high and shouting as he left. With a final declaration he disappeared behind a rock farther down ridge.

A fierce argument broke out amongst the Indians. What in heaven's name was going on? Had Patrick just declared war? Her pulse pounded and she felt ill.

"Come, Señora, NOW!" Alejandro had her arm and was dragging her away by the elbow. "Stay low and get away as quickly as you can." Alejandro scooped Duncan up in his arms, still cursing whatever it was Patrick had done. Deborah protested when he began to head off in a direction exactly opposite of where Patrick had gone.

"But Patrick . . ."

"We will find him soon enough, they aren't going to kill him—at least not yet. That loco husband of yours has just . . ." Alejandro didn't even finish the sentence, just made a low, disgusted sound in his throat.

Alejandro slashed a path through the undergrowth until they were down the hillside, hiding in a grove of trees. You could still hear the shouts from the village.

"Alejandro, what is going on?"

"When the men of the village have gone inside we will go to him. And if you are very lucky I will not kill him for his lunacy." Alejandro spat on the ground.

This had gone too far. Deborah had to know what Patrick had just done. "Alejandro! I demand you tell me what just happened. Did Patrick just declare war on those men?"

Alejandro pushed his hat farther down on his head

and peered up toward the village. "It would have been better for him if he did, Señora. Your husband was *supposed* to declare himself the Sky King. The god to whom the pearl belongs. To say he is here to take it back." He turned to look Deborah in the eye. "But he just told them he is an ordinary man. Mortal. As the kind who *can be killed.*"

Deborah's stomach dropped out through the bottom of her feet. "He *what?*"

"A damn poor time for *Gigante* to decide to be truthful. He was supposed to convince them he was the Sky King." Alejandro drew the X-shape from Patrick's cut onto his hand. "Now I can only hope he has convinced them not to kill him for insulting their legend."

Deborah's vocabulary failed her.

"If you are not a praying woman, now would be a good time to start." He headed up the ridge to watch the village.

Fifteen minutes later, after the village men took what felt like centuries to disperse into the common house, Alejandro motioned that it was safe to head toward Patrick. Deborah wanted to be the first to reach Patrick, but Alejandro's anger drove his footsteps far faster. Deborah was practically running to catch up to him by the time they reached Patrick.

He looked awful. He was sweating, shaking, and his hand was bleeding at an alarming rate. The handkerchief he had tied around the wound was already soaked with blood. His expression told Deborah he was in considerable pain.

Alejandro stood a few paces off, seething. Duncan shot to his father's side, frightened.

The bleeding had to be stopped right away. "Dear God, Patrick, why?" she said, half angry, half dumbfounded. Then, seeing Duncan's eyes, she realized the boy needed distracting. "Alejandro, take off your shirt." Alejandro was none too pleased about this, but began to unbutton it anyway. "Duncan, go over to that rock and start tearing it into strips."

"Go, son." Patrick said through gritted teeth, wiping the knife clean on his pant leg and handing it to the boy.

"You weren't bleeding at all when he cut you," Deborah said, staring at the soaked handkerchief. "What happened?"

Patrick pushed up his shirtsleeve. An ugly blue ring circled his upper arm. Then she spied a strip of leather on the ground. The fool had tourniqueted his arm in advance of the meeting. It must have been tied for a good half-hour before they got to the Indian camp. No wonder his arm and hand were pale. It was a wonder he could move it at all.

"Yes," hissed Alejandro from over her shoulder. "The Sky King does not bleed. It is why he needs the red pearl. Why go through this if you aren't claiming to be the Sky King? *Jesús*, Patrick, you've just signed your own death order by doing this!"

"I did no such thing. The legend in the document you gave me says 'being,' not 'God'," Patrick groaned.

"I doubt vocabulary will save you there," Alejandro sneered.

"It will work, Alejandro." Patrick was gritting his teeth again.

"A *being* who does not bleed is a being who *dies*!" Alejandro threw his hands up in the air in frustration.

"Stop it, both of you!" Deborah angled herself between them. "You can kill each other later if you can't resist the urge, but let's calm down and get this bleeding to stop."

She had been pressing her hands to the wound with no effect. The rush of blood down his arm once Patrick had loosed the tourniquet had evidently done damage. It must have been incredibly painful. Surely his arm must have been injured by going so long without any blood supply.

Duncan returned with the bandages. Deborah went to tend the wound, but her own hands were too encumbered by her own bandages. The cloths on her hands were now soaked in Patrick's blood. Without thinking about it, she tugged at the last two layers of her bandages with her teeth and peeled them off. She didn't even look at her hands as she peeled the blood-soaked rag from Patrick's hand. His hand was shaking. She went to start bandaging it, but Patrick put a hand out to stop her.

"Wait," he said, reaching into his vest for a small leather pouch. "Put this on first."

Deborah worked the pouch's thong with her fingers, still not thinking, and reached inside. It was the pearl salve Cochara had used on her hands. She poured it out into Patrick's hand and rubbed it in.

It was then that she realized her hands were bare.

The sight of the salve, now turning pink from Patrick's blood, forced the realization to her mind. She stopped for a moment, staring at her naked fingers.

Her naked, unscarred fingers.

She was touching him.

Her fingers, covered in the shimmering substance, stained by his blood, were touching him.

She felt the shake of his hands, the gritty texture of the salve, the warmth of his blood. Her fingers had feeling.

Deborah's breath caught in her throat. She looked up and watched Patrick recognize her touch. He understood what had just happened.

"Dear God," he said softly.

Short sobs started in Deborah's stomach and found their way up her throat. She could not hold them back as she wound the bandage around his hand. She wanted to bury her face in his hand for not telling the lie and slit his throat for placing himself in such danger. The warring emotions finally erupted out of her.

She shook him, pounding at his shoulders. "I don't care about the blasted pearl! I don't want it!" she screamed at him. "I need you. Duncan needs you. How could you . . ."

Patrick grabbed her hands and held them still. "Stop, Deborah. Not now."

"No," she said, wrenching her hands free, "Why do I have to be quiet? I don't have to be anything! I . . ." It was too much. Her hands, this jungle, what he'd just done, his blood still sticky on her fingers. She sank onto the ground in front of him.

Patrick's eyes remained locked on her, holding her. "Deborah, look at me. *Look at me.* I will be all right. It will all be all right."

Deborah pulled her face away from his hand. Alejandro cut in between them. "Can you walk, you fool?"

"Yes."

Patrick struggled to his feet, falling against Alejandro when he finally got upright. His face looked pale and pained. Alejandro hoisted Patrick's arm over his shoulder. "What time did you tell them you would be back for the pearl, you enormous idiot?"

"Sunset tomorrow."

"That will give me plenty of time to beat you senseless for your honesty. Why did you change the plan, *Gigante*?" Alejandro swore heartily in Spanish. "Let us get you to camp so I can yell at you for a few hours."

Deborah stood up slowly. The plan had been for Patrick to claim to be the Sky King, but he hadn't. So that is what he had been wrestling with all night. Whether or not to deceive the tribe to gain the pearl. Hanging his life on a single word in an ancient, musty document. "Being" or "god." So many emotions were boiling through her she didn't even know if she could walk. She felt a tug on her skirts. When she looked down, there was Duncan, holding a rag. "Your hands are all dirty, Ma. Do they hurt?" The child held the rag up toward her. There was as much fear and confusion on his face as there was in her heart.

"No," she said softly. "They don't." Slowly she began to wipe the dirt and blood from her hands. The skin was raw, alive, sensitive to the wipes of the rag and the feelings of her fingers moving.

Duncan fetched a canteen of water and held it up over her hands. He poured some water over her hands and she continued to wipe them. The sensation was powerful on the tender new skin. She forced in a trembling breath as she dried her hands off.

"All better?" Duncan's eyes were pleading.

"Much." She attempted a smile. It seemed to come out as more of a choked grimace.

The boy carefully slipped a hand into hers. The plump, small fingers ventured a gentle grasp. Her eyes squinted shut at the astounding touch. "Is it gonna be all right?" he asked with fear in his voice.

"Yes." Now who bent the truth?

"Are you mad at Pa?" Duncan ventured as they began to walk.

"I don't know."

"Alejandro sure is."

"Yes," replied Deborah, "he is."

Duncan gave a large sigh. "Pa's gotted lots of people mad at him b'fore. He'll be fine, I reckon."

Deborah didn't answer.

"I mean," continued Duncan, applying a grown-up sound to his still-quivering voice, "he's really big and strong. And he's got us. So it'll turn out."

Deborah's vocabulary failed her again.

❧ Chapter Twenty ❧

Patrick was leaning against the side of the cave, his hand propped up on one knee, eyes closed. Deborah had heard him and Alejandro shouting at each other for a good twenty minutes before Alejandro had stormed off down to the stream. She could hear him cracking his whip in the distance. Truthfully, she had no idea if the men had reconciled. They had, at least, chosen to cool off away from each other. When Duncan trotted off in the direction of the stream, Deborah didn't stop him. Duncan was an effective distraction, and while Alejandro was impressive with his whip, she knew he wouldn't wield it around the boy. If nothing else, the need to stay calm in front of the child would serve as a good safety valve for an angry man.

Deborah stared at Patrick in silence. His body language showed he knew she was there, but his face was still turned away, leaning against the wall. He looked drained. Unsure. Like a man who had just jumped off a very high cliff and had no idea where the bottom was.

"Why?" she said, finally.

"Because it was the only way." Patrick didn't move his head.

"Only way to what, Patrick?"

"The only way to keep the pearl . . . and . . . keep you." She could tell he wanted to look at her but couldn't.

"You have me."

"Would I have you if I told that fantastic tale Alejandro and I had planned?"

Deborah was silent for a long while. "I don't know."

"I do. You'd no sooner live off the fruits of that deception than . . . than . . ." He didn't finish the sentence, only let out a jagged sigh and threw a small rock across the cave floor. All the bravado was gone.

"I don't need that pearl. Duncan doesn't need that pearl. What we need is you, alive, with us, not hacked to bits by natives." She took a step toward him. The fingers flexed on his bandaged hand.

"Why doesn't anyone else see this? There is a way." He turned to her, his body stiff with pain and fatigue. "The text of the legend—that document Alejandro had—says 'a being who does not bleed.' We've all assumed it's the Sky King, assumed it's a god. Only it doesn't have to be. Why can't a being not bleed, want the pearl, and give them the future of protection the legend says the pearl will bring? Why can't I be that being? If I can do this, we get the pearl with the truth."

"The truth is, Patrick, that you're taking a huge risk with your life for one small gem."

"No!" he shot back, wiping the sweat from his

forehead. "That's not it. Not at all. It's not about one small gem. That pearl is a future. A secure future for Duncan—and now for you—no matter what happens to me. If my mind goes, if I end up like Michael or Mother or any other of the endless line of insane Blacks, you'll be cared for. And no matter how sick in my head I get, Dunc will always have one great achievement to hold in his memory. One great adventure to remember. I need to know Duncan has that. And I was willing to pay any price to get it."

Patrick pulled himself up the wall, standing unsteadily. "But I couldn't risk you. You know parts of me I don't even want you to know yet. You won't stay at a safe distance. You're everywhere. You're inside me, Deborah. Looking at me when I close my eyes. Bumping around in my head when I'm trying to think."

Patrick reached out and held her hand.

He'd never actually *held* it before. Pulled her, clinched her hand, pinned it even, but he'd never *held* it. He ran his fingers across the back of her palm. The sensation of it shocked her before she could hide it. "I *need* you," he said, and in those three words she understood what it had cost him not to be the Sky King.

He pulled one of her hands to his face, pressing the fingers to his jaw. Forcing her to touch him. Knowing what it meant to her. She remembered, in a flood she was powerless to stop, how she had yearned to touch him, to feel his skin under her fingers.

Before she could take another breath he took her other hand and laid it on his heart. It was painfully intimate to touch him there. To feel the heave of his breath, feel the cool moisture on top of the warm skin, feel his heart beat.

Patrick put out his hand and laid it gently over her heart. She felt the heat of his palm through her blouse, felt the pressure of his hand amplify the pounding of her own heart. She loved him.

Dear Sweet Jesus, she loved him. It was irrefutable. She loved what he and Duncan had become to her, she who had spent so long on the fringes of a family. She loved how he took her ordinary life and recast it in a fantastic, larger-than-life setting. He had given her adventure.

"Say it," she asked quietly. *Tell me you love me.* The way Patrick looked at her, his eyes glistening gold and deeper than she'd ever thought them to be, he hardly needed to say it. He'd just shown her in front of a host of Indians ready to cut him to ribbons.

Patrick's bandaged hand came up to stroke the side of her face. The hand was shaking. Slowly, he whispered a few soft words in Gaelic.

No translation was required.

A tender smile spread across his face when her own expression registered understanding. "And I you."

"Give me a few hours," he said, "and I'll give you all the translation you'll ever need."

"I believe you." Three small words, imbued with such power. And, as difficult as it was to fathom, she did. She believed him. Moreover, she believed *in* him.

"Stay here," Patrick said with a sudden sense of

urgency. "For the love of God, don't move until I get back. I swear, I'll only be gone a short time, but please swear to me you'll wait."

His pleading sounded ridiculous on a man of his size. Deborah could only nod, amused and still shell-shocked from their admissions to each other. Patrick nearly leapt from the cave despite his injuries.

She leaned against the wall, near dizzy. She loved him. He loved her. It solved absolutely nothing. Senseless. Priceless.

"On my life, on all we've ever been through, give me two hours with her, Alejandro. Two hours alone."

Alejandro tossed a rock into the stream. "How can you stand there and ask a favor? Of me?"

"God bloody damnit, Torres, I *need* this. If not for me, for Duncan." After a pause, Patrick kicked the moss at his feet and added, "Please."

Alejandro looked up. "*Dios mio.* He knows the word."

In any other circumstance, Patrick would have shot back a cutting retort. Instead he just stood in silence. *Come on, Torres, if you've anything close to blood running through those veins . . .*

"You will owe me so much when this is over, *Gigante.* So very much."

Patrick could only exhale. "Right. Watch Dunc, then, won't you?"

"Don't worry, Don Juan, your boy will be safe. It is the lady who has my concern now. Does she have any idea just what she's married?"

"More than you know, Torres."

"More's the pity I fear, *amigo*," Torres called from over Patrick's shoulder as he made his way back to the cave.

Patrick pulled the ring from inside a handkerchief. The wedding band. It had not left his keeping since Duncan's accident on the ship. Slipping it back onto that tiny pale finger was the most important thing in the universe at this very moment. And not just slipping it on. This time it was going to be placed on. With affection and reverence. They knelt together, on a spread blanket by a fire far into the cave, and he held her hand.

"Wife," he said once the ring was in place, savoring the word on his tongue. He brought her hand to his lips and kissed it. It was smooth and soft. He closed his eyes and breathed. He'd cracked open that long-closed part of him, and it stood wide and gaping before this woman. His wife. And, to his amazement, he could stand the vulnerability. He could even welcome it. He gazed at her, almost shaking his head in disbelief. It was the most astounding thing.

The color of her eyes struck him anew. He reached out, touching her lashes. Her eyes fell shut at the touch, her head swaying to meet his palm. He leaned in and kissed her. A soft, gentle kiss. An invitation.

She responded. And when her hands came up to touch his neck and bury themselves in his hair, the world gave way around him. After weeks and weeks of hungering for her touch, the actuality of it lit him on fire. He pulled her close, fumbling once or twice because his injured arm couldn't hold their weight as they lay back onto the blanket.

The act of finally touching him ignited her as well, for behind the awkwardness he could feel her frantic urge to touch him. Her hands wandered across his jaw, lingered around the corner of his ear, found a spot on his neck that made him nearly gasp. And when her fingers came to the first button of his shirt, he thought he'd die of impatience.

The fluttering touch of her hands across his chest sent Patrick reeling. Whether it was the wound, the fever, or the sheer intensity of his desire for her, it mattered not. He was drowning in a wild, swirling sensation that spun the universe down to just two people. Man and woman. Husband and wife. She pushed the shirt off his shoulders and let her lips wander over the skin. Patrick drew in a ragged breath, astounded at what she could do to him.

She was touching him. The power of it surged through Deborah like lightning. She slid her hand slowly over his chest, feeling the heat of his skin as it glistened in the firelight. She drew her caress across his ribs and down to his stomach. As she let her fingers round the corner of his hip he was nearly fighting for air.

Patrick wrapped his good arm around her and pulled her into a long, slow kiss. A velvety, time-stopping kiss that set off fireworks in her chest. Sitting up, Deborah began undoing the buttons of her shirtwaist. She watched his eyes as she pulled the fabric back, feeling her own skin ignited by his hungry gaze. When the blouse fell away, she pulled at her hairpins. She ran her fingers across the hair of his chest, luxuriating in the sensation. He tugged at her shift with his good hand, and with her assistance it slid to the ground.

With a delighted, intimate laugh, she rolled off the rose-colored stockings that were his first pledge of affection. Her absurd betrothal into his ludicrous family. She felt beautiful and desired.

He gave a low moan when she set herself at unbuckling his trousers. How many nights had he helped her out of her clothes, enjoying every wicked moment of it, delighting in how he could awake her passion so easily? Tonight she would give it back to him tenfold.

"Husband," she purred as the last of their clothes fell away. Now, finally, she surrendered to the long-awaited pleasure of touching him. Now, at last, it was she who made love to him. Her hands followed the planes of his hips, exploring. She slid her fingers along the column of his thigh, relishing how the teasing scrape of one slow finger made him shudder. His good hand fisted in the blanket. She was touching him. She had ached for this, craved it even more than she realized. She watched Patrick's eyes cloud over with passion as her caresses grew more bold. His body tensed and flexed, strung taut with the need she knew she was building in him.

Deborah pulled herself on top of him and joined their bodies. At that moment, that lush, fantastic moment of union when man and wife cleaved not only in body, but in soul, he stared into her eyes and said, "I love you."

No hiding behind the Gaelic this time.

He pulled her close as she began to rock against him. His skin was intoxicating. His strength captivating. She could not touch enough of him, take him in deeply enough, get close enough. They lost themselves in the pulsing, perfect rhythm of their bodies. "I love you." He called it again and again as the rhythm built and pulled them over the edge, tumbling happily until it felt as if they landed at the gates of heaven itself.

⊰ Chapter Twenty-one ⊱

Jake Napson looked up from his steak. "What if it *is* real, Arch?"

"I'm not saying it isn't. Exceedingly rare is a long way from impossible." Archibald Morton ground out his cigar. "I reckon a legend like that has to come from somewhere."

"You've a point. A find like that's a loss in the hands of a small-time operator like O'Connor."

Morton poked a finger at his partner. "O'Connor's no small-time operator. He's eccentric, odd if you will, but he's not small time. I've been angling after his holdings for a few years now. No one's got a stronger hold on some of the smaller ports on the Mexican coast. And, as you can see, he's gone farther into South America than most of us."

"You've got that look about you, Arch. You got a plan."

Morton leaned back in his chair and took a long swig of wine. "Indeed I do."

"Well, then, out with it, man," replied Napson behind a mouthful of steak.

"For one thing, we let O'Connor do the hard work

for us. Let him bring the pearl back from wherever the hell he is. He'll be all on his high horse thinkin' he's made the deal of a lifetime."

"But," prompted Napson.

"But a pearl is only as good as its buyer. It shouldn't be hard to convince everyone that the pearl is a fake. Most people don't believe it exists, anyway. Now we just fold our little friend's family history of 'less than sound minds' into the mix and we're cookin'. Feed the right information into Galveston's top-rate rumor mill and Patrick O'Connor goes from a hero to a desperate lunatic. Folks have been waitin' for him to go over the edge for years now. We'll just help things along. You and I just have to make good and sure anyone who can verify its authenticity can't be found right away. When the price drops through the floor, we'll grab it up out of sympathy. Out of kindness for a man down on his luck. And, when things get really bad, we can offer to purchase a few of his other deals at a kindly but below-market price."

"You do know how to craft a plan, Archibald."

"I do indeed, Jake. I do indeed." He stabbed his own steak with an easy viciousness. "Oh, but I forget myself. There's more."

"More?" Napson fished in his pocket for a cigar of his own.

"Just in case that isn't enough to bring our friend to his knees, I've come across some most fascinating news about his wife."

Jake clipped off the end of his cigar with a careful eye. "Now why don't that surprise me?"

"Seems the new Mrs. O'Connor has herself a bit of a past. And someone who ain't so eager to see her leave it all behind." Morton pointed his fork for emphasis.

"Really?"

"Mrs. O'Connor was once a Miss Edgerton. But more importantly, she was almost a Mrs. Hasten. There's a rather unstable fellow named Samuel Hasten who is currently cooling his heels in prison up in Austin and claims to have married her in secret."

Napson stopped in mid-puff. "How the hell d'you find all this out, Arch?"

Morton gave a fat, greasy laugh. "Now, you know a man of honor never reveals his sources, Jake."

"I'd know that," replied Napson with his own laugh, "if I knew a man of honor."

Morton leaned over his plate. "Now, I've arranged for our dear Mr. Hasten to find his way out of his, shall we say, 'unfortunate confinement,' for which he is all too eager to help us in our little cause. Seems our friend wants his lady back. And we're always on the side of true love, aren't we, Jake?"

"Most assuredly."

"It will take several weeks," said Morton as he stuffed himself with a forkful of mashed potatoes, "for us to get the arrangements worked out. I imagine, if we're lucky, we should be able to bring Mr. Hasten to town just before our hero returns with his treasures. A few whispers into some well-placed ears, a few jewelers' palms greased, and we should be able to stir up a storm just before Mardi Gras."

"I do like a celebration!" smiled Jake.

"It's all in the timing, my dear boy." Morton licked his fingers with a predatory air. "All in the timing."

The setting sun began to wash the greens of the jungle with pinks and golds. Deborah plucked a heart-shaped leaf from a nearby plant, twisting it on its stem between her fingers. "I don't see how this is going to work, Patrick."

She heard him shift his weight, leaning against a stone behind her. "I've been importing and exporting for years. I can do this."

"Alejandro doesn't seem to think so. He's down there calculating how much you're going to owe him for expenses and ruining his good name. I don't see how you're going to convince them to give you the pearl."

"I'm not."

"What do you mean?"

"Everyone's spent years trying to find a way to steal this pearl. I'm going to buy it."

Deborah stared at him. "With what? I doubt these people care much for the value of a dollar. That pearl is priceless. How could you have enough money to buy it?"

"Because I'm not going to use money. You're right about one thing: these people couldn't give a fig about a stack of hundred-dollar bills. That doesn't mean I can't give them what they want. What the pearl is supposed to give them. What the Sky King is supposed to give them." Patrick turned to Deborah, his eyes gleaming. "I've read that text a hundred times. Look at how they live, Deborah, there are things they need that money won't give them. I can give them those things. I know it."

"*Dios*," Alejandro swore as the three of them moved closer to the gathering collection of natives. "It is bad enough God has seen to make one of you, now I have to find out you are both *loco*. This is bad. Plain madness."

When Alejandro, Deborah, and Patrick reached the outer limits of the camp, Patrick put his hand out to signal Alejandro to stay behind. Deborah and Patrick walked into the camp alone.

The welcoming party seemed surprised at Deborah's presence. He didn't want her here, just in case something went wrong, but the look on her face told Patrick there'd be no dissuading her. The Indians gawked at her pale and fragile appearance—not to mention her spectacles, which seemed to fascinate them endlessly. Taking her cue from Patrick, she stood in silence.

Finally, Patrick spoke to the chief. "Your people are good caretakers of the pearl," he began. "Strong and careful. I admire you and your people. The pearl is of great value, and I want to give you things of great value in exchange."

A ripple of murmurs went through the men, but the chief held up his hand to silence them. He regarded Patrick with a narrowed eye. Patrick waited, returning his stare with all the power he could muster, until the chief finally gave a small nod for him to continue.

Patrick motioned for them to move over to a small stump by the common fire pit. He needed a table and it served the purpose. The group of men followed. Out of the corner of his eye he caught Alejandro making sure the man on the ridge still had a clear shot.

"The pearl has power, so I give you power in return." He pulled a pouch from his vest and put it on the table. From it he produced one small cream-colored pearl and a mirror. That alone seemed to impress the gathering—a good sign. Then he took out a split stick and some twine, rather like a miniature ax handle. That brought grunts of curiosity. He had their attention.

Patrick took a breath and began his explanation.

"You know this," he said, holding up the pearl. "It is useful and beautiful. And it is strong. But I bring you something which you have not yet seen, something with more value and power than all your white pearls." He opened the second pouch to pour a collection of diamonds on the table.

Patrick fitted the largest of the diamonds—the one from his own stickpin—into the miniature handle. Once in place, he brought the newly created tool down with considerable force upon the small pearl. It crushed the pearl easily. "It has great strength," explained Patrick. The men remarked to each other.

Patrick waited until the talk had died back down before moving to his next demonstration. Placing the mirror on the table, he drew the diamond across the mirror in a straight line. He showed them the scratch it left. "It is harder than wood or stone or anything

else you have here. There is nothing it cannot cut."
With that, he put the mirror back onto the table and
retraced the line two or three times. Holding the mirror up, he snapped it in two perfectly cut halves.

Patrick had shown them the diamonds' physical
powers. He knew, though, that it wouldn't be a fair
exchange if they did not believe they were getting
something of mystical powers. It wasn't deception, it
was knowing what the pearl gave them and how it
needed to be replaced. He held one of the diamonds
up for the chief to see. "My people say it is the color
of running water." Water was life to these people, so
they could understand such importance. Still, that
wouldn't be enough to generate the awe in these people that the red pearl had. Searching for the perfect
place, Patrick walked to a patch of sunlight and held
up the large diamond. When he found just the right
angle, the diamond sent a shower of rainbows onto
the ground. A rainbow on command was a very
powerful thing. Watching their faces, Patrick knew
he'd hit the mark.

All this was still pure display. Patrick knew he
could never pay them what La Roja was worth—not
yet. He could, however, give them what the Sky King
was foretold to give them: a bountiful future. "I will
purchase this land for you so that it belongs forever
to your people. I will send goods and medicine and
whatever you need for as long as I am alive. And I
will see to it that my family after me will do the
same." He could create a trust fund with some of the
sale proceeds. A pledge he could pass to Duncan, and
Duncan to his own children.

"People throughout the world place great value on these stones," Patrick continued. "They are respected. If you choose to use it to gain things for your people outside the jungle, it will bring you many goods." Patrick placed the large diamond in the chief's hand.

The chief examined the stone, finally holding it up to the light. The rainbows reappeared.

The chief was silent. He regarded Patrick suspiciously. "You are not the Sky King," he said.

Patrick's stomach twisted. How much easier it would have been to say he was. Deborah didn't know the language. She would never know if he claimed to be the god. They would give the pearl to the Sky King. Without the pearl, he would return to Galveston in debt, and empty-handed. Was it worth it? When he turned to look at Deborah, he knew the answer. Even if she never discovered his deception of the Indians, he would know how he had deceived her.

The trip *had* been the treasure hunt he made it out to be. Only the treasure he found wasn't the one he came looking for.

It was her. And she was worth everything he had.

Patrick stared into the eyes of the chief. "No," he responded, "I am not. I am a man."

"You would be guard to our people?"

"As best I can, but I am no god."

"Many have filled my ears with lies. How can you prove we can trust you with La Roja? That you will do all you say?"

Patrick had known this question was coming. He'd

dreamed up a thousand ways of backing up his claims, conjured every conceivable form of guarantee he could imagine, but none of it would mean anything to these people. The plain fact was that all he had was his word.

That was worth nothing to them.

He felt the dream slip from his body with a quiet whisper. He would return home without the pearl. And the hole it left was not as jagged as he would have thought. It would be enough to have Duncan and Deborah for as long as fate allowed.

"I can prove nothing," he said simply.

The old man stared at him with eyes as wise as Cochara's. "It may be you have proven much."

Patrick looked up.

"I know La Roja has worth outside this place," said the chief.

"Great worth," replied Patrick. "Very great worth." There was no point, now, in clever negotiation.

"What else have you to give in exchange for it?"

"Nothing. I have given you all I can, and promised you all I can."

"It is worth more." The chief rolled the diamond in his palm.

La Roja would go to the next adventurer with deeper pockets. Not him. "Yes, it is."

"Then it is good to place something of such value in the hands of a man who speaks truth."

Patrick's heart stopped.

"My people are fewer now. We are not as powerful. It has always been said the pearl will give us what we need. It will give us what we need now as

well, Sky King." With that he motioned to a man behind him, who produced a beaded pouch. Inside the
pouch was La Roja. The most astounding thing
Patrick had ever seen in his life. More glorious than
he had imagined it. Rich, red, glistening.

"I am not the Sky King," he said, his voice near
breathless with awe over the seemingly impossible
gem.

The chief raised an eyebrow. "Who is to say you
are not?"

⇥ Chapter Twenty-two ⇤

Home.

The reaction surprised Deborah as she stood on the steamship deck and watched Galveston Island come into view. In point of fact, she'd only been on the island a matter of days before the tornado that was Patrick O'Connor hurled her off on this adventure. Yet, the Island's status as home to Patrick and Duncan had rubbed off on her. Even now she felt their hunger to set foot on shore.

It wouldn't be a fairy-tale homecoming.

The anonymity she and Patrick had enjoyed on ship, the luxury of creating an identity for themselves as husband and wife without the baggage of their pasts, would disappear with their first step on solid ground. She would return to being Patrick's bizarrely acquired wife, he would return to being—well, the colorful list of adjectives that was how Galveston viewed Patrick. They couldn't simply ride into town triumphant, brandishing the rare pearl, for as Patrick had wisely ascertained, few people would believe its authenticity without expert proof. This pearl just wasn't supposed to exist.

Then again, men weren't supposed to abduct their wives. Potions don't heal scars. Six-year-old boys did not get magical Ma's. Entire cities did not rise up on sandbars. *The world has become a place where the impossible happens,* thought Deborah as she heard the distant cries of seagulls.

She heard the familiar rhythm of Patrick's footsteps come up behind her. When he slid his hands over hers on the rail, you could barely see the marks of the cut he'd carved into his palm. Nor the scars of her own hands. They had healed, both of them. *On the inside as well as on the outside.*

"How shall we tell Madge?" came his voice, soft and teasing into the nape of her neck.

Deborah gave a soft laugh, imagining the look that would erupt over the woman's face when she saw them. "That will be great fun. Except I believe she already knows. I believe she knew all along."

"Madge's crazy dreams. She's more daft than I'll ever be." Patrick left a collection of delicate kisses along the curve of her ear.

"I rather like to think she's wiser than both of us put together," Deborah countered. "She's certainly the first woman I've ever seen make you do anything against your will."

"The *second,*" Patrick teased. "And just what did she make me do against my will?"

Deborah turned to Patrick. "Why, she practically twisted your ear like a schoolboy's to make you kiss me."

"Untrue. I kissed you entirely of my own free will. And the force you speak of was used on *you,* to make you let me. As if any woman's ever needed co-ercion to submit to my charms." He pulled her in tight against him.

"Really? Was I not married at supposed gun-point?"

"Irrelevant," murmured Patrick, pushing his hips up against her as he pinned her to the deck rail. "You know, we're still on our honeymoon." His fingers tunneled up the back of her hair and began conquer-ing the hairpins one by one. "I believe we've a good half-hour before we dock."

"Trick! Stop that!" Deborah pushed away, shaking her all-too-quickly-clouding head.

Patrick halted and stared at her with an odd look on his face. He had stopped far too easily.

"What?" she inquired, fixing the wayward pins.

"You've never called me 'Trick' before," he said slowly.

Deborah hadn't even realized she'd done it. "Did I?" She wasn't quite sure what it meant or how he was taking it. "Well," she ventured, "you deserved it."

"Say it again," he teased. "Say it a dozen times."
Say it again. Say it again.
Deborah's spine went cold. That phrase.

The dark memory erupted before she could stop it. Samuel Hasten used to ask her to repeat his name just like that. The deceptive reporter had convinced her it was music to his ears to hear her say it. "No." Her voice wavered with the word.

"Deborah?" He picked up on her horrified re-sponse.

"Don't ask me that," Deborah said sharply. "Don't ever ask me that again."

Patrick moved in, concerned. "Ask you what? What are you talking about?"

Deborah shut her eyes. She fought the panicked chill that had suddenly overcome her and reminded herself this was Patrick standing next to her, not Samuel Hasten. Her husband standing next to her. A man who had proven himself to her, who had earned her trust. Every irrational doubt she'd tamped down over the last two months jumped to life. With a shaky breath she forced her eyes open and stared into Patrick's. She waited until the warmth of his eyes pushed the doubts away. Then she turned her gaze out to sea and tucked herself in safely beneath his chin and began to speak.

"The man who . . . who caused all the trouble in Austin. The reporter. Samuel Hasten. He used to do that. Ask me to say his name. Over and over. Like it was some kind of music to him, like it was magical to hear me say his name." She paused a long time, fighting the sting of the memories. "I believed him. I believed so much of what he told me and it was all so false." Deborah turned her head up to look at Patrick. "Do you know why I care so much about the truth? Well, Samuel Hasten is why. The lies he told hurt me more than you'll ever know."

Patrick touched her cheek. "You did a selfless thing out of love for your son. He had no right to use that against you."

Deborah felt the heat of one tear slip down her

cheek. "William calls some other woman 'Mother.' I wonder if he even knows I exist?" It was a long time before she added, "He may not even be called William at all."

Patrick pulled her in close, planting a quiet kiss on the top of her head. She felt him sigh. "I can't change that," he said, wrapping his arms more tightly around her. "And it is an awful thing. But you *are* mother to Duncan. He loves you. I love you. You are our family now. Come home."

Madge Cooney just about laughed herself off her settee when Deborah hoisted her skirts to show off the rose stockings. Just for the fun of it, they'd stopped at her house before even reaching home. The prospect of her joy was just too strong to resist.

"Well, Trick O'Connor, have you ever known me to be wrong? I declare! You surprise even me." She turned her sparkling eyes to Deborah, who was playfully posing her ankles. "And, Deborah honey, I didn't think the woman even *existed* who could take the red out of the O'Connors. Pink! No, wait, I think Trick called them rose. Rose. Yes, I do believe they suit you just dandy." She bubbled herself up off the settee and took each of their hands. "You suit each other, children. And there ain't no finer thing in the universe."

Deborah could only smile.

Madge touched her sleeve. "There's something about adventure that just makes a woman fairly glow. Travel changes one's perspective. Broadens one's horizons. 'Course," she added in a low voice, patting her bustle, "my horizons seem to be broadening very well all on their own these days."

"Madge," countered Patrick, "you're still the second most beautiful woman on the Island."

"I used to be the *first*," teased Madge in reply, "but I'll secede gracefully in the name of true love." She stared again at Deborah's face with delight in her eyes. "Oh, sugar, you love him, don't you? It's plum all over your face and I just couldn't be happier."

Patrick and Deborah declined an invitation to stay for tea—even though Duncan managed to parlay his short visit into a considerable stack of cookies—insisting they needed to get home.

At the door, Madge's face took on a darker hue. "Trick, honey, somethin's afoot. There's been entirely too much speculation on where you were while you were gone. A few too many casual questions, one or two well-chosen idle remarks, that sort of thing. You got somethin' up your sleeve, deah?"

Patrick arched an eyebrow. "When don't I?"

"Well, I don't expect you to tell me anyhow, but just promise me you'll keep an eye open."

Patrick planted a kiss on her cheek. "Believe it or not, Madge, I plan to fill you in eventually."

"Uh-huh." Madge's eyes narrowed in disbelief.

Patrick tossed the letter onto his desk in disgust. The fourth jeweler he'd contacted found some reason not to receive him. Why did every reputable jeweler from both here and Houston suddenly have a full schedule? Madge was right, something was afoot.

Even at last night's dinner party the stares were odder than usual. Patrick was grateful he'd kept his find a secret. One needed to know the landscape before firing off a cannon like the one he had wrapped in velvet in his pocket.

Ah, but Patrick O'Connor had a new weapon. His wife. She was perhaps the greatest asset he had against anything the world might choose to throw at him now.

What a woman she was. Once she had found her courage, allowing her hands to roam over him there in the cave, a new woman had awakened. Deborah's sensibility had gained a second side; a lush, smoldering, knowing side that could reduce him to pudding in a heartbeat. It was as if she had spent so much time as a victim of false affections, that to find a true love had given her newfound power. It showed in the way she carried herself. The way she spoke. The way she would run her hand down his thigh.

She had changed. Bit by bit, she was conquering her past with the power of her future, and that conquest was blooming a new vitality into her that took his breath away. She was twice the woman he'd married. It never ceased to amaze him. He hoped it never would.

Patrick took the stickpin—the one now missing the diamond—from an envelope in his desk drawer. Best to keep this from view for a while. Locking the study door, he walked over to the bookcase and pulled out the fourth book from the right. *1001 Arabian Nights.* The book fell open to the correct page, and he lifted the key from the spine. He twirled the red ribbon between his fingers as he moved to the second bookcase and turned the wooden figurine around.

He stopped.

He had just turned the elf toward the windows.

He'd always left the elf *facing* the windows, so that the leaf covering the keyhole would face the wall. The leaf that was angled off the keyhole right now, not covering it as it should be.

Patrick grabbed the book again and thumbed to the page. There was a second, fainter impression of the key, there on the page just above the first. He'd always been careful to put the key exactly back in the outline of the same impression.

Someone had found his key, and opened his box.

Someone knew where he had been and what he was after.

Life was about to become far more complicated.

"No, sir. You've had callers by the handful, but I've let none of 'em in the house. And some of them was bloody insistent, I can tell you. You were gone a mighty long time, you were." Mrs. Doyle thickened her brogue with a touch of resentment. " 'Course it didn't help matters not knowin' where ye' were and when ye' were planning on comin' home. And where on earth you were takin' a wee lad like Duncan as if there were no danger in it at all."

"The boy was in no danger. He's just fine," Patrick countered in frustration.

"Oh no, no danger at all." Mrs. Doyle began banging cupboards as she put a set of dishes away. "Not a bit. Swinging from the top of ships, to hear him tell it. Marching through jungles. Cavorting with natives. Thirty-foot leeches. Not a wee bit of danger." She turned to look at Patrick, hands clenched at her hips. "He's six. A strong six, mind you, but six all the same. A *lad*. Are you daft, sir?" She waved a dishtowel at him. "Oh, I forget myself. You're an O'Connor. You're all bloody daft, the whole lot of you."

Patrick glowered at her. "Mrs. Doyle, consider yourself the only woman on Earth who wouldn't pay dearly for saying what you just did."

He pulled himself up to his full size, but she just jutted her chin out and up at him, standing her ground. Damn her. It never worked with her. He couldn't stare her down, the woman had blasted changed his diapers.

"Lucky me," she murmured under her breath.

"Can you think of anyone who was especially eager to know my whereabouts?" Patrick said as calmly as he could.

"Other then your *own mother*, perhaps?" Her voice took on that all-too-maternal tone.

"Mrs. Doyle . . ." His patience was wearing thin. It would serve him precious little good to have her mad at him, for she was the best source of information he had. But the woman could vex a saint, much less an impatient Irishman.

"There were two or three that just didn't seem to know the likes of the word 'no.' That roundish man, the one with the partner, well, he seemed especially annoying, if that's what you're askin'."

"That's what I'm askin'. Did he leave a card?"

"A fair stack of 'em. But not the last two times."

Well, now he was getting somewhere. It sounded like Archibald Morton. And yet, he'd never be allowed in Patrick's study. Not even to leave his card. Not with Patrick away from home. No, if it was Morton, he'd gotten the information from someone else. Someone calling on Patricia? There were precious few easy answers. Perhaps it was time to consult that insightful wife of his. "Where's Mrs. O'Connor?"

"Which one?"

Patrick blew a breath out through his teeth. He'd clean forgotten there were two of them now. This was going to take some getting used to. But it didn't change the fact that Mrs. Doyle knew damn well which Mrs. O'Connor he was referring to. The old biddy just liked getting his dander up. As much, he admitted to himself, as he enjoyed getting hers up. They'd been at it for years. They didn't know any other way to behave toward each other.

"My *wife*," he ground out with irritation.

"Ah, yes, well you know, there . . ."

"There are two of them now, yes, damn it, I know that," he finished for her.

"There'll be no need for that kind of language around me, lad . . ."

"Where *is she*, Mrs. Doyle?" It was more of a demand than a question.

"She went calling to Miss Cooney's place earlier this morning. She told me to have you come call there when you came looking for her. She didn't want to be disturbin' you in your business but wanted you to come by when you were done."

"Thank you, Mrs. Doyle." Patrick exaggerated the words and squelched the urge to test a dishcloth's strength as a gag. "I'll be going out now."

"Indeed, sir."

Patrick wondered who was the more irritating old woman—his mother or his housekeeper. He called it a draw and headed off down the street.

⇥ Chapter Twenty-three ⇤

"Not more than ten minutes ago. It's a wonder you didn't see each other." Deborah dismissed the notion that Mrs. Doyle looked as if she actually enjoyed the mix-up. One could hardly blame the old woman; she'd done exactly as she had been asked. She'd given instructions for Patrick to join Deborah at Madge's when he was done. Only Deborah hadn't counted on his business taking until well into the afternoon, and she'd grown tired of Madge's flagrant questioning of what it was like to be a wife to Patrick O'Connor. Wife in the, well, in the *I really don't care to discuss such intimate details with you no matter how much you seem to enjoy hearing them* sense of the word. Good Lord, the woman's sense of privacy knew no bounds. When Madge began to sing the praises of a local woman's garden, Deborah took the opportunity to find an end to the visit, saying she would take a detour on the way home to inspect the plantings.

Now, that detour probably meant Patrick was just now arriving at Madge's, and sure to be undergoing his own personal interrogation at the hands of Madge Cooney's insatiable curiosity.

Would he talk about their nights together? Admit to Madge the unabashed hunger with which they tumbled amongst Patrick's fine linens? She had to wonder. Had Deborah's newfound passions bewildered him as much as they had her? Had he been surprised or pleased to discover the boldness that could so suddenly overtake her when he looked at her a certain way? What did he think of her when just the slow stroke of his hand could ignite such an intense craving that she could think of nothing else until she lay next to him? Did it show? Could others see the near-constant smolder when their eyes met?

The hall bell pulled her from the torrent of questions. For diversion, she told Mrs. Doyle she'd see to the caller herself. The door swung open to reveal an unfamiliar young lad bearing an envelope.

"Message for Mrs. O'Connor," the boy chirped, offering the envelope in one hand while scratching his grimy chin with the other.

"Thank you, I'll take it to her." Deborah took the envelope, not giving it a second thought until she realized the intended "Mrs. O'Connor." The envelope was addressed to Deborah Marie O'Connor. To her, not Patrick's mother.

Who knew her well enough to know her middle—and now married—names? No one in Galveston knew her middle name, no one in Austin yet knew she had married. Who could have sent this?

Deborah slipped into the front parlors and pulled the door shut behind her. Swallowing an inexplicable fear that crept up her spine, she sat slowly on the couch. She stared at the envelope a long moment before working up the courage to open it.

She was instantly sorry she'd opened it at all.

It was a note. A short one—direct and unwelcome. From Samuel Hasten.

Deborah crumpled the note at once, clenching a fist around the foul memory. Neither the note nor the memory went away. They refused to surrender. She spread the note back out and read it again:

My dearest Deborah,

Her mind balked at the salutation. How could he dare call her dearest? Even pretend that he meant anything to her after all he'd done? The affectionate greeting gave an unreal, sinister air to the message. This man was incapable of affection. Only the pretense of it as it suited him. She continued reading:

The pearl is a ruse. O'Connor is a swindler.

Who knew about the pearl? Patrick had told no one about La Roja and bid her do the same. Patrick was no swindler. Eccentric, perhaps. Extreme, even, but not a swindler.

Let me prove it to you. Then, I shall prove it to the world.
S. W. Dry Goods, four o'clock tomorrow afternoon.
    I remain yours,
    Samuel

Dear Lord. Samuel Hasten was out of prison and here in Galveston. *Here, in Galveston.* The Samuel Hasten who'd wooed her to her downfall. The Samuel Hasten who'd lied himself into her life and then shredded it for his own gain. A man who'd set fire to the *Austin City News* out of spite and cruelty, happily letting the blame fall to another man.

Who was she fooling that she had conquered her past? That she had won back her ability to trust? Her past and all its darkness rose up like a ghastly specter, hungry to rip her apart yet again.

No.

No, she challenged herself. It wasn't like that.

She wasn't the same woman Sam Hasten had charmed. She wasn't even the same woman who'd pulled herself up straight and forced a new life out of the wreckage of the old. She'd beaten Sam Hasten down once as a far lesser woman. She'd do it again as the woman she was now.

The sudden urge to run to Patrick shot up within her. It was a welcome reaction—it meant she trusted him. Yet within an instant, her urges were at war. Old doubts leapt up to challenge her frail new trust. As she tried to shake them off, a sharp conviction took hold. A powerful need to deny Sam Hasten every blessed inch of her new life.

"No," she said aloud, crushing the paper back into her fist. She'd give that animal no foothold into her future. She wanted to turn to Patrick for help. The allure of watching Patrick crush him was powerful. Yet the need to crush him *herself* overpowered them all. She needed to slay her own demons.

Tomorrow afternoon, Samuel Hasten would learn he had no hold on Deborah Marie O'Connor. And never would.

During that evening, Patrick seemed as distracted as she. Evidently he, too, had something weighing heavily on his mind. Perhaps the strain of grafting this new life into his old had borne down on him as well. It was all good and easy to become husband and wife in the isolation of the trip. Here, with the constant pull of family and friends, reputations and business, it was harder to hold onto the magic. Real life was rearing its head at every turn.

After dinner he suggested they walk along the beach. It was a welcome respite. Soothed by the rhythm of the waves, they fell into companionable silence. Deborah couldn't bring herself to ask Patrick if there was something wrong. If he confided in her, she would surely end up confiding in him, and she couldn't—not yet.

Heading back toward the house, Patrick pulled her body tightly inside the circle of his arm. After a moment he began to sing. The act caught Deborah by surprise. He sang soft and low, in a rich a capella lilt of Gaelic. The tune was haunting. His voice amazed her. Deep and clear, but with an edge that spoke of the tight corners of her own heart. She'd heard him sing silly ditties to Duncan, even heard a precious lullaby or two as he tucked Duncan into bed, but this carried an altogether different tone. It hung powerfully in the air. It pulled her with him as they walked, the vibrations of his baritone seeping into her wherever their bodies touched. He wrapped them in the persistent repetitions of the verses, binding them together as they made their way back to the light of the house.

Deborah barely noticed the rest of the house as they came in the door. She wasn't even sure her eyes were open as Patrick softly sung them through the hall and up the stairs. She let his voice carry her. When he pulled the bedroom door shut behind her, she envisioned herself falling into that voice, surrendering to it.

He stopped. She opened her eyes to see him staring at her. There were no flecks of brilliant gold in his eyes tonight; rather she saw the dense tones of topaz and burning embers. Heat. Tension.

Eyes still locked, he wrapped his arms around her and lifted her against him. Patrick kissed her passionately, her body suspended against him as if his kiss were the only thing holding her to the earth. Deborah was falling yet floating all at the same time. Locked to him, anchored to the frenzied connection that radiated out from his lips and tongue.

They tumbled onto the bed, pulling off their clothes with desperate urgency. His touch was hot and fierce, his skin salty under her tongue. There were no endearments, no gentle stroking, only the speechless plea of raw need. Need was the word for it. This was not want, this was not desire, this was need.

A sizzling intensity sprang everywhere as skin touched skin. No gentle rhythm grew between them tonight. Instead, she and Patrick were running, rushing, scrambling together toward the potent, life-giving place where they were one.

It seemed like only seconds until Deborah cried out and arched against him, Patrick's own body giving a great surge mere moments after. They fell, sweaty and gasping, into the tangle of each other's bodies with gratitude. Exhausted, emptied, grateful for the respite of each other.

When she looked into Patrick's eyes, the gold had returned. His gaze held a mind-dazzling power. A strength she knew she had given him. The same strength he gave her. In that moment, Deborah understood that the love she had with Patrick had already conquered Sam Hasten's wounds. There was not anything that could come between her and Patrick.

Certainly not Sam Hasten. She needed to tell him about Sam's note. She drew in a ragged breath and shut her eyes for a moment.

"Tell me," Patrick said quietly as he lay on his back and pulled her against him. "Tell me and then I will tell you."

Of course. He knew she was wrestling with something as clearly as she could see it in him. It was wonderful, soothing to be known so well. She used to think the term "soulmate" was silly, a dreamy-eyed romantic term. She understood now.

"Samuel Hasten is in Galveston," she said simply, the words holding their own weight. "He wants to see me. He knows about La Roja and claims it—and you—are false. He's out to bring us down, Patrick."

Patrick considered the facts for a moment. He

graced her forehead with a tender kiss. It felt exquisite after the maddened passion of moments before. "I thought you said he was in prison in Austin."

"He is supposed to be. I don't know what's happened."

Patrick's eyebrows furrowed in thought. "I believe I do." She knew by his face that he was about to tell her what had pressed down on him this evening. "Someone's been into my safe and found the letters from Alejandro. I don't know how—or who—yet, but I'll find out. Someone's also been making sure there isn't a jeweler within a hundred miles willing to certify that pearl. Madge told me this afternoon there's an undercurrent of rumors running about regarding you and me. I'd bet your friend here has been given some help from whomever got into my papers. My dear Mrs. O'Connor, I believe we're being preyed upon."

⊰ Chapter Twenty-four ⊱

"This is far too obvious." Deborah stared at the outlandish necklace draped across her chest. "Everyone will know. It's lunacy to wear this out in the open."

Patrick finished the clasp from behind her. "My point exactly. The foolishness of it is what will protect the pearl. Wearing it like this only feeds the rumor that it's false—no one would wear such a rarity in a Mardi Gras costume."

"No one, that is, except the wife of Trick O'Connor."

"Well, I won't deny I enjoy having a good excuse to keep my eye on your bosom all night. All day. All afternoon . . ."

"Enough." She pushed his chin up to return his gaze to her face. "It's bad enough to know you're leering at me, now I'll have to contend with all of Galveston whispering and wondering." Deborah readjusted her glasses nervously.

"That started long before the pearl, my love," replied Patrick. "And it will continue long after.

You've joined a long, distinguished line of jaded spouses—us Blacks and O'Connors are a hard lot to be wed to. Only the finest and the strongest can endure it. And you've a whole family of O'Connors to keep on the straight and narrow now."

"Lucky me." Deborah adjusted her skirt a third time. "You'll be there?"

Patrick walked over to a small corner cabinet. "You won't see me. I don't want him to see me. But I'll be there." Deborah nearly gasped as he unlocked the cabinet door and withdrew a sinister-looking pistol. She'd avoided thinking about the danger until now. "He'll not hurt you, Deborah. On my life. But we need to know what he knows, what he's up to, and he won't tell you if he thinks you're not alone."

"Oh, Lord." Deborah put her hand on her galloping heart. I'm not sure I can do this. He'll see how frightened I am."

"That's all right. I think, actually, that it's better that way. If you appeared calm and unruffled, he'd be more suspicious. Your reactions will be perfectly natural. In fact, the more in control he feels, the more he's likely to reveal." Patrick walked over to her and took her hand. "Ready?"

"No."

"That'll do just fine."

Four o'clock in the afternoon felt like the dead of night as Deborah put her shaking hand on the back door handle of S. W. Dry Goods. On the northeast side of the Island, at the fringes of the docks and warehouses that lined the rail tracks, the location was dusty and quiet. With Mardi Gras festivities due to start just hours from now, Sam had timed the appointment well, for no one was about. Nearly the entire Island's population was either at the parade site or home preparing. She pushed open the door with a trembling breath.

Inside, strips of light fell across the dusty floor from cracks in the dilapidated walls. The sharp creak of the door hinges echoed in the huge room. Piles of crates jutted high around the outer edges of the space. Deborah lifted her skirt slightly as she stepped over a small lump of empty burlap sacks. The glimpse of her rose-colored stockings gave her a shred of comfort. She was not alone. Somewhere, somehow, Patrick would be behind her, watching, protecting. Deborah took a deep breath and twisted her fingers around each other.

"I'm here," she said as calmly as she could. She didn't want to say his name.

She heard a movement behind one stack of crates. Her eyes snapped to the spot where a man's shoulder slowly appeared, then Samuel's fire-red hair came into view. It was just plain awful to have to look at his face again. The betrayal, the hurt she thought she had conquered, returned with full force in a heartbeat. Every wound he had cut sprung open, raw and stinging. Her stomach churned.

He was still Sam Hasten, but altogether different. The boyish charm that had once amused her was completely gone. In its place was an aged hardness that cut sharp edges into his features. He looked mean. Dangerous. Her eyes focused on the hand behind his back, and she panicked, wondering what kind of weapon he was hiding.

Seeing her gaze, Sam smiled and drew the hand around into view. He was holding a cone of peppermints. He used to bring them to her every time he called. Their engagement brooch had been in the red-white swirl shape of the candy. There was a time when they were her favorites. Now even the smell sent her stomach in circles.

"For you," he said, walking toward her. "I remembered how much you like them." He was looking at her with affection.

No fear rose up in her, just an odd, sad pity. "I don't like them anymore."

"Nonsense," he said in a soothing voice. His shirt, clean but damp with sweat, was tucked into his trousers in an effort to appear neat. He'd combed his hair, washed his face, but his hands were dirty. Like he was trying to hide any desperation. "You just need to try them again. You'll remember." He held the paper cone out to her. "Take them. I bought them special, just for you." His voice was gentle, eerie, as he placed the cone in her hand. He made sure he touched her when their hands met. Even through her gloves, Deborah's skin recoiled at the contact.

She said "Thank you" just because he looked so dreadfully unstable. As if just the mere omission of such a pleasantry might make him very angry.

He gazed at her, looking like he wanted to touch

her. "You look as beautiful as I remember. The color
of your eyes. The way you push your glasses up. I remember all those things."

"Why are you here?"

"You haven't said my name yet, Deborah. I want
to hear you say it again."

Deborah's ears strained for the sound of Patrick
cocking his pistol. But there was only silence.

"*Say it*," Sam said, the request turning into a command.

"Why are you here . . . Samuel?" It made her ill to
say his name, to see in his face how much he liked it.

"Music. Pure music." He waved his hands in the
air.

She remembered his doting courtship. How she
had believed so much in him. Believed she could have
a happy ending, only to have him do what he did.

He took another step toward her, putting out a
hand she refused to take. "I know I hurt you, dear,"
he said. "I tried to stop them from running that
newspaper story because I realized I loved you. Don't
you see? I know it was bad, but it can be better now.
There isn't anything I wouldn't do now to make you
happy. I told them we were married. We *should* be
married, you and I." He stared into her eyes.

This wasn't about Patrick or the pearl at all.
Samuel Hasten wanted his girl back.

"Why did you tell them that? And who are you
telling? What's going on, Samuel? You know we
never married. I'm married to Patrick now," Deborah declared with strength in her voice.

"You were mine, first," he countered. Sam ran his

hand through his hair in growing agitation. "You were betrothed to *me*." He reached for a piece of paper sticking out of his shirt pocket. "I have a marriage license here. I went and got it the day the *Austin City News* burnt down."

"It didn't just burn down. You set it on fire."

Samuel continued as if he'd not heard her. He unfolded the paper and handed it to her. "I've got some new friends here in Galveston and they did some looking for me. Seems no one can find a marriage license for you and that man you call your husband." He narrowed his eyes. "I'm not at all sure you two are even really married. He's unworthy of you, Deborah. You're supposed to be my wife. *My wife*."

"I am not. We never married. Stop this." Deborah pushed the document back at Samuel. "I don't want any part of you. I want you to go away."

Samuel ignored her. "He's got some pearl he thinks will make you all rich. He's convinced you it's real, I bet. Well, this reporter has a news flash for you, my dear: it's *not real*." His control was slipping with each sentence. "No one will believe it's real, either. Archie Morton is a powerful man, and if he doesn't think it's real, no one else will believe that fraud of a man you claim you married. He's going down, Deborah. Morton's bringing Trick O'Connor down, and I don't want you to go down with him. That's why you're coming away with me. We're going to pick up where we left off. Start over. Make that happy ending I always promised you. And I brought you something else, honey. I found William for you. I know he's not my son, but we'll make us a happy family, us three. And maybe a few more, don't you think?"

Deborah gasped. "William?"

"You've forgotten how good I am at snooping, haven't you? I told you I could get information out of anyone. I knew you'd come with me once I told you I could take you to William. I just knew it."

"Where is he, Samuel?" Her voice grew urgent. "Tell me where he is."

"Now, you don't think I'd let a juicy tidbit like that go without some commitment from you, do you?" He took a step closer. "I want to know you love me before I give you that." His eyes grew hard and dark. "I *need* for us to be together, Deborah."

"Stop this. I . . . I don't believe you. How could I ever believe you? Even if . . . even if you do know where William is, I won't let you near him." The thought of Samuel going anywhere near William drove Deborah over the edge, her anger getting the best of her. "Don't you touch that boy. I'm not listening to you. I'm not going anywhere with you!" All Patrick's plans for pulling information out of Hasten fled her mind and she turned toward the door. "I'm getting out of here."

"No you're *not*!" Sam's hiss came over her shoulder as he grabbed her.

"Patrick!" Deborah shrieked. *"Patrick!"*

"He's here, isn't he? I thought I told you to come *alone*!" Samuel's hands jabbed into her ribs as he pinned her to his side. "Come on out!" he called in a sinister voice. "Morton'd probably be pleased I picked up his garbage for him."

There was no response. *My God, where was Patrick? He said he'd be here.*

"I said come on out, O'Connor. Or isn't she worth it to you?"

"Patrick," she called, the silence frightening her, "help me."

There was a movement off to one side, behind a row of crates. Patrick, looking entirely too calm, walked into view. "She don't look like she's worth much to you, the way you're holding her like a sack of potatoes." The tone of his voice was apathetic. Disinterested. Deborah stared at him in shock. Patrick didn't even have his gun drawn. He was absent-mindedly looping a rope in his hands. "Let the lady go, Hasten."

"She's mine." Hasten pulled her closer to his side for emphasis. It hurt.

"Patrick, stop him," Deborah urged, Patrick's casual attitude was disturbing her.

"Doesn't seem to me like she wants to go with you." Patrick wasn't even looking at Deborah. He was staring at Hasten. Why wasn't he protecting her?

"She just needs time. We've been through a bit, she and I." Samuel thrust Deborah back behind him, his hands still firmly around her chest.

"Let the lady go, Hasten." Patrick took another step toward them.

"Back off, O'Connor."

Patrick spread his hands wide so his jacket opened up. It revealed the pistol stuck inside his belt. "Don't make me use this, Sam."

"Don't call me Sam!" She didn't know where he

pulled the gun from, but Samuel suddenly produced a pistol of his own. Deborah watched the muscles in Patrick's neck tighten as Samuel cocked the pistol. "I'd enjoy shooting you, O'Connor."

"I imagine you would. But word is, you aren't much of a shot, so I'll take my chances."

Deborah couldn't believe her ears. If Patrick had wanted to anger Samuel, he'd done it. Sam let out a loud yell and fired a shot over Patrick's shoulder. Patrick stood still.

Deborah screamed. Why on earth was Patrick letting him do this? "Patrick! Do something!" Samuel pushed her farther back, knocking her glasses off into the folds of her skirt.

Deborah couldn't see quite clearly, but it looked like Patrick continued to loop the rope. "She's annoying at times," he said in a tone of disgust.

"Patrick!" Deborah couldn't believe what she was hearing.

"Feisty," he continued. Patrick was making no moves to save her.

"Tempermental." Samuel suddenly agreed.

"You know, I've gotten what I needed. I'm thinkin' maybe I should let you have her." Patrick's voice was casual and resigned. He was doing something with his free hand but she couldn't see what it was.

Holy God. He's not going to rescue me. He never was. Deborah's heart burst into a thousand pieces. It had all been a lie. She'd believed in Patrick, only to have him deceive her as cruelly as Samuel had. "Patrick," she moaned, "you don't mean that."

"Well, I know it hurts to hear it, honey, but I think

I do. Not too much in this world is worth being shot for."

Sam looked as shocked as Deborah was. Sam shifted his feet, seemingly forgetting Deborah was still locked in his grip. The jostle sent Deborah's glasses sliding down her skirts onto the floor. She looked up at Patrick. He was still putting his hand up by his head, only she couldn't see. What on earth was going on?

"You've knocked the lady's glasses, off, Hasten. You know she needs them."

"She'll live," Sam replied coldly. He kicked them away with his foot.

"I don't want to stand here rubbing my sweaty neck all day."

What a ridiculous thing to say. What on earth was Patrick talking about? Rubbing his sweaty neck.

Rubbing.

Rubbing his neck. What was it Patrick had said about rubbing his neck?

It came to her in a jolt. On the ship. On the deck, that night they'd argued the truth of his stories. He'd asked if he should rub his neck to signal her he was lying. *Of course.* Patrick had been rubbing his neck! Only he hadn't realized her glasses were off and she couldn't see. Once the glasses had slid into view he had found a way to tell her what he was doing when she couldn't see it. Patrick *was* saving her. Granted, he was taking his blasted time about it, but he *was* planning something. It would be all right. Deborah started to cry from anguish and relief.

"She's upset, Hasten, let's get this over with. Tell

me who put you up to this and I'll see to it you get out of Galveston nice and quiet."

"Why should I trust you?" Sam retorted.

"Because if I had wanted to kill you I'd have already done it when I had a clear shot, now, wouldn't I?"

"Patrick, how could you do this to me?" Deborah asked, looking straight at Patrick. Even though she couldn't judge his expression from this distance, she trusted that her own expression would let him know she understood.

Samuel thought it over for a moment.

"You'll both have passage out of here by midnight on *The Thorn*. I know the ship's captain," continued Patrick. "He'll take you to New Orleans and you can go wherever you want from there. Think about it, Hasten, here's that chance for the happy ending you promised her. I doubt she wants to go home with *me* now, don't you?"

"I can't stand the sight of either of you!" Deborah hissed, pulling against the grip Samuel had on her arms. "Haggling over me like some sack of potatoes."

"She can be annoying at that," Hasten replied. "But I've a soft spot for those lilac eyes of hers. You say you can get us out of here by midnight?"

"Sooner, maybe."

Hasten considered his options once more. "All right then. It's Morton and Napson. They're going to prove your little bauble a fake and then buy your business out from under you when your clients start deserting."

Patrick's voice was tight. "I figured it was something like that."

Sam waved his pistol. "Now get us outa here."

Deborah saw Patrick put his hands up. "Easy, fella. You won't get two feet if I'm bleeding. Now just let the lady get her glasses and we'll be going. Pick them up *carefully*, Deborah honey, they're about six feet to your left, and the floor's mighty dirty."

When Hasten loosened his grip on her, Deborah lunged for the ground in the direction Patrick had given her. She heard a shot, and then something flying in the air over her head. Patrick gave a loud yell, and she heard something overhead give way. Pulleys screeched, things toppled. She flattened herself against the ground and heard Sam shout behind her. Then she felt hands grab her and pull her forward. Patrick's hands.

Wood splintered. Dust billowed up. More shouting. Metal clanging, then a sharp moan. Deborah screamed and pulled her hands up over her head. Two more loud thumps that sounded like more crates falling. Patrick's hands pulled her close and she clung to him. There was an eerie silence as the tumbling stopped. She felt Patrick exhale.

Deborah looked up to see blood running down Patrick's sleeve. "You're hurt. You've been shot. Patrick, you've been shot."

"Only grazed, I hope. It hurts, but I'll live." He looked at her. "I'm sorry you had to hear that. I didn't know how else to get his guard down. When I realized you couldn't see, you must have thought I . . . I'm sorry."

Movement from the crates drew their attention. "My God, Patrick, is he dead?"

"Not nearly, but he's not going anywhere soon." Patrick brushed off her glasses and handed them to her, wincing at the movement. "If those crates had been full, he might have been."

Deborah put her glasses on and surveyed the scene. As near as she could tell, Patrick had thrown the rope to catch on a pallet of crates. When he pulled, the crates had crashed down onto Samuel, crushing him underneath. The wreckage lay only yards from where she had lain.

"That was awfully close," she said, eyeing the frightening proximity.

"I knew I could pull you away in time. I can't risk my son losing his new mother so soon, can I?"

"You never gave a thought to the prospect of losing your wife?"

"Not one," Patrick smiled, rubbing his neck.

Patrick's quick work had the unconscious Hasten bound in no time. As he tied the last knot, he kicked the crushed cone of candy on the floor. "Is it safe to say I shouldn't be buying you peppermints anytime soon?"

"Never. Patrick, you're still bleeding."

"I'm well aware of that. He's secure, and he'll have a nice long night to consider his options. Let's get out of here."

❧ Chapter Twenty-five ❧

"Ouch! May I remind you I received that wound whilst saving your life? Stop grabbing my arm, Deborah." Patrick winced and pried her fingers off his upper arm.

"Sky Kings don't bleed," Deborah countered.

"I'm no Sky King." Patrick held her hand tightly. "And they only don't bleed. No one ever said anything about them not hurting when pummeled."

"I did not pummel you."

"Enough. We've got to get to Morton. He's big enough to find him in any costume." Patrick pulled her hand into the crook of his arm, keeping her against the wound so that the bustling crowd wouldn't bump it. He scanned the partygoers to no avail. Morton had to be here. It'd be a serious social mistake not to attend the Mardi Gras ball, and Morton never missed a social occasion. There was a gazebo outside; perhaps he was there. "Let's look around in the gardens."

Galveston's particular mist—a thick, almost animate gray haze, swirled around the gardens. It squelched the revelry inside, giving the night an intimate feeling. Bursts of laughter echoed from the lit gazebo. Patrick recognized one of the laughs as Morton's. He nodded to Deborah.

"He's in there. You remember what to do?"

Deborah nodded. Deborah raised the feathered fan that was part of her gypsy costume as Patrick slid his pirate mask down over his eyes. He stayed out of sight, for his size, like Morton's, would surely give him away in any disguise.

From under a tree, he watched Deborah ease her way into the circle of people inside the gazebo. He saw Deborah move next to Archibald Morton, then lean in as if to speak a confidence. Morton's thick fingers drummed against his silk vest. God, you could practically see the man's greed. With a broad smile, he took Deborah's arm and excused himself from the conversation. Deborah and Morton walked down the steps just past Patrick.

Quietly he slid up behind them and skewered the man with the end of his pistol. "Evening, Arch." He cocked the hammer for emphasis.

"Well, well," Morton said after a moment of surprise, "ain't this interesting? It seems your husband has other plans, Mrs. O'Connor."

"That is where you would be very much mistaken, Mr. Morton." Deborah pulled her hand from his arm. "I'm afraid we're quite in agreement on this. It is you who will be having the change of plans."

"You mind tellin' me what all this nonsense is about?" asked Morton, with enough sense not to try and turn around.

"Funny, I had the exact same question on my

mind, Arch. Keep walking. You mind telling me why I can't seem to locate a cooperative jeweler these days? Surely it can't be the sheer strength of my charming reputation. I'm sensing some greasy palms, Arch, and a little red-headed bird told me you'd done the greasing."

"Hasten? You believe that unstable young man?"

"It didn't take a lot of faith to believe this of you, Morton." They'd reached the edge of the park, so Patrick pushed the pirate's mask up off his face. He could tell the rage in his eyes frightened Deborah, but he was in no mood to hide it. "You've been gunning for my holdings for some time," he said into Morton's ear, "and don't think I haven't noticed it. What I want to know is how'd you get into my papers?"

"I haven't the faintest idea what you're talking about."

"Perhaps my pistol can refresh your memory?"

Morton made a sound as Patrick pushed the barrel further into his ribs. "A fired shot here in the park would not help your cause, O'Connor. You can't shoot me now. I'm too valuable to you."

"You've a point there, Morton," Patrick leaned his face right up beside Morton's, "but let me simply remind you I can do it slowly and very painfully later when I've got the time. And Lord knows, I've the inclination. But right now you and I have an appointment to keep at the telegraph office." He jabbed the pistol to spur Morton onward.

"The wire office? At this hour?" With pleasure Patrick noticed the huge man had begun to sweat.

"I've made some special arrangements, Arch. Not to worry. I'll apprise you," Patrick continued as they walked, "of your current situation as we go. Your associate, Mr. Hasten, is in knots in the warehouse. He was mighty forthcoming, once properly persuaded." They turned the corner onto a side street. "You of all people ought to know you can't count on the loyalties of someone like that. And if you really think a few well-placed rumors can hurt the likes of me, you're mistaken. I've been whispered about since I was born, Arch. Now my clients, well, you've got one on me there, but I aim to fix that right about . . ." he kicked open the wire office door, ". . . now. Evenin', Eddie."

"Evenin', Trick," said the man behind the desk.

"I've a friend here who needs to send some wires." Patrick knocked Morton off his feet and into a chair. With his foot, he pulled up a desk and leaned on it, crossing his long legs in front of him. He pointed the pistol directly between Morton's eyes. "Deborah, honey, would you kindly take the sheet of paper Eddie is holding and hand it to Mr. Morton here?"

Deborah slid the paper across the table to where Morton was sitting.

"You'll recognize the names, Morton. Six jewelers who seem particular friends of yours. Which one would you like to wire first?"

"I'd sooner die than help you."

Patrick took aim. "Don't tempt me. I've had a long night and I'm short on patience. Now, we're going to wire each of these fine experts to say you've gotten your hands on a certain item, and requesting that each of them high-tail it down here to verify it right away. I'm trusting they'll know what it is and why they ought to get here on the double. Have I made myself clear?"

Morton only nodded. "You can't make me."

Patrick cocked the pistol and stepped up to Morton. "You know, I can still send the wires with you dead on the floor, Morton, now that I think about it."

The incentive proved sufficient. Morton pointed to the third name on the list.

"Excellent choice. Take this down, Eddie. I want it word for word. And then, Arch, you're going to tell me how you came in possession of a letter from a certain Alejandro Torres."

Deborah and Patrick left Morton in Eddie's care and returned to the ball to keep up appearances. Patrick's arm was throbbing, but he wanted to make sure Morton's partner Jake Napson couldn't muddy the picture. Napson wasn't worth coercing, he was never the leader. Getting him good and drunk should distract him long enough for the wires to go through.

Napson was sauced enough already that it didn't take much. While suspicious of Patrick's generosity, he was all too happy to have someone buying him a string of drinks. By nearly midnight Patrick was worried he was swaying as much as Napson as they poured the man into a carriage and sent him off for home.

An hour later, Patrick walked through his darkened house. His wound was freshly bandaged, and his free hand held the last remains of a hefty brandy prescribed by his wife. Pain and exhaustion pulled at him. He opened the door to Duncan's room and stood looking at the boy. Unsteady, he leaned against the doorway. There was something so lasting, so timeless about watching Duncan sleep. Listening to the sound of his breath. Duncan was a fine boy. He'd make a fine man. Tall. Proud. Defiant. It was almost over. The profits from the sale of that pearl would set Duncan and Deborah for life, if anything happened to him.

Patrick bent and kissed the boy's head. "I'd take on the world for you, Dunc."

The boy turned and mumbled, recognizing his father's voice but still asleep.

"The whole wide world." Patrick shut the door and headed for bed.

Chapter Twenty-six

"Holy mother of God, it's real." The jeweler's loupe nearly fell out of his eye. "I can't believe my own eyes."

Patrick smiled. "I've four other sets of eyes who can't believe it either. I reckoned this needed a blasted consensus for verification. Six jewelers ought to do it, don't you think?"

"Mr. O'Connor, where did this come from?" The jeweler turned it over and over in his palm, much as the other four had done. It was downright gratifying to watch each of them gawk in astonishment. He'd done it. Trick O'Connor had brought the red pearl back. Pulled La Roja fresh out of legend and plunked her down, shiny and marvelous, into the halls of history. And now he had the family to enjoy what that gem would bring. It was a fine, fine day.

"That one may go with me to my grave, Mr. Charles." Patrick kicked his feet out in front of him, folding his hands back behind his head in triumph. Even though it hurt.

"I don't think I need to tell you I have well over a dozen buyers who might be interested."

"Music to my ears, Mr. Charles. What will your firm pay to handle the auction?"

Charles looked up in surprise. "You are aware, Mr. O'Connor, that we generally *take* a commission on an object. We don't pay *you*, you pay *us*."

"I have two other offers that indicate you might want to reconsider." Patrick pulled his hands down and leaned in. "Think of the press, Mr. Charles. Think of your employer. There isn't another pearl like this in the entire world. Do you think he'd want it sitting on someone else's auction block? Are you sure he'd let a small issue like money keep your firm from its place in history?"

The man narrowed his eyes. "Mr. O'Connor, why do I get the impression that money is *never* a small issue to you?"

"Indeed."

"This may take some time. It's Sunday."

"Look at that color. Look at that size. This is a one-of-a-kind gem, Charles. I'll give you four hours. The telegraph office is just across the street. I happen to know they're just waiting for you."

Mr. Charles took a long, last look before handing the pearl back to Patrick and heading toward the wire office. Patrick ran his fingers with admiration across the lustrous, blood red orb. Red was indeed the O'Connor signature color. Destiny couldn't have chosen a better man to bring back La Roja. Or a better gem to give both his family and those people on Margarita a bountiful future. Today, he felt like the Sky King.

⇥ Chapter Twenty-seven ⇤

The Mardi Gras parade had the most lavish favors anyone could remember this year. O'Connor Exporting's profits provided for the excessive generosity. Patrick enjoyed it when a gaggle of Galveston's social hens swept Deborah off for a moment of newfound adoration. Morton and Napson had been outwitted. Fiona had been exposed and she was gone, even though it pained Patrick to tell Mrs. Doyle of the betrayal her daughter had committed. It was astonishing that Mrs. Doyle had chosen to stay. But then again, that was Mrs. Doyle. She was loyalty personified. Samuel Hasten was back rotting in jail where he belonged. They'd gotten what information Samuel Hasten had collected about William—if such facts could be trusted. Even if Hasten's information turned out to be a red herring, they'd find William. If it took another seven years to find him, Patrick would.

Everything was conquered, his family was safe and secure. Tonight, Trick O'Connor was on top of the world.

"Pa! Look at that!" Duncan ogled at something

new every moment from his perch atop Patrick's shoulders. It didn't matter that his sore arm burned like coals from the load. Hoisting a son was a man's privilege.

"No, Pa, over there! I'm gonna go see." Like a monkey, Duncan scrambled off Patrick's shoulders, predictably digging his shoe heel into Patrick's wound on the way down.

"Ow! For God's sake, Dunc . . . watch what you're . . . Duncan!"

The boy shot off into the crowd before Patrick could catch him.

"Duncan! Come back here!" He caught sight of Duncan's dark hair zipping around a corner. Cursing boyish exuberance, Patrick set off after him. Mardi Gras was no time to go speeding off into the night. Things got crazy on the Island this time of year.

Patrick turned the corner where he had seen Duncan go. There was no sign of the boy. "Duncan! Son!"

Out of nowhere, a hand shot over Patrick's mouth and a rope coiled around his hands. Patrick fought with all his strength, but his injured shoulder left him at a disadvantage. Someone pulled a cloth over his head and bound his hands behind his back. Before he could kick the assailant, a second rope pulled him off his feet and held them fast.

"What the hell is going on? Where's Duncan? What have you done with my son?" Two hands grabbed him and hoisted him onto a . . . it felt like a wagon. In seconds he was careening off down the street. Two right turns, three lefts, he tried to calculate where they were taking him, but he hadn't paid enough attention to the intersection when he'd sped off after Duncan.

Minutes later—too short a time to be off the Island—Patrick was pulled from the wagon, dragged up some stairs, and unceremoniously dumped onto some floor. Carpet. Warmth. He was inside somewhere, but he had no idea where.

"I swear to you I'll have your skin, whoever you are." He let out a string of expletives as he fought against the ropes. "If you so much as harm one hair on my son's head . . ."

"*Potatoes*, Pa," came Duncan's all-too-amused voice, "you're supposed to say potatoes. It's all right. I'm right here." Patrick exhaled in relief as he felt Duncan's small hands pull off the cloth from over his head. The ropes around him weren't ropes, but the coils of a whip.

Patrick looked up and nearly choked.

He was lying on the floor of Madge's front parlor.

At his head stood Deborah, smiling. Tapping her foot. A foot he could see was encased not in rose stockings, but in red. Deep, rich, ridiculous, O'Connor red. And holding a length of copper piping.

As a matter of fact, everyone in the room was holding a length of copper piping. Except for Alejandro, who was still holding his whip.

"I hope I never have to do that again, *Gigante*. You put up too much of a fight for being a soft, old, married man."

Patrick ran his tongue across the split in his lip.

"Torres, I could have bet you'd have a hand in something like this. I'd ask what the hell is going on, but I don't think I want to know."

"Welcome to your own abduction, dear." The smile on Deborah's face could have lit the room. "Why don't you tell everyone why they're holding pipes?"

"I don't know why they're holding pipes. Perhaps you'd like to fill me in on what the potatoes is happening here?"

"You're getting married."

Patrick gulped. He didn't like where this was heading. "I'm already married."

Deborah nodded to Alejandro, who untied Patrick's feet. He stood up. The room was packed with friends and family, all looking rather bewildered but highly amused. Most amused of all was Madge, who was barely containing a laugh.

"Well, yes," said Deborah, her voice ringing with satisfaction, "that is true, but I feel it's important to point out that *you* married *me*. I feel it's high time *I* married *you*. I do, however, have a few requirements."

Patrick shifted his weight. *God bloody damn.* "I can only begin to imagine."

"Oh, no, honey," chuckled Madge, "I don't think you can."

Oh, he really didn't like where this was heading. Patrick cocked an eyebrow at his wife. She put up a single finger, counting.

"First, you shall actually *ask* me. Propose, in true gentlemanly fashion, here in front of witnesses."

Well, that wasn't too bad. He could do that. But Deborah didn't look at all like she was done. He shifted his weight again, trying not to look like he was pacing.

"Second," oh, he knew that was coming, "you shall tell everyone in this room the complete truth of how we were married."

"You're serious," he gulped.

"Quite."

He rubbed his chin on his shoulder to get off some of the grime. "I'm done for."

"Hardly."

"Is there anything else?" Not that he really wanted to know.

"If I think of something, I'll be sure to tell you." The glint in her eyes was like fireworks.

Patrick knew at that moment that he wanted this woman more than every gem the universe had to offer. He wanted her next to him for the rest of his life, if not longer. "Torres," he called, wiggling his fingers. "I'm going to need my hands to do this."

"Only if the lady says so, *Gigante*. I'm under orders."

Patrick glared at him. "Traitor."

"I only prefer to be on the winning side, *amigo*."

Deborah, thankfully, nodded her approval.

In the split second that Torres undid his hand, Patrick grabbed Deborah and pulled her into a long, wet, passionate kiss. A man had to keep the upper hand whenever he could. He was pleased to see her fluster when he finally pulled away. "Now, let me see."

With a flourish, Patrick got down on one knee. Deborah didn't know he'd had her pearl bracelet restrung upon their return to Galveston. It had been destroyed in the ship accident, but he'd managed to gather the pearls and keep them. He had planned to give it to her later tonight, but this seemed a delightfully perfect time.

He took Deborah's hand. Her beautiful, strong hand. The hand that had hung on to him, hung on to Duncan. Sweet Jesus, he loved those hands. "Deborah Marie O'Connor, I love you to the depths of my wild Irish soul. Would you, *please*, do me the honor of marrying me?"

He produced the bracelet. Gasps of astonishment fluttered through the gathering, and Deborah's other hand flew to her chest. He put the bracelet around her wrist, finishing it off with a tender kiss once the clasp was closed. He stared into her eyes, his heart galloping at the tears that welled there.

"Generally," he cued with a mile-wide smile, "one expects an answer to that kind of question."

She blushed. A splendid shade of rose. He'd become so fond of that color. "Yes."

Well, that was pretty much the most delightful word he'd ever heard. The world was looking rather wonderful tonight. He kissed her again, just because it gave him such enormous pleasure to do so.

"Forgive the intrusion, *Gigante*, but I am rather looking forward to this story of yours. I have a feeling it is going to be a . . . how do you say it? A whopper?"

The room laughed. Deborah smiled. "The truth, Patrick. All of it."

He realized what a gift it would be to her. Perhaps the truth did have power after all. How could he deny this woman anything?

"You see," he began, taking Deborah's hand, "Deborah didn't exactly come to Galveston of her own free will . . ."

He told the entire story. Every last detail, down to the copper pipe, for which he was sure he'd be ribbed until his dying day. And then he told them, in the best, most heartfelt terms he could muster, about how he had come to love her. About how fate had taken his plan and turned it into a gift he could have never imagined.

"Deborah, I love you. I'll say it as many times as you want me to in front of as many people as you want. Here, now, in front of all these *accomplices*, I promise you: nothing will ever come between us. I'll make you glad you married me every single moment of your life."

"Every *single* moment, Trick O'Connor? That's a rather impossible promise to make."

"Wife, I don't make any other kind."

Don't miss Allie Shaw's delightful romance:

THE IMPOSSIBLE TEXAN

*The War between the States might be over,
but their battle is just beginning. . . .*

Bold and strikingly beautiful, Marlena Maxwell
dislikes playing the part of a Southern belle. She
would much rather run her father's reelection bid
for Senate. That dream vanishes with the arrival
of Tyler Hamilton III, a Harvard-educated Boston
blue-blood hired to rejuvenate her father's cam-
paign. Now a slighted Lena plans to teach this
Yankee a thing or two about Texas politics. But
neither expected an election rife with desire!

Published by Ballantine Books.
Available wherever books are sold.

Subscribe to the new *Pillow Talk*
e-newsletter—and receive all these
fabulous online features directly in
your e-mail inbox:

♥ Exclusive essays and other features by major romance
writers like Linda Howard, Kristin Hannah,
Julie Garwood, and Suzanne Brockmann

♥ Exciting behind-the-scenes news from
our romance editors

♥ Special offers, including contests to win signed
romance books and other prizes

♥ Author tour information, and monthly announce-
ments about the newest books on sale

♥ A *Pillow Talk* readers forum, featuring feedback
from romance fans...like you!

Two easy ways to subscribe:
Go to **www.ballantinebooks.com/PillowTalk**
to sign up, or send a blank e-mail to
join-PillowTalk@list.randomhouse.com.

Pillow Talk—
the romance e-newsletter brought to you by
Ballantine Books